DEAD MAN DANCING

ALSO BY JOHN GALLIGAN

Bad Axe County

Red Sky, Red Dragonfly

The Nail Knot

The Blood Knot

The Clinch Knot

The Wind Knot

DEAD MAN DANCING

A BAD AXE COUNTY NOVEL

John Galligan

ATRIA PAPERBACK

NEW YORK   LONDON   TORONTO   SYDNEY   NEW DELHI

ATRIA
PAPERBACK

An Imprint of Simon & Schuster, Inc.
1230 Avenue of the Americas
New York, NY 10020

First Atria Books paperback edition May 2021

ATRIA B O O K S and colophon are trademarks of Simon & Schuster, Inc.

For information about special discounts for bulk purchases, please contact Simon & Schuster Special Sales at 1-866-506-1949 or business@simonandschuster.com.

The Simon & Schuster Speakers Bureau can bring authors to your live event. For more information or to book an event, contact the Simon & Schuster Speakers Bureau at 1-866-248-3049 or visit our website at www.simonspeakers.com.

Manufactured in the United States of America

1 3 5 7 9 10 8 6 4 2

Library of Congress Cataloging-in-Publication Data has been applied for.

ISBN 978-1-9821-1073-4
ISBN 978-1-9821-1074-1 (pbk)
ISBN 978-1-9821-1075-8 (ebook)

PROLOGUE

March 24, 2018

Bad Axe County, Wisconsin

As she watched the shivering band set up to play the farmers market at the corner of Kickapoo and Main, Bad Axe County sheriff Heidi Kick found herself counting days again.

How many days since she had danced?

Pink-cheeked Augustus Pfaff was the bandleader. His cold hands were full of tuba, so he shot the sheriff a nod and a wink. She waved back, recalling that the last time she had hopped and twirled to a polka was to Pfaff's band at the bowling alley, with Harley, her husband, at Family Fest on the afternoon of New Year's Eve.

So, that was—to calculate, she used an app on her phone—eighty-one days.

The number made her wince. She loved to polka. She *needed* to polka. Polka was sheer and simple joy.

Sheriff Kick sighed, feeling she had lost track of herself. She and Harley had been banging heads lately. Last night things had gotten heated. Then she had a nightmare. At times like these, she tried to take a hard, clear look. *Wow. Long time, no polka.*

Augustus Pfaff, tuning up, pushed a lungful of air out his old silver tuba and delivered the first oompah of spring. She smiled and made a decision. *OK, then: today.*

Hungry for a two-step, her feet drifted. She found herself gazing at a bushel of yellow onions that had overwintered in an Amish root cellar and were not too awfully shriveled. *Right. Today.* She always looked for markers in time—points after which things would be different—and Mr. Pfaff's oompah would mark a new beginning. *Family repair begins today. For real this time. Keep it simple. No new conflicts.*

"I'll take a half dozen onions. Not the muddy ones, though."

"Dem muddies dunna kept better." An Amish boy, one of the Schrock kids, with a dirty face and bright blue eyes, looked behind him for the support of his granddad. "Eh, Dawdy? Ent dem muddies dunna kept better?" The elder Schrock nodded.

"OK, I'll take a half dozen muddy ones."

Sheriff Kick passed the boy a five-dollar bill. He passed it to his sister. She showed it to the granddad, who pointed a bent finger across the market, and the girl sprinted away with the bill gripped tight and her bonnet strings and long black dress flapping.

Waiting for her change, the sheriff used her phone app again.

She put in April 15, 2016. The app came back with 707.

So it had been 707 days since she had shot Baron Ripp, a local guy who had been rearing back to club her with a steel fence post. Secretly, improperly, she had shot to maim, and she hadn't killed Ripp, who deserved worse than death. He had lost his left leg at mid-thigh before heading off to manage two life sentences as a one-legged rapist, sex trafficker, and killer of other people's daughters. She hoped he was popular.

The little Amish girl, breathless and smiling, put three one-dollar bills back in her hand.

"Danke!"

"You're welcome, sweetheart."

She had been the interim sheriff at the time, and three months later, the Ripp case had swayed a special election in her favor. Now she put the date of the election into her app and it came back with 619. So anywhere between 707 and 619 days is exactly how long she and Harley had been debating the impact of her job, the drain of her workload and her trauma, the fallout from her absence, on the family.

"Mommy . . ."

As if to score a point for Harley, their daughter, Ophelia, tugged on the cuff of the sheriff's new dusty-rose Carhartt jacket.

"Did you forget me? I said I'm cold."

"I know, hon." She marked the place in her thoughts. "How about chase the boys? That'll warm you up. We'll go inside the library in a few minutes."

With an emphatic roll of her eyes, Ophelia, they called her Opie, seven going on seventeen, rejected the suggestion to chase her twin little brothers around the first farmers market of the season. She had chosen not to wear her winter coat because the coat, like her mother's new jacket, was also pink. So either Opie was no longer liking pink, or she was no longer liking her mother, or both. Whatever it was, life was choices, and the oldest Kick child had chosen to be cold.

Augustus Pfaff's entire band was tuning now, bleating and plinking, wheezing, thumping and rattling—five goose-bumpy old men in lederhosen and short-sleeved white blouses—tuba, clarinet, banjo, accordion, bass drum, and snare—the Principals of Polka.

"Or, sweetheart," the sheriff suggested, "how about you go sit in Rosie Glick's buggy? I'm sure that would be OK. You'd be out of the wind."

Opie glowered her refusal. Against the trembling girl shoved a raw wind from the northeast. On fields beyond the parking lot, sunshine strove against the last dregs of snow. Flocks of starlings whorled above the muddy void. Opie turned her blue-lipped scowl toward Main Street. The state highway as it bisected the town of Farmstead was winter-fatigued, rimed with sand and broken into chuckholes by heavy trucks barreling elsewhere. The banners installed last summer by the Chamber of Commerce—VELKOMMEN! WE'RE GLAD YOU'RE HERE!—snapped and frayed against their poles.

"Or," Sheriff Kick tried, realizing Opie might have heard her fight last night with Harley, "you could think about how much Daddy and I love you and your brothers, no matter what. But maybe that would make you so hot from love you would sweat."

"Mommy."

"What?"

"Stop that."

She returned to her thoughts: her workload, her trauma, her absence . . . *and the pressure on her to perform*, Harley had reiterated last night. In the special election, she had defeated "Olaf the Handsome"—her popular chief deputy, Olaf Yttri, a good guy and a great deputy—by eleven votes to become the first-ever female elected sheriff in Wisconsin. Olaf the Handsome had left the Bad Axe to become a police chief up north. He was mourned and missed by the same people who judged and tested Sheriff Heidi Kick.

"Two rhubarb jams, please," she told Eli Glick. "And two quarts of mustard pickles."

The granddad of Rosie, Opie's Amish friend, nodded and through his bushy salt-and-pepper beard muttered something inaudible but no doubt pleasant.

She moved on to the beekeeper, Amos Yoder, and his honey. Then the Zwickle family and their maple syrup. Opie tagged unhappily along in jeans and an old flannel shirt that was actually a pajama top because she didn't have a real flannel shirt, yet she was determined to wear one. Her brothers, Taylor and Dylan, now four, were dressed as if for sledding and played happily on the parking cleats, leaping between them.

"*Eins, zwei, drei!*" whooped Augustus Pfaff, and his chilly little band burst into "Happy Valley Polka."

But instead of tickling her feet, the tune sent Sheriff Kick right back to numbers. A lack of happiness at home, in their own little valley, was her issue. Last night Harley had complained that she "never" took days off. He had wondered: Was it that she *couldn't* take days off? Was she not capable?

"*Never* is a big word," she had told him. "*Never* is a fighting word."

Like the baseball guy he was, he had answered, "Bring it. Hit me with the stats."

Well, by light of day, her contract with Bad Axe County gave her two of every ten days off, so in the 619 days since her election, that came to 124 days—a far cry from "never."

"Let's see," she said next to Sara Bontrager. "I think I'm out of butter."

She was never out of butter. Opie snorted, crossed her arms and shivered.

"I'll take five pounds."

It seemed like a good comeback: *124 days is a far cry from "never."* But just after she imagined this response, a text the sheriff had been waiting for arrived, from her night dispatcher, Denise Halverson. She had called Denise at 3:00 a.m. in a post-fight lather and asked her, when she had time, to count up the days that she had actually taken off. Denise had needed to check with Payroll at the county clerk's office, open nine to noon today.

Denise's text said: *27 total out of 124*

The sheriff stared, not believing.

Denise added: *Only 6 so far this year*

That could not be right. She reached to take her five pounds of Amish butter, a roll wrapped in wax paper. But no, that could not be correct.

Yes, hon, that is correct . . . and not good for you

Then her phone rang.

"OK, Heidi," Denise said, sounding nervous, "I have to tell you something that I swore I wouldn't tell you, but now, since you asked for these numbers, and you and Harley are having this fight, I feel I have to tell you."

Sheriff Kick turned away from Opie.

"Tell me what?" she said. She bit her lip and felt her pulse speed. Denise was a good friend who watched her back.

"I shouldn't . . . Oh, shit. Heidi, I know it's not my business. But you're my business. OK. Well, I saw Harley with somebody up at the Ring Hollow Dam."

"Somebody? You mean a woman?"

"A woman, yeah."

"When? Doing what?"

"Last Friday about lunchtime. Remember that day when it was weirdly nice out and we all thought spring was here? Harley and this chick were sitting in the sunshine on that concrete dam spout. It looked like they were having a picnic. Long blond hair—" Denise paused as if to mute herself. "That is completely all I know. I have no idea who she was. Hey . . . are you at the farmers market?"

"Yes."

"Is that bastard Jim Raha there selling eggs? I cracked one, it had a chicken inside it. I'm sorry, Heidi. Maybe I shouldn't have said anything. I don't know. But I said it."

"I appreciate it, Denise."

"It's nothing, I'm sure, because—" She stopped short again. "Well, what do I know? Anyway, do you want to know how to tell if a man is cheating on you?"

The sheriff was fighting a primal scream.

Denise said, "He starts bathing twice a week. Ha! At least the kind of men I hang with. Not Harley, of course. Heidi, I'm sure it's nothing. I'm so sorry. But it's nothing."

"Thanks, Denise." She ended the call and made her cold lips smile.

"Opie, let's get a pie. Let's get two pies. No, three. Take one to Grammy Belle and one to Uncle Kenny. Can you pick out three pies?"

She heard the polka stop abruptly, the way polkas do. That was it for "Happy Valley Polka," an instrumental, short and sweet. A cold gust carried away the final notes. Augustus Pfaff spoke to the meager crowd through a portable PA system.

"Thanks for coming out and showing winter who's boss. This next song is to kick the devil in his scrawny patoot on his way out the door. It's called the 'Hoop Dee Doo Polka.'"

As the band rollicked into it, the sheriff turned stiffly to look at Pfaff, a roly-poly retired teacher and high school principal, dancing nimbly with his instrument, man and tuba like an old married couple still in love.

Hoop dee doo,
Hoop dee doo,
I hear a polka and my troubles are through

"Three pies costs twenty dollars, Mommy."

"That's OK." She fished another bill from her jacket pocket. "Give this to Mrs. Zook. Hon, take the wagon with you."

Last night, on the subject of days off, she had accused Harley of underhandedly complaining about a lack of sex. With the "stats" now on the table—*only six days off so far this year*—her claim sounded defensive and stupid. Of course her husband wanted more of her. The whole family did, for a whole variety of reasons. And Harley had begun the conversation by talking about Opie's new issues. He was worried about the possible impacts of an overworking mother on their seven-year-old daughter. That was his stated concern, not how often he was getting laid. It was wrong of her to put words in his mouth. She had been projecting. She missed sex too, and the stats were beyond grim: three and thirty-nine.

They had made love three times this year.

And the last time was thirty-nine days ago, February 13, on Harley's birthday.

As Opie pulled the wagon back with three pies, the sheriff felt her heart twist. Here was her problem: everybody had to be safe. *Everybody.* And safety came from action, not reaction. Safety came from leadership, from presence, not from the sirens of her deputies screaming up to a crime scene. Safety was a climate of respect, and climate constantly changed, and constant change kept fear and hate constantly looming in the sky.

As Opie parked the wagon, the sheriff realized she had felt this way for exactly as many days as her polka-dancing drought. The Kicks had come home from Family Fest—eighty-one days ago on New Year's Eve—and Opie, at the dinner table, through a mouthful of meat loaf, had asked her mom and dad what she had to do to change her name from Ophelia to Oscar.

What do you mean, sweetie?

Because I'm probably a boy.

The sheriff squelched a grimace at the memory. After the shock, she had responded instinctively. In eighty-one days, she had showed her face at every one of twenty-five township board meetings. She had attended either mass or some other event at every church in the county. She had spent time at all the schools. She had driven night-shift patrols, making herself visible to the drinkers and the druggies in the taverns. She had spoken to the Lions, Kiwanis, and Rotary clubs, she had attended countless wrestling, basketball, and volleyball contests, and she had invaded the den of the Farmstead VFW post, where she was generally not welcome. *I am here.*

"Whee!" shouted Augustus Pfaff against the chilly breeze. His lips were off the silver tuba in a wide smile. He put them back, puffed out the oompah beat, skipped and twirled and marched in place as the lyrics resumed.

Hoop dee doo,
Hoop dee dee,
This kind of music feels like heaven to me . . .

She wasn't done with the market yet—she wanted to look at Hans Lapp's birdhouses made from gourds—but she took the kids inside the library so that Opie could warm up.

She sat in a comfortable armchair between the children's books and the window. The sudden warmth made her groggy. She could still hear the next polka coming from Main Street, even though the window looked out on Pool Street, one block west and parallel to Main. She found herself studying the town that was hers to take care of. Establishments along Pool Street mingled run-down old Farmstead with tentative new Farmstead. Mindy's Repair had been there forever behind its shabby front. Next door to Mindy's was River of Oz, something new, a freshly painted sign depicting a wizard on a flying dragon and offering "body work and supplements." Then there was the Farmstead Eagles Club, Aerie 3409, a dull cinder-block building she had visited just last week. Next door was probably the most exotic place in Farmstead these days, a dingy little grocery, Mercado Chavez, occupying a former insurance office and catering to the influx of Spanish-speaking people who mostly lived in trailers on the grounds of Vista Farms, the factory dairy operation that had appeared last fall on Belgian Ridge.

Staring out at Mercado Chavez, her stomach tightened. Hardly more than a cow-chip toss away on Main Street the banners read, VELKOMMEN! WE'RE GLAD YOU'RE HERE! But there had been friction. She had heard nasty grumbling about "invasion," about "speak English," about jobs stolen from locals. Not Harley, but his family—his mother, Belle, and his brother, Kenny—were of that persuasion, she knew.

Pausing for these thoughts had allowed fatigue to catch her, and she spent the next minute fiddling inside her coat pocket and feeling furtive.

As an avowed teetotaler, nothing stronger than coffee, she had a secret, and here was one more tally to note: It had been ninety-eight days since she had bought her first pack of Nicorette gum, in the midst of a marathon search for a runaway junior high school boy. Before she got to day one hundred, she had sworn to herself, she would quit.

She touched the pack secreted in her inner coat pocket. But her kids had a spooky sixth sense about the presence of gum. She didn't dare.

Without nicotine, she drifted, seeing her face reflected in the cold skin of window glass. Then she sank into sleep, and in sleep she began her nightmare again, inserting Denise's update that Harley was doing his cheating on the Ring Hollow Dam spout, and the woman had long blond hair. In the dream, it was her zeal for everybody's safety that had pushed her husband too far, created too much conflict. He was a fucker, not a fighter. She had lost her marriage.

Then Opie was tugging her sleeve.

"What, honey?"

Opie said in a library whisper, "Uncle Kenny just drove by with a big flag in his truck."

"What?"

"That big red flag with the blue-and-white cross and stars on it."

"Uncle Kenny?"

"He had a flagpole standing up in the back of his truck."

She roused into a wakeful dread.

Uncle Kenny . . .

More often than she dared to count, Harley's troublemaking older brother had taken a piss on their marriage. Kenny Kick brawled in the taverns, trespassed and poached, yelled crude things at high school games—always a story, always an excuse—constantly putting his sister-in-law on the spot and pitting her against her husband. Most recently, back in September, she had busted him for OWI at a blood-alcohol level of .09, which Harley had argued was *Just one swallow over legal! And you're his family!* As if Kenny wasn't usually a whole lot drunker behind the wheel, as if laws should not apply when one was related to their enforcer. Harley had assured her that no amount of punishment was ever going to change Kenny. Kenny's whole life history proved that shaming him would only make him worse.

"Here he comes again," Opie whispered.

Sheriff Kick gaped in stunned denial at the old two-tone Ford pickup roaring down Pool Street, showing off windshield cracks, rust craters, a mud beard . . . and a statement. A ranting voice started inside her. *Goddamn you, Kenny! You can't be bullying around Farmstead with a giant Confederate flag posted up in your truck box!* The flag caught a cold gust and preened out perfectly behind the truck. *Goddamn it, Harley! Your dumbass brother is not really doing this to us!* Then Kenny was gone past. What the hell?

"That's the Nazi flag," Opie remarked.

"No, hon, it's not. But."

"It's a bad flag."

"Well . . ."

"He's going around and around the block."

So he was. He was flagging the farmers market. In little Farmstead, Wisconsin, in front of mostly Amish, who were immune to the politics of the English, and in front of a few nice old men playing polka for the love of it, the sheriff's brother-in-law was making a display of the Southern cross, a symbol that in the North had only one meaning.

The polka stopped dead. In the quiet of the library, the sheriff could hear her brother-in-law rip-snorting south-to-north up Main

Street, revving his dirtbag engine and squealing his worn-out tires as he cornered on First Street, cornered on Pool Street . . .

And now here he came once more, past the library windows, past the Eagles Club and the Mercado Chavez, doing laps.

Opie stomped her foot very quietly but with real force.

"Mommy," she whispered hotly, *do something.*

ROLL OUT THE BARREL

Bad Axe County 51st Annual
Syttende Mai Festival

Friday, May 18

7:00–10:00 a.m.	Kickoff Breakfast (@ Farmstead VFD w/ Squeeze Box Three and DJ Gunnar B)
10:00 a.m.–3:00 p.m.	Volunteer Setup (@ Fairgrounds)
Noon	Grand Parade Registration Deadline (@ County Clerk's Office, 135 Third Street)
Noon–1:00 p.m.	Volunteer Brat Feed (@ Fairgrounds, Sponsored by: Piggly Wiggly, Clausen Meats, Wanstaad Implement)
3:00 p.m.	Rosemaling Workshop, 4-H Animal Registration, Lions Club Lefse Presale, Rodeo Qualifying Round, Meat Lottery (All @ Fairgrounds)
5:00 p.m.	Beer Tent and Food Stands Open, Tractor Pull Sign-Up (@ Fairgrounds); Alcohol Awareness (@ Raymond Gibbs Public Safety Building); Model Plane Race (@ Bjorn-Hefty Airfield); Troll Hunt (@ You Find 'Em!)
6:00 p.m.	Festival Grand Opening (@ Fairgrounds w/ the Principals of Polka)

No more than fifteen minutes into the festival kickoff breakfast, in the garage of the Farmstead Volunteer Fire Department, with three pale pancakes and a sausage patty on his plate, the beloved elderly Bad Axer who everyone called "Mr. Pfaff" had the terrible feeling that his house was on fire.

He handed his plate to Mrs. Einar Kleekamp—"I'm on fire," he blurted—and left in haste, without further explanation.

Only a few times in his life had Augustus Pfaff intentionally exceeded the speed limit. This was one of them. In his maroon Oldsmobile, on County Highway J, he hit eighty. On the potholed gravel of his own Pinch Hollow Road, he went fast enough to bottom out three or four times, in such a rush that he nearly hit a doe he knew personally a hundred yards from home. He was certain, absolutely certain, that his house was on fire.

It was not. When he reached the end of his steep driveway, Pfaff saw that his cozy old farmhouse along the Little Bad Axe River was just as it always was, a bit of a shambles, a bit sunken in the flood plain, surrounded by great tufts of grass that he hadn't the heart to mow because his dandelions were blooming.

He parked in his barn and rolled the door shut. He was still out of breath when he entered the house. All was well. His silver tuba was on its stand in the living room. Opposite, on the tabletop in the dining room, just as he had left them, sat the four boxes of freshly printed books that had arrived by UPS yesterday, one hundred copies, one box open for inspecting and admiring. He was an author! He passed through his cluttered bachelor's kitchen to his den. His boxes of research files, his computer, his backup disks, were just as he had left them. All of this would have been destroyed by the fire that he had imagined. Now he wished that he had taken a few deep breaths and eaten his pancakes.

Yet he had felt so strongly. He had *known* it.

He had talked to so many people in the course of writing his book that he couldn't guess exactly who had lit his house on fire. Probably someone who didn't like his genealogy work. His family trees, his own included, were accurate beyond a doubt, but he had been so wrapped up in the research and writing, in such a mood of triumph to have finished it, and he was such a stein-half-full individual by nature, that it was only as the pancakes hit his plate that a dreadful sensation had stopped his breath and made his skin burn. Now that the book was here, someone wanted to burn it, and his house was on fire.

Well, but it wasn't. He had been wrong.

He was appreciating this reprieve as he stepped back onto his front porch, thinking he would set up and practice his tuba there in the cool morning shade. But before going back inside to fetch a chair and the tuba, he paused. He heard something.

Pinch Hollow Road went past the house at roof level about fifty yards away, and with the trees now leafed out he could only tell that some kind of vehicle was creeping north to south along the road above the property. He could hear tires pop gravel. He moved along his porch until he glimpsed blue and maybe silver when the vehicle paused at the end of his driveway. He heard his mailbox open and close. Then the vehicle moved away at normal speed. After it was gone, an old-fashioned alarm clock—inside the mailbox, it seemed—began to ring.

As a retired high school history teacher and senior-class principal, Augustus Pfaff had always enjoyed the gentle pranks that students had played on him across four decades. *Don't egg me.* This was all he asked. Now, he assessed this to be one more prank for nostalgia's sake. He toiled on his gimpy old knees up the driveway, intending to get the clock and turn it off and keep it. Had the rascals forgotten how this worked?

He had just reached the mailbox and extracted the clock when from uphill on his property across the road came the hard crack of a gunshot. He flinched and stumbled. With his heart suddenly thundering he gripped the mailbox to hold himself up. The box felt strangely hot. When he pushed back he saw two holes, in and out, he believed the bullet had torn right through him and the box both.

He dropped the clock. The alarm stopped. He felt nothing. And it meant everything, he knew, that he felt nothing. Feeling nothing was the highest level, the lethal level, of pain and shock. He checked himself, his chest, his gut, couldn't find the wound exactly. But the early sunshine felt suddenly cold, while his left leg felt wet and hot. He was going to die. He headed straight back down his driveway, blind with dizziness, yet still hurrying because it was suddenly his ambition to take his final rest like a real author might, among his dandelions.

He made it, and he lay down on lush grass to bleed out among the yellow flowers.

———

For nearly one hour, Augustus Pfaff remained committed to the poetry of his demise. *Shot for his courage . . . on the very day his book was born . . .*

But eventually the sun blazed directly down and he became too hot. He noted that otherwise he felt no discomfort. Also, he felt cogent and capable of clear perception, able to note that he smelled a bit like urine. *Hoop dee dee!* He struggled stiffly to his feet. The bullet had missed him. Or perhaps it had not been meant for him at all. It was possible, even, that the holes had already been in the mailbox.

He brushed himself off and picked a fistful of dandelions. His dear departed Loralee had loved them so. *Go inside, find a vase, change your piss pants, and notify the sheriff's department*—these steps would be his next. But when he cornered the house, he was surprised by Deputy Larry Czappa skulking down his porch steps with his hairy fist around a freshly printed copy of *A Round Us* by Augustus Pfaff. Deputy Czappa, heading in urgent strides for the steep driveway and his cruiser at the top, hadn't seen the author yet.

"To what—ahem—to what do I owe the pleasure?"

Czappa put on the brakes and turned with a smile that struck Mr. Pfaff as wild and stiff and guilty. Long ago, he had tried to teach this underachieving troublemaker a bit of history along with the value of kindness toward others. Later, as the boy's principal, he had boosted Larry Czappa over a very low bar to reach graduation.

"Oh. Mr. Pfaff. You're here."

"Of course I'm here. I live here. And you?"

"I knocked," he said.

"Did someone say come in?"

"Um, I wasn't sure."

"My book is twenty dollars."

"What? Oh." He quickly switched it hand to hand like a hot potato. "I forgot I had it."

"You're not in it anyway. Would you please put it back where you found it?"

Pfaff waited, arranging the dandelions in his chubby fist. Czappa seemed to take too long. When at last the deputy reappeared, his old teacher and principal gave him an assignment.

"I was just going to call in an incident report. I may or may not have been shot at. In any case, someone was shooting on my property, and across the road. Since you're here, will you take the report?"

Later, as Augustus Pfaff was fixing his own pancakes in the kitchen, reflecting on the incident and on Larry Czappa's curious appearance, he sensed fire again, saw flames in his mind's eye, and he decided that he had been right about his house but wrong about the timing.

His house *would be* on fire.

The part he had gotten wrong was that if the goal was to kill his story, to keep the past dead and buried, then it did no good to burn his house and his books *without killing him first.*

"Have Sheriff Kick call me," Pfaff told Rinehart Rog, Bad Axe County's daytime dispatcher.

"She's in court most of the day. Can I help you? Or how about one of the other deputies?"

"No. Only her. Have her call me as soon as she can."

After that he ate too fast. Then he sat on the porch before his music stand, burping pancakes and feeling anxious, unable to push air into the tuba. At first, he had only meant to write about the round barns in the Bad Axe—their fascinating and forgotten history—but the story had become bigger than he planned.

When he finally put his lips to the tuba, it was with a frown and the hope that Sheriff Kick would call him right away . . . because in some unhappy person's design—*oompah!*—he was dead.

2

Ivy Kafka could see the Bad Axe County Courthouse out the post office window, with Sheriff Kick's brown-on-tan Dodge Charger parked in the reserved spot out front. Ivy's old high school pal Kenny Kick was over there for a hearing today, and in his mind, Ivy was talking to Kenny.

"*Cigar Aficionado!*"

"Please stop that."

Emily Swiggum, the young postmistress for Farmstead, spoke to Ivy with her back turned as she expertly fed the PO boxes.

Ivy complied as long as he could, about one a minute. Then he read more mail to Kenny Kick.

"T. Rowe Price Quarterly Investor Report! And oh, look, a hot tub catalog!"

This time the postmistress turned, a milk-skinned, raven-haired, blue-eyed Norwegian beauty, hardly out of college, the age a daughter would be if Ivy had ever had one. She fixed him with a prim smile.

"Francis?"

His real name . . . She waited for his pouch-saddled eyes. When they lifted and connected, she squeezed her smile a little harder. He could see this pained her, scolding him again.

"We don't snoop in other people's mail. And when we can't help but see things, we don't comment."

His nickname, Ivy, came from the Roman numeral four: IV. He was the fourth Francis Kafka. Four generations of Kafkas had built an impressive dairy farm, a minor empire on a thousand acres in Bohemian Valley, out in northeast Bad Axe County.

"*House Beautiful*!" he blurted soon enough. "*Yoga Journal*!"

"Francis!" The postmistress turned upon him sternly. "Do you need this job or not?"

She asked because Ivy had lost the farm. A messy and mostly drunken decade ago, he had lost Kafka Acres. After one hundred years and four generations, after his dad's death and under Ivy's management, the farm had slid into a debt crater. Overnight, the bank had owned everything.

"I do need this job, yes, I do."

"Have you been drinking?"

"Not yet."

"Please focus on your work."

"Work?" His mouth came open. His unshaven jaw hung from his face like some querulous, salt-and-pepper possum. As a farmer, Ivy knew work. This was not work.

"OK, Francis. I know how you feel about the word. Please focus on your *job*."

He tried, but today was a special challenge. A few irregular times a week, in a substitute capacity, he sorted mail, then applied his occupational license and drove left-footed from the wrong side of his wheezy Kia Sportage, delivering the rural post. Today's route was his most painful one. Over the next hours he would deliver *House Beautiful* and *Yoga Journal* into the mailbox of his ex-fiancé, Kristi-Jo Babb, who had two little ones now with her real-estate-broker husband. He would ferry a cigar magazine, a hot tub catalog, and a quarterly investment report out Kafka Road to his family's former farm, now owned by a personal injury lawyer from Chicago who vacationed on the property two or three times a year.

"*Metamorphosis*," he said next.

The postmistress released a long sigh but kept her back to Ivy, her pretty arms feeding the boxes.

"Have you heard of that?" he asked. "Have you read it?"

"Yes, Francis. I read that in college."

Because lately he had heard a new term sniggered by some wiseass in a tavern on the river. *Kafkaesque*. From a storybook. Out of nowhere, a guy wakes up one morning and he's not a man anymore, he's an insect. A man-size insect. And he is reviled.

Sometime in early March, Ivy had visited the Bad Axe County Library to check out the book and see what happened next.

Nothing.

Nothing happened next.

"Nothing happens in that book," he said now to Emily Swiggum.

But it was a very slow and very bad kind of nothing, and after he had finished the book it had seemed obvious to Ivy that if Gregor Samsa had possessed a pickup truck and a flag, he might have driven, like Ivy's pal Kenny Kick, up and down his own Main Street, saying, *Look at me, I am not an insect, I'm a man.*

———

In the glove box of his Sportage, Francis Kafka IV kept his old varmint gun, a loaded Colt .38 revolver, ready for instant relief whenever the day came that he completely lost his shit.

At lunch, under the Lions Club pavilion along Amish Mill Road, he accessed the glove box and slipped the .38 into his mouth for a deep taste.

When Kenny Kick came along, showing off his new blue-and-silver monster pickup, he saw the wet weapon on the bench. He sat down beside Ivy. He installed a dip of Grizzly and worked it into place, meticulously ejecting wayward nits of tobacco.

"Innocent," he said.

"Really?"

"The DA dropped the charges."

"That's not the same as innocent," Ivy said.

"My snowflake sister-in-law couldn't make that shit stick."

"But that's not the same as innocent."

They sat a while. The cottonwood beside the pavilion had just broken out of its buds. New leaves rattled in the breeze.

"Well, at least you look like roadkill," Kenny said.

Ivy shrugged. He didn't care. Of late he rarely looked in a mirror. On occasions when he did shave, he steered the blade by feel, often cutting himself and missing large tracts of stiff gray whiskers. So what? Was he trying out for Man of the Year? And he would always dress like he was born in a barn—because, guess what, goddamn it, he *was* born in a barn.

He glanced over. Beside him, Kenny was a bit of a peacock. Kenny was bald beneath his hat, but he allowed the hair he had left to grow thickly on the back of his neck, red brown and lustrous curls, like a well-fed weasel heading down his shirt. Today that shirt was a snappy new item featuring an image of Mount Rushmore replaced with the heads of NASCAR drivers, Dale Earnhardt, Richard Petty, and two others Ivy didn't recognize.

"So," Kenny said in time, "I'm going to ask you the same question as before. Same exact question. When you gonna wake up? What's it gonna take?"

Ivy shrugged. Since he had done that thing with the flag, Kenny had some new friends. Or maybe Kenny had done that thing with the flag *because* he had some new friends. Either way, this was new Kenny.

"I'm out there making a difference, brother."

New Kenny said *brother* all the time.

"I'm out there fighting back. What about you?"

Ivy shrugged again. Kenny squirted brown spit through his front teeth.

"It'll cure what ails you, brother."

"I'm what ails me," Ivy said. "I never had a brother. If I did, I wunta lost the farm."

"Hell with that. You're losing your culture. That's what ails you."

"My culture? The Department of Agriculture. Archer Daniels? The goddamn bank? They ain't lost. I am."

"Listen to you. Playing right into their hands. Invasion, brother. That's what ails you. You're under attack."

Ivy watched a kingbird chase a small yellow butterfly across the mowed grass in front of the pavilion. Kenny began saying words as if he had borrowed them and had to take them back unbroken.

"Annihilation," he pronounced, "of your kind. Treason by the globalist powers that be, leading to usurpation"—relieved to have managed the word, he discharged spit—"by the browns and the blacks."

"Wow," said Ivy. "Back in school, I had to give you all the answers."

"You face extermination, brother."

"I do?"

"Question is, do you fight back or not? Question is, are you a man or a mouse?"

"More of an insect," Ivy said.

Screw Kenny, he thought. His mind felt sour and drifty and like he could use a drink. He remembered in high school tapping code on Kenny's chair leg from behind, giving him every single answer on their Spanish tests. But lately Kenny acted like he was the one with all the answers. He leaned close to Ivy.

"I'm gonna let you in on something, brother. Crawford Toyle is coming to the Bad Axe."

"Who?"

"You mean you don't know Crawford Toyle? Crawford Toyle is one of the big guns. He's one of the heavy hitters."

"OK."

"He's coming to the Bad Axe. All the way from south Indiana. Stang invited him to march with us on Sunday."

"Stang?" Ivy knew some Stangs, sketchy river folks, a father and a son. "To march? March where?"

"The parade."

"The festival?"

"Hell yeah," Kenny said. "Right down Main Street."

"Who's coming again?"

Kenny squirted. "Fucking A, brother, you never heard of Crawford Toyle? He's international. He's marched in Austria and France. Crawford Toyle is coming right here to march with us in the Syttende Mai parade on Sunday. And hell, little old me—"

Kenny's cheeks had turned pink. He rubbed his palms on his thighs.

"I'm the reason, me, that Crawford Toyle is coming here. My right to free speech. My brother's wife . . . Sheriff Snowflake . . . Disturbing the peace, show of force, fucking intimidation . . . bull-fuck . . . innocent! . . . and my shit went viral."

The word *viral* triggered old associations for Ivy: infectious bovine rhinotracheitis, bovine viral diarrhea, bovine spongiform encephalitis . . .

When he came back from these wandering thoughts, his friend Kenny was saying, "I will not back down to oppression. I will not be exterminated. You see that truck? That's a fucking 2018 Ford F-350 XLT, brother. Stang hooked me up with some guy who put my story on the internet. People believe in me. People like me, and they give me money. . . ."

"I get it," said Ivy. "You lose a farm, go fuck yourself. You fly a flag, GoFundMe a truck."

Kenny glared wet-eyed at him. "Man, fuck you. The blacks and the browns, man, no way. They ain't eating Kenny Kick's cookie."

"OK," Ivy said. "That's good."

"I have manned up. I am making a difference."

"OK, Kenny."

"You shoulda seen me—"

Ivy waited. Kenny took a whole bunch of deep breaths. He finally said, "Stang, man, he is so jacked that Crawford Toyle is coming. Totally big-time shit, man."

They sat a while longer. Kenny hooked his chew out and ate a candy bar. Ivy never ate much anymore. His stomach seemed to have a kink.

"So what's it going to be, brother? You going to get with us and make a difference?"

"Well, I don't know," Ivy said. "We Kafkas got some past with Stangs. And if something seems like a good idea to me, then probably it's not, probably I ought to run the other way. . . ."

Kenny looked at him and snorted. He stood and aimed his key. His truck went *beep-boop* and the engine started.

"Man-oh-man," he said. "Look at you, brother. Belly up. Just lay-ing there. *Please exterminate me.* What's it gonna take to wake you up?"

After Kenny ripped away, Ivy sat a few minutes longer thinking about the Stangs he knew. The mother ran off when Ivy was in junior high school. After that, Rolf Stang Sr. got life in prison for killing a man in a drug deal along the river. So Kenny had to be talking about ringwormy little Rolf Stang Jr. Join him? He tried but failed to imag-ine what it would take for him to tolerate all that "brother" talk from an angry little river rat like Rolf Stang Jr.

But it was time for him to get moving. Since tonight was opening night, draft beers in the festival beer tent would be going for a buck apiece from four to six.

He replaced his .38 in the glove box, aimed his left boot to rev up the Sportage, and headed out to finish his route.

3

"I don't recognize this group," said Sheriff Kick when she met with Syttende Mai parade comarshal and county board chairperson Bob Check. She was worn-out and ornery after several hours at the courthouse, but it was protocol to sit down and review the organizations scheduled to march, ever since a group from Madison had shown up riding bicycles in the nude and waving signs about climate change. If the festival could not deny legal applications, at least they could be ready for whoever came down Main Street.

"Who are the 'Sons of Tyr'?" she asked Bob Check.

"Heck if I know."

"Who is 'Tyr'?"

She watched the eighty-year-old retired farmer begin to peck a thick finger at his brand-new smartphone.

"Tell you in a minute," he said.

She tried to clear her mind. At the courthouse, in discovery, the public defender had floated the argument that Kenny did not intend to intimidate because he did not understand the cultural context of the Confederate flag. This was all too believable, actually, and when Kenny wouldn't say who put him up to it—his innocent idea, he maintained—the DA had decided to withdraw the charge, making Sheriff Heidi Kick look like a fool. Like a *snowflake*.

Still grinding on it, she scanned the rest of the groups registered, mostly the same that always marched in the Syttende Mai grand parade, now just two days away. The list included the Lions Club, the VFW post, the ladies' auxiliaries to both, the high school cheerleaders, the 4-H kids, several volunteer fire departments from the townships, the Bad Axe Rod and Gun Club, and . . .

"The Sons of Norway," she read from the list. "Is Sons of Tyr like Sons of Norway?"

"I'm working on it."

The Sons of Norway kept alive such old-world practices as eating lutefisk, getting schnockered on large quantities of aquavit, and belting out Norwegian cow-calling songs. Her Irish dad had belonged.

"Almost there," said Bob.

Also marching were the Bad Axe County Humane Society, the Little Britches rodeo team, and the 1999 Class 5A state high school baseball champions, the Blackhawks, which included their star player, her husband, though Harley didn't care for nostalgia and she doubted he would march with his teammates.

The parade would go down Main Street on Sunday morning. Within the marchers would proceed several floats on wagons pulled by vintage tractors. The most important and familiar float would bear Augustus Pfaff's band, the Principals of Polka, which provided the main soundtrack for the entire three-day festival. Then there was the maiden voyage of the heritage float, sponsored by the Bad Axe County Library, which would "celebrate the history and culture of under-recognized peoples in the region."

The sheriff skimmed the description of the heritage float. It was just as Opie had told her. The sheriff's daughter would ride the float as a bearded Amish man. A little boy in breechcloth and turkey feathers was going to play Blackhawk, the high school mascot and secondarily the leader of two thousand Sauk renegades massacred in the Bad Axe two centuries ago. An adopted African American kid would represent the escaped slaves who settled in the coulee region in the 1850s. The

Hmong population, a small group of truck farmers in the northwest Bad Axe, would be represented by a Hmong child in ceremonial dress. A child of the couple who ran Mercado Chavez would ride the float in a sombrero.

"Is it *T-Y-R*?" Bob asked her.

"That's how it's spelled on the parade permit."

"Got it. Tyr, pronounced *tear*, as in *tear in the eye*."

He cleared a squeak from his throat.

" 'Tyr, a god of war from Norse mythology who presides over law and justice. The god Tyr is normally represented as having one arm, the other having been ripped off by a wolf—' "

"Hang on a sec, Bob."

Her day dispatcher, massive Rinehart "Rhino" Rog, had eclipsed her office doorway.

"Sorry," Rhino said, holding out a small box and an envelope. "The mail just got here. I know you were waiting for this."

Sheriff Kick tore open the box and sighed in relief. Here in the nick of time was the chin beard to go with Opie's Amish costume. Opie needed her beard to look right, and this one seemed to. It was reddish-blondish, decently close to Opie's hair color, and to the sheriff's own. She paused a moment to mentally argue with her husband. Nearly five months after Opie's dinner-table announcement that she was probably a boy—"It'll pass," Harley had said—their eldest child still insisted on riding the heritage float as an Amish man, not an Amish girl.

Sheriff Kick put the beard aside. Things had only become more turbulent at home. She had not been able to work less, and Denise had seen Harley twice more on the Ring Hollow Dam spout with his blond girlfriend.

"And what's in the envelope?"

"Um. Well. Junk."

"Who's it from?"

Rhino flushed and tugged his own beard. "It's just some whack-job," he assured her. "It's nothing."

Bob Check, still absorbed, continued, " 'The wolf, called Fenrir, was the child of Loki, another war god, who with the giantess Angrbroda also fathered the serpent Jormungand, who slays Thor during Ragnarok—' "

"Give me the envelope, Rhino."

She held it, studied it, and entered an uneasy state of puzzlement. It bore her name and the address of the Bad Axe County Public Safety Building. In bigger letters it declared its purpose: A BOUNTY ON YOUR HEAD.

"A bounty? On *my* head? For what?"

"Yes," Rhino said, "your head. It says, if you read it, for treason."

Bob stopped reciting from his phone. "Treason?" he repeated, scowling.

She smiled at him and said, "I guess they finally caught me selling cheese recipes to North Korea."

A grimace tightened the old farmer's weather-beaten face. As her champion on the county board, Chairperson Check was protective.

"Yeah," she said, still trying to defuse him, "and I confess to once owning a Honda. And loving it. They finally caught up to me, Bob. I'm a traitor. Sorry to let you down."

"Horseshit," he growled back. "A bounty on your head? Paper terrorism. Isn't that what they call it?"

"I guess. Yes."

She touched the envelope with all ten fingers and took a deep breath. The enhancement of her conflict with Harley was one aspect of her attempt to charge Kenny with intimidation for his stunt with the flag. Here was the other: she had become an internet topic and a target. While she was working last Saturday, Opie had sprinted back from the mailbox in tears, holding a postcard addressed to "Sheriff Heidi Snowflake" with a handwritten excerpt from U.S. Code § 2381, the one that reads *Whoever, owing allegiance to the United States, levies war against them . . . is guilty of treason and shall suffer death . . .* On the other side of the postcard was a picture of a kitten. It had taken Harley all afternoon to settle Opie down.

But for now, for the sake of Bob Check's blood pressure, she needed to make the bounty into a joke.

"Whoever this is, they overestimate me. I'm way too busy to sell out the people of the United States. Maybe when I'm retired."

"Malarkey. Pure horseshit malarkey."

She touched his arm to calm him. One heart attack was enough for the sweet old man. "It's OK, Bob. It's called trolling. We're going to ignore it."

Rhino stepped between her and Bob and opened her office window to a cool spring breeze that carried canned polka music from the fairgrounds across a just-planted soybean field. The festival would kick off in just over an hour. She and Bob Check were due to appear at the grand opening ceremony.

"Oh, and I forgot to tell you," Rhino said. "Augustus Pfaff called while you were in court. He wants to talk to you. He doesn't trust the rest of us. Only you."

"What about?"

She glanced at last week's newspaper, still in the pile on her desk. Mr. Pfaff had been interviewed in the *Bad Axe Broadcaster* about a self-published book he was going to launch tomorrow at the festival. She had skimmed the article. The book was about the region's unique round barns and how their story led the author into discoveries about the Underground Railroad and fugitive slaves who once settled in the Bad Axe.

"He said he's been threatened. He doesn't feel safe."

"Threatened by who? Why?"

"He wouldn't say. He wants you to read Czappa's incident report from this morning, and then he wants to talk to you."

"Czappa's report? What report?"

"Same question I had," Rhino said. "As far as I know, Czappa was on patrol along the river this morning. There is no report."

She glanced at her watch. Deputy Czappa was now on duty at the fairgrounds, until eight.

"I'll see both of them soon," she told Rhino. "I'll catch Mr. Pfaff when his band is on break and find out what's going on."

At last she focused on *a bounty on your head*. The envelope was postmarked two days ago in Oklahoma City. Inside was a single sheet. Bob Check leaned in to read along.

ATTENTION: SHERIFF HEIDI SNOWFLAKE. A BOUNTY
HAS BEEN ISSUED FOR YOUR DELIVERY DEAD OR
ALIVE FOR PUNISHMENT ON CHARGES OF DER-
ELICTION OF DUTY AND FAILURE TO UPHOLD THE
CONSTITUTION, CRIMES OF TREASON AGAINST THE
SOVEREIGN CITIZENS OF THE UNITED STATES. ADDI-
TIONAL CHARGES YOU MAY FACE INCLUDE ELECTION
FRAUD AND HATE CRIMES. HOW DO YOU PLEAD?

"Pure horseshit malarkey," the county board chair fumed. "Who
the hell?"

"Some whack-job," Rhino assured everyone again. "The flag thing
again. Some nutcase entertaining himself."

"How do I plead?" she asked.

"In what court?" Rhino wondered. "And how could you plead anything if you were delivered dead?" He took the document back. "And
why tip you off about it? This idiot can't even watch TV correctly. I'll
file it with the other stuff."

For a moment she stared away toward the window and listened
to the happy canned sound of the "Tick-Tock Polka" carried on the
sweet spring breeze. This was her favorite time of year. The Syttende
Mai was her favorite festival. She had two days off starting at 6:00
p.m., and she had sworn an oath to herself: take the two days off, for
real, and have fun with the family. Fortified by that, maybe she would
feel valid enough, as a mother and a wife, to straight-up demand that
Harley come clean: *Who is the blonde?*

"How do I plead?" she asked again. "I plead polka."

By late afternoon, a rattled Augustus Pfaff had taken three game cameras out of retirement and used a ladder to install them out of reach on trees along his driveway, for surveillance, and, if needed, for the recording of evidence. Into a fourth camera, already aimed conspicuously at the driveway but only for show, he loaded a battery.

He had found his shotgun in the barn, had cleaned it and loaded it, and had tried it out on a stump. The old double-barrel kicked harder than it used to. After four test blasts he could hardly raise his tuba shoulder. But the stump was nicely shredded.

The notion that he was needed to lead the Principals of Polka was self-aggrandizing bunk. He had eventually admitted this to himself under the calming influence of some chilled schnapps. Those old farts would be just fine without him. But they did need a tuba.

The cord on his phone receiver was so long that after he dialed Royal Strander, Pfaff could walk through his pantry into the dining room and touch a fresh book on the table. His do-it-yourself cover design featured his clever title—*A Round Us: Once Upon a Time in the Bad Axe*—over his own photograph of one of the lovely round barns, designed a hundred years ago by a son of slaves, Alga Shivers.

"It's here!" he said when Royal answered.

"I'm happy for you, Gus. Congratulations."

"One hundred beautiful copies."

"And may you need to print many, many more."

"And thanks to you for all your help. But listen," Pfaff told his friend, "there was a bit of an incident this morning. I may have been attacked. I'm concerned about my books. I'm going to stay home tonight and guard the fort."

He heard no reply for a moment. Royal ran a gravel pit. Pfaff could hear a crusher working in the background.

"I was worried about that," Royal said at last. "Not everybody wants to know who they are."

But Pfaff was feeling brave and hearty on the schnapps. "Tough nuts," he said. "Anybody who wants to kill my story has to kill me too, right? First? Because it's all in my big old dizzy brain?"

His friend was quiet again. The rock crusher gobbled and spewed in the background. Royal had helped him parse out the clues to one of the juicier side stories in the history of the round barns.

Royal said gravely, "Call the sheriff, Gus. Don't take potluck with deputies like Czappa. Call her directly."

"Done," Pfaff replied. "Awaiting her response. And I'm loaded up for bear here. The only problem, my friend, is the festival. Somebody else has to play the tuba tonight."

————

When the call was over and Royal had agreed to take Pfaff's place at the festival grand opening, Pfaff was cleared to guard the fort. He dressed in his lederhosen, knee socks, and blouse, put on his suede shoes and his Tyrolean cap, for the defiant fun of it. He would party at home. He positioned himself on the front porch with his tuba, his loaded shotgun, and his chilled schnapps. The approach of hostile parties down his driveway would be discouraged by the game cameras. The shotgun would clean up any leaks. He committed to a regimen of vigilance, playing only twelve bars of oompah at a time before he stopped, took schnapps, and listened for gravel popping on the road.

Safe so far, he believed.

And so he oompahed and he sipped and he basked in his new authorship . . . until, at about 5:00 p.m., he flubbed a note and thought about the river behind his house.

The waterway.

Bad Axers drove everywhere. They drove to their mailboxes at the ends of their driveways. Never walk. Always use an engine and a road. But that was the good Bad Axers, the normal ones, not the ones with criminal intent.

Then his phone rang inside. The sheriff, finally. He left his shotgun on the porch. Just as he answered the call—"Gus Pfaff, author, speaking. With whom do I share the pleasure?"—he looked out beyond his kitchen window and saw the cell phone that made the call dropped into the pocket of a man wearing a blaze-orange three-hole ski mask.

Then a rifle rose to aim through the glass.

5

Syttende Mai meant the "seventeenth of May."

What it referred to was Norwegian Constitution Day, a declaration of independence from Sweden that had occurred a little more than two hundred years ago. The Syttende Mai Festival in the Bad Axe, in Sheriff Kick's Irish German opinion, had been always been the best party in the coulees.

She loved it. When she was a kid she would drive up from Crawford County with her mom and dad and overdose herself on dance contests, costume parades, rodeo, carnival rides, pig wrestling, mass quantities of the Norwegian pudding rommegrot, fireworks, rosemaling and tatting and quilting, everybody's 4-H animals on display. The biggest thrill was seeing the hardworking grown-ups in her life, farmers hustling to get spring crops in, taking time off to roll out the barrel and, like the song said, have a barrel of fun.

She felt like a girl in a cop costume as she climbed the main festival stage before the microphone to perform the county sheriff's traditional duty.

First she counted down the kickoff in Norwegian: *"Fem! Fire! Tre! To! En! Festivalen!"* Next, she pointed to the band and shouted in German, *"Eins, zwei, drei . . ."*

And wham! Trumpet and tuba and trombone and flügelhorn and accordion and banjo and clarinet and drums, the full Principals of Polka exploded into "Roll Out the Barrel." A breath, a hop, and a happy whoop later, the sheriff was whirling across the stage in the embrace of county board chairperson Bob Check.

The celebrity duo tore it up. Quickly the spectators paired off and got busy. Up came the hoots and the hollers. The opening fireworks popped. The beer barrels were tapped. Bratwurst hit the hot grills. They danced! Bob Check was a dervish, almost frighteningly strong, just like Sheriff Kick's dad and grandpa had been. On one whirl, she glimpsed her three darlings in their father's care. On the next spin she threw a quick wave. A few twirls later, dizzy and flushed by the rusty joy inside her, she reminded herself: talk to Augustus Pfaff.

But as she skipped close to the Principals of Polka, expecting Mr. Pfaff's red face and puffing cheeks, his happy feet, she realized he wasn't there. Royal Strander was playing the tuba. Not Augustus Pfaff.

As the song ended, the kids raced to embrace her.

"Mommy! Mommy! Mommy!"

She stiffly hugged Harley. Over his shoulder she saw his mom, Grammy Belle, behind the snow fence surrounding the beer tent, already with a cup in hand.

"You smell good," she told her husband. "Is that cologne?"

"I just took a shower. Are you off duty?"

"Yes, I'm off."

"Are you *really* off duty?"

"I said I was, Harley." It was like this every day now. "Why do you ask? Did you have other plans?"

A camera flashed, caught their faces. Harley put his arm around her, as if to deny their bad vibe. He felt her phone buzz beneath her badge.

"Go ahead," he said.

"Do I need permission?"

"I just mean don't feel bad about it."

"Thanks." She hit TALK. "Yes?"

By now Rhino was off duty. Denise was on.

"Heidi, I know, I know, I know," Denise began, sounding a little out of breath. "I'm so sorry to bother you. I know this is family time, and you really need that, but I think you should take the call that just came from the ER at the hospital."

Her heart both sank and accelerated. This seemed like her job in a nutshell. She stepped away, stood against the livestock barn.

"I'm listening."

"Wait, it's the hospital again. Hang on."

She leaned back against the rough boards. Harley was watching her. Then he tried to distract the kids by pointing toward the teacup carnival ride. Was this about Augustus Pfaff?

"OK, Heidi, are you ready?"

"I'm ready. Is it Mr. Pfaff?"

Denise paused.

"No," she said. "No, not Mr. Pfaff. We have another assault. Some Hispanic kid got beat up and dumped behind the hospital. He's unconscious. He's got no ID. We have another Juan Doe."

Harley was already leading the children away.

"Have Morales meet me there," she said.

6

"Gus Pfaff, author, speaking. With whom do I share the pleasure?"

The bullet had crashed through the window above his kitchen sink, slugged his right shoulder, and knocked him to the floor on a spurt of arterial blood.

Augustus Pfaff had crawled, dragging the phone, beneath his round kitchen table and braced his back against the wall, gasping from his glass-shredded face as the blood puddle from his bullet wound grew larger. His shoulder felt enormous and hot.

The back door slammed in.

"*Author speaking.*" The voice mocked him. "Lying bag of dicks."

From under the table Pfaff saw muddy knee-length boots and a red plastic gas can with a yellow spout. A flashing ax hacked the phone cord in clean pieces. The boots stomped away, leaving the gas can. He heard his computer tip over in the den, then a sound like harsh wing-beats as his precious books and papers began to fly about.

Slow him down, Pfaff thought, feeling his own blood expand around his legs. *Somehow slow him down.*

The attacker tore the den apart. Then he went upstairs. Maybe he was looking for a fireproof safe box, Pfaff thought, that should exist but didn't. He had never thought about security. Every year for three decades the senior class had toilet-papered his trees or tied cans to his car bumper or put strange items in his mailbox, but he had never once been the target of anything serious, and he had never once felt insecure.

He found himself staring woozily at the gas can left behind on the kitchen floor.

His attacker stomped back downstairs. Pfaff's first words came out too feebly to be heard. He drew a painful breath and used his tuba lungs.

"It's all!" Another breath. "In the cloud!"

This was a lie. He had put nothing in "the cloud." He was unsure what "the cloud" was. He was only sure that people would now tell him "you should have put your data in the cloud." He sucked another breath.

"You can't destroy my work!"

His voice was a sticky, fading thing, a splutter and a croak.

"It's all . . . in the . . . cloud!"

He heard a mutter: "Fucking cuck. Sit there and bleed. You'll be in the cloud."

Sinking back against his kitchen wall, looking up for help but seeing only leaf struts on the underside of the table, Augustus Pfaff heard the whir and grind of his old computer booting up.

7

"We found him right there by the dumpsters."

She had stopped her Charger on the wide asphalt driveway behind the brand-new Blackhawk Memorial Hospital building, on a rise at the east end of Farmstead.

She stepped out, chewing Nicorette, four milligrams. It was that time of day. The rush filled her chest and crinkled up her neck into her ear canals. Sunset across the ridgetops turned her freckled face a tangerine hue and cast shadows a hundred feet across the cornfield beyond.

"Who found him?"

"Lucas. He's our radiation tech."

"Get Lucas, please."

Out into the sprouted corn trailed the knobby tire ruts of a vehicle with a narrow axle. The ruts flowed inward with the rows, then broke across them toward the dumpster and stopped ten feet short of the asphalt.

The sheriff squinted against the fiery orange at the corner of the building. The security camera was about twenty feet up, aimed directly at the dumpster. She turned back to the field. She was raised on a farm. She knew dirt. The little curds kicked up by the vehicle's tires were dry. The ruts were hours old. They went back the way they came. The victim had been dropped off, and not recently, by someone driving an off-road vehicle.

"This is Lucas Larsen, sheriff."

"What were you doing out here, Lucas?"

"Calling my girlfriend."

"Show me the call, please."

He had made a call and discovered the injured man at 5:37 p.m., less than forty minutes ago.

"Take me to the security office, please."

The footage from the camera on the corner of the building told a harrowing story. The recording had to be reversed all the way to 4:34 that morning before there was anything to look at. At this point, a pair of close-set headlights appeared out of a swale across the field. Just as she thought, it was an off-road vehicle. In fast motion, the ORV's headlights raced forward, paused, and raced back, the vehicle retreating in reverse. A pale gray lump remained beside the dumpster.

"I must have been taking a break," the security guy mumbled. "Twelve-hour shifts and all."

"Now play it in slow motion."

But there wasn't much more to see. He had lain there for the next fourteen hours.

Inside the ER, Sheriff Kick's stomach tightened. The young man had been mauled. His eyes were swollen shut, his nose was busted, and his top lip was split.

"Can you hear me? This is Sheriff Kick of Bad Axe County."

His eyes split, then closed again.

Did he speak English? If not, she was stuck until the arrival of David Morales, her new chief deputy, replacing Olaf "the Handsome" Yttri. By chance, Morales, whom she had hired away from Dallas County, Texas, was also handsome, but more the point of her hire, he was from outside the Bad Axe, he had experience and a good record, and he could speak Spanish with the new immigrants who worked at Vista Farms.

She came closer to the injured young man, lifted the sheet, and saw deep bruises and dried blood on brown skin that looked scratched by the gravel and glass beside the dumpster. The wicked-looking contusion on his right side was familiar: broken ribs. Inexplicable to her were the shreds of white tape on his wrists. She cleared her throat.

"Can you tell me your name?"

He shook his head faintly side to side.

"*¿Nombre . . . tu nombre?*"

That was bad Spanish, but clear enough what she meant. He shook his head again.

"*¿Qué pasó?*"

Or was it supposed to be *pasa*?

"*¿Quién te . . . quién tu . . . ?*"

Come on, Heidi. Morales had been teaching her. She had made "language facilitation" part of his job description.

"Who did this to you?" she blurted.

"*¿Quién te hizo esto?*" came the voice of Morales from behind her as he hustled into the room, small and sleek, with a nifty chinstrap beard that he drove two towns over to get properly trimmed. As chief deputy, he handled the night shift, and he had just come on duty.

"*Gracias,*" she said. "You saved me."

"*De nada.*"

"But he's not talking."

She walked around the bed and studied the multicolored skull tattoo on the young man's left shoulder. Her nod told Morales to look at it.

"Is this a gang thing? A skull?"

He paused about two seconds, a thing he did when she said something he considered uninformed. "Sure, if you consider the Aztecs a gang."

"Hey, you promised not the beat me up," she said. "Down in Crawford County we had a cow named Queen Isabella. That's about all I knew of Hispanic culture coming into this."

"Latino. Or Latinx."

"OK. I'm working on it. But what do you make of this?"

"Well," Morales responded, "two beatings of Latino men, both cases where they appear to have been helpless and beyond fighting back. I'd say we have a situation."

"Yes. I agree," she said.

These were heavy words she had to pry from her heart. Last month, about a week after Kenny's flag stunt, an undocumented Salvadoran had been ambushed on the Great River Road outside the Pronto station, his face smashed with a blunt object. As their investigation produced his name—Nelson Flores, employed at Vista Farms—but no suspects or motives, not even robbery, Morales had developed the theory that someone driving past the Pronto had seen a little brown man standing there, alone and defenseless, and for philosophical reasons had pulled over and teed off.

"Who would do that?" she had asked at the time.

"*Que linda eres*," Morales had answered after his trademark pause.

"What does that mean?"

"You're so cute."

So naïve, he had meant.

She said now, "I do agree, but also this seems different. These are multiple wounds from a sustained beating. Maybe multiple attackers. And nobody bothered to drop the first guy off behind the hospital."

Morales moved to the other side of the young man's bed and peeked beneath the sheet.

"Maybe another boat anchor," he said.

She gnawed her gum and felt annoyed by his attachment to the idea of a boat anchor as the weapon in the first assault. He got the idea because last week a Crime Busters tip had come in. A mushroom hunter had reported finding a small boat anchor, a ten-pounder, bell-style, not much bigger than a cereal bowl, on a rope that could swing it, and possibly with dried blood on it, in a ravine near the Pronto station where Flores was assaulted. The citizen had attached a cell phone picture of the anchor and its tail of yellow rope. Rhino had put the tipster's information out on the closed channel, and Deputy Larry

Czappa had radioed to say that he was close by. The tip was a hoax, Czappa had concluded. There was no boat anchor.

"Can we let go of the boat anchor?" she asked Morales now. "It's a clumsy thing to hit somebody with. And Deputy Czappa didn't find one."

"Didn't he?"

"What do you mean?"

"Why would someone make that up, stage a photograph, and call us?"

Morales dropped the sheet back over the young man and looked at her. "We have two assaults now," he said. "So, OK, if we think the boat anchor is a fake tip, then the tipster is deliberately obstructing our investigation. We go after him, or her. If it's a real tip, and Czappa didn't find the anchor, then somebody else is obstructing. Why don't we follow up?"

"Are you saying Czappa tampered with evidence? Why would he do that?"

He muttered something in Spanish.

"Am I being cute again?"

"*Tal vez.*"

Maybe.

Morales touched the young man lightly on his shoulder. He spoke quietly at some length into his ear. The young man's lips split painfully, and he began to whisper back. They spoke for only a minute before a nurse interrupted.

"Time to go," she said brusquely, snapping up the brake on the bed. "He's going in for X-rays and an MRI."

The nurse steered him out.

Morales said, "His name is Carlos Castillo. He's twenty-one, from Mexico. He overstayed a work visa two years ago and was recruited up here from Texas in March. He shovels shit at Vista Farms. He got hurt trying to earn extra money in a prize fight."

"A prize fight? What does that mean?"

"At a fight club."

"Here, in the Bad Axe? A fight club?"

"They're everywhere," said Morales. "Eight hundred percent increase in the last five years. Back in Dallas County we had six of them. Some were just fight clubs. But three were whites only, white-power supremacists, and considered themselves paramilitary training camps. The FBI was watching them. They recruit in online chat rooms. They provoke. They incite. They troll. They pick fights, but only easy ones they can win."

She nearly said, *Paramilitary training for which war? Here, in little old Bad Axe?*

But that might be cute.

Instead, she said, "I'll talk to Czappa."

8

Back at the post office in Farmstead, during the disposition of his collected mail, Ivy Kafka discovered yet one more in his endless parade of mistakes.

He double-checked.

Damn it, *now* he was seeing it correctly.

The plain white business envelope was clearly sent *FROM: Mr. Augustus Pfaff*, who lived along Ivy's substitute route that day, in his old farmhouse on Pinch Hollow Road. But the letter was also addressed *TO: Mr. Augustus Pfaff*, at the same address on Pinch Hollow. What he had failed to notice earlier was that it was postmarked already. Thinking he had nothing to deliver, he had skipped Mr. Pfaff's mailbox. The envelope was therefore a failed delivery, not a collection.

"Dummy."

Emily Swiggum frowned at Ivy across the sorting room. Her little nose crinkled. She was sniffing. He put his head down and, breathing shallowly, resumed disposition of his mail. Before returning to the post office, rather than risk missing beers for a buck, he had spent forty minutes and four dollars in the beer tent.

"What's the problem, Francis? Let me see."

She took the envelope to examine it. Ivy held his breath and drummed his dirty fingers. He listened to live polka racketing from the festival grounds. Any minute now beers would be three-fifty.

"You didn't collect this."

His postmistress used a neatly trimmed thumbnail to underline the postmark.

"You were supposed to deliver it."

"My fault," agreed Ivy. "I didn't look at the postmark."

"Mr. Pfaff sent it to himself. Probably a poor man's copyright. Are you familiar with that? It's really an old-fashioned concept."

Ivy spoke with care. "I am not familiar, no."

"People do a poor man's copyright when they're trying to protect ownership of intellectual property, like when they've written a book. Did you know that Mr. Pfaff has written a book?"

"Actually, I did not."

"The U.S. Postal Service does not recommend this practice, however, since it's not legally binding."

She looked at the back of the envelope. An *X* was inked across the sealed flap.

"Sure enough. It must be something related to his book. He's launching it tomorrow. He's got a stand set up at the fairgrounds. I can't wait to get my copy. Did you know that escaped slaves used to live here?"

"That would be new information to me," said Ivy to the back of his fist. Her small cute nose was reeling in the scent of his one-dollar beers.

Thankfully her phone rang. Ivy's thoughts drifted back to the festival. Mr. Pfaff led the Principals of Polka. He could take the letter there, right? He still had ten bucks. That was almost three more beers.

"Francis?"

When his attention resurfaced, Emily Swiggum was handing back the letter.

"You have to redeliver it."

"Can't I just take it to him at the fairgrounds?"

"Have you been drinking?"

"OK, OK, I'll take it back to his mailbox."

9

A long season of narrowing darkness had ensued, of slow and muddled thought, of freezing cold and impossible thirst. During this time, the round tabletop over Augustus Pfaff's head had come to be a shelter and a comfort.

Round barns.

This is where his research had begun.

Alga Shivers's round barns were truly lovely artifacts for their architecture alone. But he had found the round barns to be things of beauty for other reasons too.

Ah, beauty. Ah, yes, reasons. His beloved house had been torn entirely apart, he guessed, in search of passwords to the cloud, for safe boxes, for anything from his research that might survive a fire. Now at last the boots approached. Their mud was dry. The ax broke the plane of the tabletop. Suddenly Augustus Pfaff understood its higher purpose. The ax would record a truth. It would extract evidence against future forgetfulness and lies. His attacker wanted boasting rights, proof of the story that he would tell later.

Well . . . he couldn't save himself. That was obvious. Pfaff drifted into wider, softer worries. Who would ever know his careful history of bygone harmonies, of a lost time in the Bad Axe when white and black families were united by the power of the round . . .

Of the lovely round . . .

Alga Shivers's astonishing and revolutionary round . . .

Ancient now, but still standing . . . still connecting, uniting, reminding . . .

"Time to shut your lying suckhole."

Had he been talking?

"You'll never find what I buried where it won't burn," lied Pfaff.

A hot hand closed on his cold ankle and yanked him out through the slick of his own blood. The ax flashed down again and halved his left arm at the elbow. A boot kicked the arm away. He hardly felt it leave.

The rifle reappeared. From a straight-down angle its barrel probed his face. So it was time. His journey ended here. His final brainwork was a fantastic, futuristic image: a larva breaking up from deep earth, rising into human form, and singing.

Hurry! Hurry!

On muscular instinct he scooted backward under the shelter of the round table. The rifle muzzle followed, found his teeth, shattered them, and touched his throat.

Then it was all blown away, bloody bits into the mists of history.

10

"There's a lotta old barns."

"I mean a round one. Still standing. I'm looking for a round one."

The young man is jittery and dry-lipped, his whole body buzzing from the longest ride he's ever taken. He is getting close, he hopes. A nearby gunshot startles him, hurries his pulse, raises his chin and his eyebrows.

To which the old man, who seems like every old white man, cranky and hostile for no apparent reason, somehow offended and defiant, answers, "Turkey season."

"OK. Good to know."

"Turkeys everywhere these days."

"Sure. I see. So, yeah, an old round barn, still standing, somewhere near here." This is his habit, not letting things go. "My granny told me so. In Lyric Valley, she said." He points. "And the sign on the store says Lyric Valley Pit Stop. So—"

Another gunshot. "Take that, you turkey bastard," says the old man.

He hopes to get out of Bad Axe County by dark. He should leave this old man alone and ask someone else, but he has this sticky thing, this stubbornness that comes from inner anger.

"You haven't heard about a round barn?"

"Nope."

"An old one, a historical barn, like a hundred years old?"

"Nope."

"Near here somewhere. Lyric Valley?"

"Nope."

"Seriously?" He points where the intersection spills gravel onto the highway, where the sign reads SHIVERS ROAD. "Round. Designed by somebody named Shivers."

"Nope."

He floats a wise-ass test question: "Does the bear shit in the woods?"

"Nope."

"OK, well, thanks. You keep on having a nice evening."

"What kind of nutjack doesn't wear a helmet?" the old man answers him.

He feels the milky eyes on his back as he rolls his stepdad's yellow Honda Valkyrie away from FREE AIR and toward the gas station store, offering turkey permits and thirty-packs of beer.

There he kickstands the heavy bike. He's a big, strong kid, handsome, but softer than he looks and less sure than he acts. His mid-tone brown skin is infused with a dry-lavender pallor that suggests his recent struggles with drugs and depression and displays his general lack of vitality. He has copied an NBA hairstyle that he knows would look better on a self-assured multimillionaire. Up close, beneath the kinks and curls, his face is distinguished by a scattering of large, vaguely rusty freckles. His eyes are gray green with dark circles underneath.

He takes stock. His odometer tells him he is 189.7 miles from Milwaukee. His phone tells him it is 71 degrees at 6:12 p.m., with sunset at 8:19 p.m. He has two bars of reception. He has one text message from his mother, a busy radiologist, sent two hours ago.

Where r u?

He puts the phone away in his jacket pocket. He is at the intersection of Highway 53 and Shivers Road, the borderline of Bad Axe County, immersed in a landscape so green that it looks warm to the touch. He sniffs sharply, intakes a sweet smell. He turns and finds pink-white blossoms on old apple trees climbing a grassy hillside. His granny said she remembers that Bad Axe County was pretty as a picture. He'll give her that. Pretty as a picture.

The door of Lyric Valley Pit Stop opens with a harsh buzz. He keeps his hands out of his pockets. Then he clasps them behind his back to show he's not grabbing stuff. Then he shoves one hand into a pocket because he thinks he looks nervous. With the other hand he carries a can of Rockstar to the counter.

He begins, "Nice evening. Sure can smell those apple blossoms."

Though the clerk has been watching him, she answers, "Any gas?"

"No, ma'am, just the drink. And directions, if you don't mind."

She drops change from a sanitary height into his palm and says, "Do my best."

"I'm trying to find a place called Lyric Valley."

"You're in it."

"I saw online there's a historical marker somewhere."

"Never saw any historical marker."

"Also there's supposed to be a round barn built by Alga Shivers. I figured I might be close to it, since that out there is Shivers Road."

"Oh," she says. He perceives an eye roll in her voice. "That."

The barn survives on a ridge a half mile up Shivers Road. It is smaller than he imagined, only about sixty feet in diameter. It glows like an old ember in the strong early sunset. It might have once looked taller. For sure it once was level. Now it slumps away from the sun, sunken into a fold of bursting grass and closing dandelions, surrounded by a windbreak of stunted evergreens and brown waves of tilled earth.

His granny has commanded him to take a picture, since she has never actually seen one of Alga Shivers's barns. When she was younger she was out here twice, she said, first trying to uproot her cousin, Vernice Freeman, and bring her to safety back in Milwaukee, and a second time to help Vernice when she was sick. She was reminded of the round barns, his granny said, by a man who came from Bad Axe County to ask about her cousin, because he was writing a book about the barns, and Vernice Freeman was going to be in the book.

"OK, Granny. A picture. Here goes."

He turns the bike off and stands it. He readies his phone and takes a few steps to get the best angle—and sure enough, the thing is round. That seems weird, but cool. The barn's stone foundation is spaced with wooden doors that seem the right size for trolls. The structure builds upward in russet bricks laid in perfect curvature to a ribbed silver roof. At its peak, the roof sprouts a brick mini barn, then a mini silver roof, then a weathervane, bent and still.

KEEP OUT.

As he aims his phone, he wonders: *Keep out of what?*

———

Several hundred yards away, in a sunken turnout littered with beer cans, he finds the historical marker. It is overgrown and faded. Some kind of thriving brier has thrust its tough stem between the marker's leg posts and pried it unevenly from the ground. The raised lettering once stood out in white paint.

> NEAR HERE LIES LYRIC VALLEY, WHERE, IN THE 1850s,
> FUGITIVE SLAVES SETTLED AND FARMED, SOCIALIZING
> WELL WITH EUROPEAN IMMIGRANTS AND ESTABLISH-
> ING THE REGION'S FIRST INTEGRATED SCHOOLS,
> CHURCHES, AND SPORTING TEAMS. IN LYRIC VALLEY
> AT ONE TIME COULD BE FOUND SEVERAL EXAMPLES
> OF THE ROUND BARN, THE INNOVATIVE DESIGN OF
> ALGA SHIVERS, SON OF A TENNESSEE SLAVE. THE AD-
> VENT OF THE AUTOMOBILE, AND OTHER ELEMENTS
> OF CHANGE, LED TO THE GRADUAL DECLINE OF THE
> RURAL AFRICAN AMERICAN POPULATION.

He takes a picture for his granny. *Decline* seems an odd word. Other than his own partial and inadequate dose, he hasn't caught one whiff of blackness in the hundred miles west of Madison. *Decline* and *disappear completely* seem like two different things.

And *the automobile* caused the blacks to leave? How? And what does this mean: *other elements of change?*

But the sun is dropping quickly. If he's going to find the man who interviewed his granny about her cousin Vernice, he needs to move. His granny said a strange thing before he left the nursing home in South Milwaukee. Maybe it was just one of those random things that an old woman utters. As he left, she had said to him, "Maybe you're the one."

"The one?"

"Her jar fly," she had said, and closed her eyes, adding, "Mm-hm."

"What's a jar fly, Granny?"

"Long time after it's been buried, a jar fly comes back."

That was all she said. Just now, the moment spooks him.

He gets lost then. He rides back down Shivers Road to the highway intersection. But he doesn't want to bother the clerk. He believes his phone can find *RR512 Pinch Hollow Road.*

He has no idea where he is when his reception drops off. He is a suburban kid, all digital, no innate powers of navigation. The red vector of the sunset tells him nothing. He turns away from it, thinking he'll retrace his route back to Lyric Valley Pit Stop, but by accident of disorientation he drops into a different, deeper coulee, threaded with a single gravel road and already dim with evening shadow. He feels the cooler air against his nervous sweat.

He stops on an iron bridge across a creek. Bats and swallows veer about his head. He feels annoyed now, endangered when he didn't choose to be. But it's not fair to blame his granny. In the first place it was Dr. Aster who insisted that he pay her a visit. Maybe the ninety-five-year-old granddaughter of slaves could help him figure himself out. Maybe a woman with his granny's wisdom could help him answer his big question: why—when so many other mixed kids like him just deal—why is it that his black self and his white self are tearing him apart?

In two-tone dusk light he raises his arm to flag down a battered red pickup that hammers around a curve, coming at him. The truck tows a strange-looking trailer, spined and ribbed upward, like a place to stack something, but empty. The truck's windshield is dust-caked and rock-starred. Too late the driver sees the Valkyrie taking up too much space between the iron rails. The truck screeches on bad brakes, clips a bridge post, and skids to a stop. The trailer racks its bones and jackknifes into the ditch. Dust chases over.

"What in the goddamn hell."

The man's face is bloated, sheened with sweat and tufted with a tobacco-stained soul patch. He wears a dirty green hat and blue-mirrored sunglasses. Red-blond hair grows thickly down the back of his neck. Both hands grip the twisted wheel.

"You own this road, do ya?"

"I'm sorry."

"Goddamn. This ain't even my own truck to bung up."

"I'm sorry. I got lost. I'm just looking for a man's house."

After a long stare, the driver says, "A man's house to do what?"

"I'm supposed to give him something. And meet him, I guess."

Dirty hands slide back to center on the steering wheel.

"Meet who? Who's him?"

"Uh, just a second."

He paddles with his heels off the bridge and dismounts the bike to open its saddlebag. The man's book tells about the fugitive slaves, like the historical marker said, including the family of Alga Shivers, the man who built the round barns. The author had mailed the manuscript in a box for his granny to approve. His granny is mostly blind and never looked at it. *Take it back to him and have a visit out there,* she said. *Look around and learn. It's just pretty as a picture.*

"Augustus Pfaff," he reads from the box. "On Pinch Hollow Road."

The man puts one hand out his window. "I'll take it to him."

They meet eyes for a few long seconds. There's a certain kind of white man's face that is a fun-house mirror to him, where he sees his true self distorted. But he will not survive, Dr. Aster advises, if he lets others define him.

"No, thanks. I just need to get pointed in the right direction."

The man responds with a slow grin. He sits with that for a weird few moments. He lifts a beer can from between his legs and spits into it. He twists and looks behind him. Then he acts almost friendly.

"OK. What you do is you turn around," he says, "same way I'm going, take this road all the way up to that ridge over there, go left, second intersection is Shivers Road, turn right there and go all the way until you hit the state highway, there's a little gas station, turn left onto the highway, and keep going. That'll put you right where you want to be."

"Thanks. I appreciate it. Have a nice evening."

He lets the truck get way ahead, gone around a corner, so the dust can settle.

But this never feels right. He reads every sign after Shivers Road along the way and never sees Pinch Hollow Road. The directions lead him into a little town called Farmstead, where there is some kind of festival underway.

He shuts down and sits at the roadside hearing polka, watching a mini roller coaster, watching a horse prance in a rodeo ring, watching tractors line up for some event, hearing a PA announcer call out names.

He gets a chill. Weird. Among all the other names, he feels his has just been called.

Of course, it hasn't been. He is positive it hasn't been. No one knows him here.

But his name is Shivers.

Same as the road sign and the historical marker.

Same as the man who built the barns.

Neon Michael Shivers.

11

Sheriff Kick found Deputy Czappa watching the ax throw, a new attraction, five throws for five bucks, adults only, prizes for bull's-eyes but no doubt the axes were wonky. Ax throwing was a tavern sport now, but this was a carnival game.

"I need to talk to you about the boat anchor."

"What boat anchor?"

Height-wise, she came up to about Larry Czappa's broom-brown mustache. She stepped in with her chin up, holding eye contact. Czappa raised his mustache over large yellowed teeth, flashing his annoying *Who me?* smile.

"Right," she said. "If there was never a boat anchor, like you said, then I wanted to get your thoughts on why someone called in and told us they had found one and marked it for us. And then that person even texted us a photo. How do you explain that?"

Czappa crossed his furry arms. Back in March, he had been the first one to wear his short-sleeved uniform shirt. He was the department's record holder for traffic stops in a month. He loved how he was hated. That kind of guy.

"Huh. Explain? Yeah, well, sometimes it's just loony tunes out there. Lotta crazies."

He watched an ax leave the grip of a big farm girl. It cartwheeled toward the target, glanced off the side, and fell into the grass. Her friends booed.

"Because the thing about Crime Busters," the sheriff reminded Czappa, "is that the tips are anonymous, *unless they are intentionally false*, in which case they become crimes themselves, and then we are allowed to trace the tipsters. Right?"

The girl pushed back boisterously as she retrieved the ax. In her league, with her own throwing ax, she *did not suck*!

"If we suspect a tip is a lie, or, a like you said, a hoax," the sheriff continued, "we can investigate and prosecute."

"I never said it was a hoax," Czappa claimed, though he had said exactly that. He turned his gaslighting smile on again and shook his head ever so faintly to suggest that once more she was being snowflakey, out of touch with the real world, like thinking she could successfully charge Kenny Kick with intimidation. "I just said I didn't find anything."

"Do you think you might have missed it? Should I send someone back to double-check? Or should we put the wheels in motion to prosecute the tipster?"

"You're the boss. Why ask me?"

"I figured you might know."

"Know what?"

"The right thing to do."

She waited for Czappa's eyes as he watched the girl's next throw. The Principals of Polka had launched into the "Too Fat Polka." Royal Strander played loud and fast on the tuba.

"Well, OK," she said. "We'll prosecute the tipster. Let's move on. Augustus Pfaff wants me to look at an incident report by you that doesn't exist. What can you tell me about that? Where is that report?"

Czappa watched the big girl chuck her third ax. He released a snort at her third bad result.

"Busy day. I didn't have time to write it yet."

"I understand. What happened?"

"Basically, someone played a prank on him. You know, one of his ex-students. He likes that. Then someone was turkey hunting on the hillside near his house and he thought he'd been shot because there was a bullet hole in his mailbox. Who knows when the mailbox got shot. Not today. Senior moment, Sheriff."

"But he didn't call us, Rhino said. You just showed up. So why were you there?"

"I heard he left the kickoff breakfast in a panic. I was worried. Welfare check."

She let her eyes say what she was thinking: *A self-initiated welfare check does not sound one bit like the Larry Czappa I have come to know.*

"File the report, Deputy. Put every detail in writing. Before you go off duty."

"Yes, Mom," he said.

"Excuse me?"

"Oops. Yes, ma'am."

She turned and saw her kids were coming.

"It's 'Yes, *Sheriff*.' "

Backing away with his hands raised, Czappa gave her more gas. "Whoa! Sorry!"

"Mommy, Mommy, Mommy!"

They bounded up with Harley on their heels. This was the replay, they all thought, of the moment after the opening polka with Bob Check, when she had been called away to the hospital. *Now* she was all theirs.

She embraced them and listened. Taylor had popped a balloon with a dart and won a plastic monkey. Dylan had dropped his funnel cake, but Opie had shared hers, and then Dylan had done the teacup ride by himself. Opie noted that she was too mature for any rides, but she had found a purse and taken it to lost-and-found. They had visited the boys' competition rabbits in the 4-H barn. Conditions there were satisfactory, Opie had determined. She had somehow dressed herself, God love her, like a retired farmer driven into town by his grandkids to the festival: her plaid flannel pajama top buttoned squarely at her throat; stiff jeans, shapeless and cuffed; her leather boots with waffled soles; and all of her pretty red-blond curls tucked under a mashed-in orange hat with black lettering declaring she was *CHORE BOY*.

"Mommy, can we all go together on the teacup ride?"

"Umm . . . just a sec."

"Hi, hon, how's it going?"

She took Harley aside. She noticed again that he smelled unusually good, extra Irish Spring, and she remembered Denise's joke: *He starts bathing twice a week.*

"I'm sure you noticed Royal Strander's playing the tuba. Something's up with Mr. Pfaff. I'm headed out to Pinch Hollow for a visit."

"Is something wrong? Can't you call him?"

"Denise has been trying. His line is out of service. That's why I'm going out there."

"Pinch Hollow, there and back, is an hour."

"Yup."

"So, we'll see you . . . when?"

She noticed that her head ached for nicotine. Gum was calling.

"You'll see me when you see me."

He winced.

"You sure do smell nice," she told him again, and then the kids invaded.

"Can we, Mommy? Can we all go on the teacup ride together?"

As she looked across their little heads at the long line to the ride, their fresh-scented daddy let them down.

"Kids, I'm sorry," he began solemnly, "but a man might need help. Well, you know Mr. Pfaff, my old teacher, the funny man who dances with his tuba. And it's Mommy's job to make sure everybody is safe. . . ."

Her job, her life, felt like balancing on a greased ball with her eyes closed while people took potshots.

"So now she has to leave again. . . ."

12

Neon Michael Shivers plunges from bright early dusk into the hollows, all in shadow.

Following his new directions, he slaloms around chuckholes as gravel rushes under, popping against the underbody of the Valkyrie. On creek-side curves he passes green meadows. He drops lower. In patches of ground fog, his visibility shortens to a gauzy few hundred feet. He is startled by a deer on the road. He slows past a fisherman ungearing at his tailgate. Above, hunching like his own tense shoulders, ridges narrow the sky.

He pauses on the same iron bridge. He was exactly here before.

If you'd just continued straight, said the girl in the Norwegian queen costume at the festival. She was tall, blond as butter, refreshingly blunt, not unpretty, a girl he might talk to. But he had rushed away.

Now, in a sink of deep fog ahead appears a flickering light, tossing and bobbing as if on waves. The image dizzies him. Is there a lake he hasn't seen, a boat approaching?

He shuts off the bike and hears a low racket, a friction of crude mechanical parts, like oarlocks. He hears a crackling, then a snort. He restarts the bike in self-defense, turns on the headlight. Just where the beam touches the fog, two pairs of bestial eyes glint and roll hugely.

He stiffens. Whatever it is, he is blocking the bridge again.

Paddling backward with his heels, he makes out two tossing black heads with smoke-spewing nostrils . . . then understands he is looking at two black horses pulling a covert black buggy, and behind the buggy on a rope trails a massive plow horse with shaggy white feet, plodding with its head down and snorting. As Neon watches, his throat fills and his heart begins to wallop with the hoofbeats of the trailing horse. For several thrilling, time-skipping moments he is seeing the Underground Railroad, the far northern end, in action. He is witnessing slaves on the move under cover of fog. Incredible!

But that can't be. In a minute more, an Amish couple peers out as the buggy passes, a slight bearded man and a slighter bonneted woman, their wire-framed spectacles pooled with indigo light from the sky.

The man hoists a limp wave. Neon nods back. When they are gone down the road, he gets the bike rolling, and a few hundred yards past the bridge he finds the place.

From the mailbox that reads A. PFAFF, a driveway cuts steeply down from the road. He can't see what's below.

He kicks the bike into neutral and coasts down, skimming gravel with his boots and squeezing the brake, still not very good at handling on irregular surfaces. The driveway descends in an *S* shape. It bottoms out in a low spot patched by hand-poured concrete, then rounds between an old barn and a ramshackle farmhouse with one weak light aglow inside.

He knows right away he should leave and come back tomorrow.

But he didn't plan to stay the night out here. He doesn't want to. He wouldn't know where. He has told his stepdad he will have the Valkyrie back tonight.

His eyes adjust. In gardens about the house nod the faintly luminous heads of closed flowers. Large potted plants clog the front-porch steps, and smaller pots balance along the railing. In the yard are several more pots that seem to have been hurled there, shattered and emptied.

If the author is home, Neon thinks, he might be sleeping. He should go.

But though it's nearly dark at the bottom of the coulee, it seems too early for someone to be sleeping. And there is one lamp on, he thinks, shining from some inner room and fanning secondhand light out the half-open front door.

Well, how about this? Just leave the box. The book. Leave it on the porch. He doesn't need to meet Augustus Pfaff. He has seen the barn and the sign. Just return the book and go.

Neon stands the motorcycle. He removes the manuscript box from its saddlebag, crosses the un-mowed lawn, and climbs the porch steps. At the top he stares until he realizes he is looking at a big silver tuba, set down on its bell. On the porch floor beside the instrument are pages of sheet music blown or fallen from a music stand. Squared to the stand is an old wooden chair.

Now the moment tightens. There is an upended drinking cup on the porch floor, and a pair of eyeglasses.

He steps toward the half-open door. The porch floor squeaks. He freezes and turns his ear to the gap. From inside come faint sounds like an old appliance, like moving fluid, like a faucet spitting through an air lock.

Then he can't hear these sounds anymore. Instead, he hears one sharp click. The fanning light is gone. He hangs there another second. On the breath of the house he now smells gasoline and, he thinks, meat. A shotgun leans against the porch rail. He sets the box of pages down on the porch floor and backs down the steps.

He hesitates on the yard. Now he sees a dozen fresh holes dug in the grass, a shovel left behind. He thinks he hears someone moving inside, coming his way. Only in moments like these is he purely a black man.

Get the hell out! he tells himself. *Go!*

He shoves the bike back up the steep driveway and arrives gasping at the road. A small car tilts at the shoulder. A dull orange flasher rotates on its roof. It's not a cop. Still, someone is seeing him, and in what feels like ancient, primal fright, Neon kicks the bike alive, gears it, and rips away.

Back in Farmstead, adjacent to the festival, he passes a motel, a place he could stay. He keeps moving. But five miles up the highway, accelerating away from Bad Axe County, his granny's voice comes back to him.

Maybe you're the one . . . her jar fly . . .

What did she mean? Long buried, it comes back? What is a jar fly?

He hates to feel afraid, hates fear, somehow lives by its rules. He would like to be so much more than what he is. He would like to have one good reason.

He kicks into neutral, coasts to a stop. Then he turns the bike around.

13

One could never be sure anymore of the correct terminology.

This was Ivy's take on the matter of race.

As in, he did not speak of it, since he surely would say a disrespectful word, and even after all his loss and damage, he was still a Kafka, and Kafkas were respectful people.

But for sure what he saw—the extended wrists pushing a heavy yellow motorcycle, the anxious face sheened with sweat—was brown skin.

Other observations he could not so handily comprehend: the young man's spotless leather boots, untied and splayed open at their collars; his cream-colored quilt jacket that looked like long underwear; his homeless-looking mop of hair.

But otherwise he had clearly seen what Kenny called a brown.

And how did you explain a brown pushing a motorcycle up Mr. Pfaff's driveway in a rush at sundown, then blasting away like a bat out of hell? Did you not wonder, using Kenny's terminology, if that brown had been eating Mr. Pfaff's cookie?

Ivy left his Sportage at the road, placed the misdelivered envelope, both *from* and *to* Augustus Pfaff, into the mailbox, and, gripping his repurposed varmint pistol, he headed down Mr. Pfaff's driveway.

Cautiously he made the steep descent. The bats were out. The frogs sang. As he took the driveway's hairpin corner, he saw head-high on a tree trunk the tiny green light of a game camera. He saw a second camera on a different tree even higher, aimed down at the driveway. Then he saw two more cameras. Mr. Pfaff was on high security.

The driveway opened up. The house was dark but just that moment one small light winked on. The Syttende Mai was underway by now, the polka band was playing, so Ivy wondered why Mr. Pfaff seemed to be home.

A whisper stilled Ivy's boots. He raised his .38. But it was only the Little Bad Axe River issuing softly through the meadow behind the house.

Then, creeping closer, he was seeing things he didn't like.

Here were broken pots, plants strewn, and holes dug all over the yard.

Here on the porch floor was Mr. Pfaff's big silver tuba, standing on its bell.

Here were pages strewn from a music stand.

Here was a cup overturned, and a pair of eyeglasses right where they could be stepped on.

Here was a small postal box, the eleven-by-thirteen Priority mailer, addressed *from* Augustus Pfaff *to* someone named Harriet Shivers in Milwaukee. The box was postmarked almost four months ago. It was still sealed. Nearby, an ancient over-under shotgun leaned against the porch rail.

Mr. Pfaff's front door was half-open. Ivy heard a slosh and smelled gasoline.

"Is anybody home?"

The light winked off. He brushed the door with his fingertips and listened at its wide gap. The gas smell was strong. He pushed the safety off the .38. His skin crawled and flushed.

No, sir, I said to myself, I said that brown did not belong there. . . .

"Is everyone OK?"

Now it was all dark inside, but the house was exactly like the old Kafka farmhouse, the one that Ivy had lost to the bank, so he knew the floor plan without thinking. Just inside the foyer, the space was neatly divided, living room to the left, dining room to the right, staircase up the middle. Behind the staircase, from left to right, would be a study, a bathroom, and a kitchen. Ivy knew right where all the light switches were.

He didn't touch any yet.

I figured that brown was in there eating Mr. Pfaff's cookie. . . .

"Mr. Pfaff? This is Ivy Kafka, class of 'ninety-nine, the substitute mailman. I saw a . . . uh . . . fellah running out of here." He gagged on the gas smell and coughed. "I think he might have robbed you. Are you in here somewhere?"

Ivy pulled his shirttail up over his mouth and nose. He led with his pistol into the dining room. On the table were four UPS boxes soaked with gas, reeking and damp to the touch. One box was open and had books in it. A china cabinet's doors were flung open and its drawers tongued out. *And you shoulda seen the mess that damn brown made. . . .* He moved through, kicking silverware and shards of broken dishes.

As Ivy stepped into Mr. Pfaff's kitchen, his hot skin sensed a cool breeze off the meadow where the Little Bad Axe flowed. He let his shirttail fall. This air was clean . . . because above the sink the window was shattered. The cabinets were open, the drainboards littered. Mr. Pfaff's phone cord lay cut across the floor.

By God, I caught him just before he burned the place down. . . .

Ivy's next step felt crunchy, then sticky.

He looked down. He stood in the outer lobe of a broad black puddle sparkling with glints of broken glass. On the floor ahead, the full puddle extended past the horizon of the kitchen tabletop and encompassed two tasseled shoes, two stout calves in knee socks, two plump knees, and the stiff hems of lederhosen. The rest was under the table, where the puddle came from.

Ivy took two sticky steps. He bent and looked into the dim space beneath the table.

Mr. Pfaff sat in the puddle, slumped against the wall, his head blown back into broken plaster. His eyes were fixed open while his mangled mouth dripped steadily into his lap. Half his arm was gone.

Ivy staggered back. He reached blindly with his left hand and found the wall behind him. He felt along the cool smooth surface for the light switch.

He had just touched the switch plate when an exhalation came from the den. Then the faintest mutter. Someone was still here.

He said, "Whoever you are—"

A metallic flash and a thump. His eyes followed to the wall. An ax was buried in the plaster next to the switch. Ivy's first two fingertips were half-gone. The tips were on the floor.

He stood in shock, feeling nothing, dripping blood.

Then he raised his pistol. He fired two rounds into the dark space of the den.

He waited through the ringing silence.

A low voice hissed, "*Vamos.*"

Ivy knew enough Spanish to know that this was another brown. He blasted two more rounds, shattering objects in the den.

Then the pain arrived. He couldn't see, couldn't breathe. His pistol hit the floor with a dull thud beside his fingertips.

He was reaching to pick them up, to save them, when he heard the voice again, a harsh and sneering whisper.

"*Vamos, Señor Ivy, vamos.*"

14

As Sheriff Kick steered her Charger southwest toward Augustus Pfaff's place on Pinch Hollow Road, the vivid twilight made all her feelings fierce. The final sky of this long and difficult day was the mingled surface of flesh and fire, racing overhead like a great inward swoop of breath, while from below the shadowed coulees reached up with black fingers.

For hours what she had tried to joke about had stung like an ember inside her: *A bounty on your head.* It felt too close, and too crazy to ignore. . . .

When the road swung directly west, she had to reach up for her visor. This is when the rearview mirror showed her the miniature flag flying from her center back antenna.

She pulled over and walked to rear of the Charger. It was the Southern Cross, the same flag she had charged Kenny for flying.

How cute.

She tore it off and drove on toward a horizon that blazed like hot coals. As she cleared a wooded rise and began to descend, she saw from down on Pinch Hollow the bright orange flames leaping up to meet her.

THE GANG'S ALL HERE

Saturday, May 19

7:00 a.m.–9:00 p.m.	Troll Hunt (Downtown Farmstead)
7:00 a.m.–10:00 a.m.	Frokost (@ Bad Axe Good Savior Lutheran Church, 121 First Street)
9:00 a.m.–5:00 p.m.	Rommegrot, Bunads, Norwegian Baking Demo (@ Historical Society, 13 Kickapoo Street)
9:00 a.m.–5:00 p.m.	Book Signing Meet & Greet w/ Local Author Augustus Pfaff (@ Fairgrounds)
10:00 a.m.–9:00 p.m.	Beer Tent, Food & Craft Stands (@ Fairgrounds)
Noon	Grand Parade Float Lineup (@ Fairgrounds Harness Track, Judging by Parade Marshals Bob and Trudy Check)
Noon–2:00 p.m.	Coulee Region EMS Benefit Brat Fry (@ Fairgrounds, Sponsored by Clausen Meats, Farmstead Chamber of Commerce)
Noon–9:00 p.m.	Music by Squeeze Box Three, DJ Gunnar B, the Principals of Polka, the Coulee Cats (All @ Fairground Main Stage)
2:00 p.m.	Rommegrot Eating Contest (@ Fairgrounds)
3:00 p.m.	Rosemaling Sale, 4-H Animal Judging, Lions Club Lefse Sale, Pig Wrestle, Kiddie Tractor Pull, Meat Lottery (All @ Fairgrounds)
7:00 p.m.	Rodeo Main Event, Tractor-Pull Main Event, Nordic Dancing (All @ Fairgrounds)

15

Augustus Pfaff's house was fully engulfed in tall and twisting flames by the time Sheriff Kick arrived. She waited helplessly for twelve minutes while the nearest volunteer fire department mustered and raced to the scene, then another ten minutes while the firefighters strung hoses across the meadow behind the house to pump water from the Little Bad Axe River.

It was too late. She knew that as the firefighters sprayed water everywhere but at Mr. Pfaff's house. All they could save now was his various slumping outbuildings and his junk-stuffed old barn. In theory they were also preventing breakout fires in the adjacent forest and along the river bottom, though in lush May there was little chance the blaze would spread. She walked the property and watched for an hour, then climbed the driveway and sat in her Charger. The fire fight had seemed almost ceremonial.

"Harley, I won't be home."

"I know. I already heard."

"And I won't be taking any time off this weekend."

"I understand."

"I need to say good night to the kids."

"We'll miss you," he said. He hesitated. "Heidi?" He sounded wary, like he had a delicate point to make, one she would contest.

"What?"

"Hon, *I'll* miss you."

"Sure," she said. "Great. Gotta make another call."

She hung up and touched her speed dial.

"Denise, do we have a laptop with an SID port?"

Searching with a flashlight, she had found broken flowerpots and several shallow holes dug in Pfaff's yard. She had found a shovel, wet and trod on by firefighters, doubtful for prints. Then she had found several game cameras trained on the driveway. In Mr. Pfaff's barn she had found a ladder that would reach them.

"Ten-four. Yes, we do."

"OK, stand by. I'll be sending Schwem in with some memory cards."

Chief Deputy Morales joined her beside the fire.

"Any ideas?" he asked.

"Vague ones. From the timing, it could be something to do with his book. He felt threatened. Something made him call his band this afternoon and say he couldn't play tonight. 'Guard the fort,' he said."

They stared into the flames and hissing towers of steam.

"Carlos Castillo won't need surgery," Morales said. "They're going to cast his right arm and left leg, straighten his nose, and sew his lips back together. His concussion is not that bad, I guess."

A cloud of orange vapor swept over them.

"You think he's in there?"

"Where else?" she said.

"Did he have enemies?"

"Everybody loved him."

"*No todo el mundo.*"

"Not everybody? I guess you're right."

She could feel his dark eyes on her. In just a few months, their relationship had become intense, almost to the point of discomfort. He could often read her mind.

"You want me to visit Czappa at home," he asked her now, "before he goes to bed?"

"Yeah. Please. This morning he dismissed Pfaff as worrying about nothing. He owes me a report. I want it now, and I want it picked apart."

"Got it. *¿No crees que debas descansar?*"

She stared blankly at his flame-lit face.

He said, "Maybe get some rest? Come back at it tomorrow?"

She frowned. Sometimes he crossed her line. "How do you say in Spanish 'You're not my father'?"

"*Tú no eres mi padre.*"

"Ditto," she said.

Morales nodded with a small smile and looked away at the fire.

She stayed with the firefighters, probing Pfaff's yard and sheds and barn with her flashlight beam, finding nothing suspicious. Within an hour Denise called back. All four memory cards were packed with ancient footage of mostly deer. Two had nothing forward of that, as if the cameras had been set incorrectly or had malfunctioned. But the other two had freshly recorded views of a male in a light-colored coat going down Pfaff's driveway on a motorcycle and pushing it back up, then another man—tall and lean, T-shirt, jeans, and hat—walking down into Pfaff's property with a gun drawn and running back up without it.

"You know everybody in the Bad Axe, Denise. Any clue?"

"I can't see faces. Nice bod on the first dude, though."

A minute later, Morales called her.

"So," he began, "the bullet hole in Pfaff's mailbox looked old to him, Czappa said. He said somebody named Duck Hubbard poaches deer on that hillside, so he thought the shot fired was probably from Hubbard. He believed Pfaff had been drinking. I said, 'But it was eight in the morning.' He said, 'Right. This is the Bad Axe.'"

"He meant *still* drinking," the sheriff said. She let that settle, watching the firefighters reel back their hoses. Morales was still learning the culture. Then she said, 'OK, so read Czappa for me. What's going on?"

"Hmm. My problem? Why was he there in the first place?"

"Right. And he said?"

"He said his belief was that Mr. Pfaff had some kind of fire emergency."

"So he came out on his own? No fire trucks or firefighters? He said that?"

"Yup."

"What was he going to do with a fire? Piss on it? Makes no sense. Even for Czappa."

"No, you betcha," Morales said. "Yup. Nope. No sense at all."

"Your Bad Axe—ese is coming along nicely." She broke a Nicorette blister and chewed. It was already midnight. "Better than my español."

"Shall I follow up on Castillo, see how his procedures went? See when he can talk to us?"

"Por favor."

After the firefighters were gone, she ordered a Bad Axe County Roads truck to block Pfaff's driveway. It would be hours, daylight probably, before she could do anything else.

As she was driving away from the scene, her high beams lit an Amish courting buggy coming toward her, the horse stepping out at full gait along Pinch Hollow Road. She pulled aside, stepped from her Charger, and waited. The buggy stopped. The horse was lathered and blowing. A round-cheeked, beardless boy peered at her uncertainly.

"Samuel?" she asked him. "Samuel Stoltzfus?"

"Leander," he corrected. "I is Leander."

"Can I help you?"

He nodded. Kept nodding.

"How can I help you?"

"I come to tell you sumpfin. I can tell you sumpfin."

"OK, Leander. Go ahead. I'm listening."

"My sister saw a red truck. Old red truck with a trailer buggy. Lizzie, she was walking on this road home. He followed her saying dirties. He had hair on his neck. He had faces on his shirt. My dawdy said tell you it was just before that fire on Mr. Gus."

He had finished. He was turning the horse.

"Thank you. Tell your sister and your granddad *danke schön. Vielen dank.*"

A guy with hair on his neck, faces on his shirt, rolling alongside an Amish girl talking dirty to her. The truck wasn't right, but otherwise she knew a class act just like that. She called Kenny Kick's cell phone and got voice mail—no surprise. Then she drove by his double-wide on Ten Hollows Road. No vehicle, nobody home. She tried to call him again. No.

"Oh . . . it's you," Harley said when her call awakened him.

She jumped on that. "Who else?"

"I don't know. My ma? Heidi, what is it?"

"Please call your brother. He won't pick up for me, and I can't find him."

"What'd he do?"

"Let's not talk about that right now. He always answers when you call. Please call me back and tell me where he is."

She steered her Charger through the night toward Farmstead.

"He didn't answer," Harley said when he called back. "I left a message. I'll call you if I hear from him. Come on, Heidi. What'd he do?"

Back at the Public Safety Building, in the wee hours, Denise located Augustus Pfaff's only living relative, his sister, Gretchen, on the roster of an assisted-living facility in Davenport, Iowa.

"I'll call her in the morning," the sheriff told her dispatcher. "Meanwhile, I want a warrant to backtrack through the Crime Busters app and find out who gave us the tip about the bloody boat anchor. Who wanted to collect that reward? Let Judge Rickreiner sleep until five and then wake him up."

"Ten-four, my queen."

But the idea of tips and rewards, of citizens getting mixed up in the administration of justice, had rung a bad bell. Sitting at her desk, gnawing a thickening wad of sour gum, she thought again about *a bounty on your head*. Bob Check had been correct. By the official definition of the FBI, this was terrorism. Paper terrorism. But terrorism all the same. *Treason? Pure horseshit malarkey*, to quote Bob Check. The message was delusional . . . ridiculous . . . stupidly written. But why did the fire at Pfaff's make it seem like paper terrorism had just become real in the Bad Axe?

At first light, she returned to Pfaff's property. She parked behind the Roads truck and walked down the driveway. The wreckage was still too hot to approach. She lingered anyway, partly just too tired to walk back up the driveway, but also sensing there was something here for her to discover. Around the smoldering heap, life went on as always, rendering exquisite beauty in the clean new sunlight. Across the bursting meadow behind the ruined house, vapor rose off the Little Bad Axe River and swirled in a low golden layer, occluding and revealing spiderwebs sparkling with dew. A bluebird flitted through this. The call of a red-winged blackbird sawed the quiet. Then a pair of male goldfinches tumbled through in a hot squabble before darting away in separate directions. The firefighters had beaten a trail across rich, black, bottomland mud, to and from the Little Bad Axe. Their efforts had chewed up the yard and the driveway too. She had pinned her hopes for easy evidence to Pfaff's game cameras. But she knew their aim was weak and narrow. By contrast, this valley around Pinch Hollow Road was a vast space, and suddenly she was moved by its isolation. She held her breath and stood completely still. This quiet beauty was crystalline, a pure and shiny thing into which Mr. Pfaff had had the good fortune to awaken every morning—until this one.

Then an odd sound broke the spell. While she held still, it seemed as if the murmuring Little Bad Axe had coughed. She looked that way. And coughed again. No, the other way—she had heard a muted echo—a puttering engine up on the road. Somebody was up there. Somebody must have arrived on a slow roll. Maybe she was jumpy, maybe the vague threats of a bounty on her head had gotten under her skin, but the tiptoeing presence of the vehicle made it feel like someone was sneaking up.

She touched her holster snap and climbed the driveway, suddenly feeling the burden of her sleepless night. The vehicle had concealed itself behind the county truck, idling. She bent to look beneath and saw small tires, one of them a discolored spare. From its faint creeping progress, she guessed the vehicle had come from north to south and was pointed at her Charger, stalling for some furtive purpose.

Or was she just twitchy and tired?

As she rounded the truck, a sun-faded silver hatchback spun its tires and tore away, throwing gravel and dust in her face. But before it was gone she had recorded three things: it was an old Honda Civic, like she had driven years ago; it was crammed to the windows with junk; and it had a yellow license plate.

She was still hearing it whine away along Pinch Hollow Road when Denise made her phone buzz.

"Heidi, we just got the weirdest call from Vernon Memorial Hospital."

Ivy Kafka had arrived in shock, the nurse explained, and he was unable to tell them what happened as he staggered through the emergency room doors last evening, his car still running in one of the ambulance bays.

He had driven forty miles, the sheriff noted. This was not the start-up Bad Axe County hospital, where Carlos Castillo was. As an ex-farmer, because farmers hurt themselves all the time, Ivy had better sense than to call 911 and wait to be taken to an understaffed new facility. He had driven himself nearly an hour to Vernon Memorial, where he knew there would be surgeons.

"Two fingers," said the nurse, "index and middle of his left hand, were completely severed. The fingertips were in his shirt pocket. We couldn't understand what he was telling us."

The sheriff followed down a corridor, listening. They had sedated Ivy, the nurse said, and prepared him for surgery. The ER staff had just assumed this was their weekly booze-and-power-saw event. Ivy's

BAC was at .121, not much by Bad Axe standards, but legally intoxicated.

"Then he got a look at Dr. Chakrabarti," the nurse said, "and, I mean, he went off."

"Went off?"

"He started ranting about Mexicans taking all the jobs and getting all the breaks, putting farmers out of business."

"Why?"

"You tell me. Dr. Chakrabarti is from Pakistan, via the University of Wisconsin medical school. But he does have brown skin."

They arrived at Ivy's recovery room. The nurse lowered her voice.

"Sure enough, when he came out of sedation, he started talking about a man who was robbed and shot and mutilated by 'the browns,' he was calling them. Where? we said. When? He said last night down in Bad Axe County. That's when we called you."

The nurse touched the door as if it were hot.

"Dr. Chakrabarti is inside speaking with him now. Unfortunately he was not able to reattach the digits. The bones were crushed, and there was too much vascular damage."

"So it wasn't a saw?" the sheriff asked.

"Well, it is a left-hand injury," the nurse said, "suggesting a hand-tool accident, which usually is a saw. But the doctor says it looks more like blunt force, a blow with something sharp, and then a follow-through that crushed the bones."

Now she whispered.

"He claims a 'brown' threw an ax at him while he was reaching for a light switch because he had seen the dead man under a table on the floor. An ax makes some sense given the injury. But keep in mind that he was drunk."

As Sheriff Kick entered his recovery room, Ivy Kafka looked stoned and placidly enraged, half listening as the Pakistani doctor debriefed him on the surgery that had been performed to close up his newly foreshortened fingers.

"Yeah," he was saying, rocking slightly, "sure. Whatever. Can I go now? I got shit to do."

His left hand was bandaged in a big oblong of white gauze and trapped awkwardly against his chest by a canvas sling. His hairy arms and legs stuck out of a lavender hospital gown. Tiny slippers hung from his toes. The sheriff felt an old grief. He looked just like her dad, the several times that Ron White had ended up in similar shape. She remembered him during her junior year of high school after his heart had stopped while he was yelling about his increased property taxes at a meeting of the Crawford County Board of Supervisors. She cringed now to see in Ivy Kafka a similar druggy, impotent fury.

"You will feel considerable pain—" the doctor was saying.

"I don't feel nothing. Can I go now?"

"—given that there are thousands of nerve endings in each finger. You can expect significant discomfort for a considerable period of time."

"Where's my clothes?"

When no one answered him, Ivy scowled out the window into a luminous spring sunrise, the perfect dawning of the Syttende Mai's second day.

"Going forward," continued Dr. Chakrabarti, "you should be aware as well that there is often a difficult emotional adjustment to be made when any body part is lost. We cannot overlook this. There may be significant grief and perhaps anger. In addition to physical pain, you may also feel the pain of loss."

Ivy snorted and glared at the doctor. His pupils were pinpricks.

"We'll see who feels loss."

"Yes." The doctor blinked. "Certainly."

Ivy turned from the window and saw the sheriff.

"I seen one brown coming out," he barked hoarsely at her. "In a white coat. Rode away on a yellow motorcycle. Didn't seem right. I went in to check on Mr. Pfaff. Smelled like gas all over in there. They'd robbed him. They shot him in the shoulder, he crawled under his table, they shot him through the mouth and chopped him up. Then the other brown chucked an ax at me."

She nodded and assured him, "We're going to talk as soon as the doctor is finished."

He snorted again.

"Talk." He turned on Dr. Chakrabarti. "That's why they call her Sheriff Snowflake. She's gonna talk about it."

The doctor spanned them with a puzzled look, then resumed.

"The good news I have to share with you, Mr. Kafka, is that outside of the pain, and presuming you negotiate the emotional adjustment, your injury, medically speaking, is not a big deal."

"Ha!" Ivy ejected the word so forcefully that it seemed to hurt him. He went still.

"Recovery is very straightforward. Your quality of life can resume just as it was. Later today, you can go home with a friend or a family member."

A slipper dropped from the end of Ivy's long, gnarled foot. He turned his head very carefully and looked out the window. As the sheriff understood it, Ivy had made wreckage of the few family relations he had left.

"Good luck, Mr. Kafka," said the surgeon. "Sheriff, he's all yours. Good luck to both of you."

———

Presuming you negotiate the emotional adjustment . . .

Aiming her Charger back toward Bad Axe County, chewing on four milligrams of nicotine gum that wasn't doing much good against her fatigue, the sheriff planned her next steps.

Step one was to strategically disbelieve everything that Ivy Kafka had just told her. Two Hispanic men had shot and maimed and robbed beloved old Augustus Pfaff, a modest widower, everybody's friend, a man not worth robbing by any rubric that she knew of, and yet they had left behind the most obviously valuable item that he owned, his tuba. She had asked Denise to look on eBay. Tubas went for thousands. Then, according to Ivy, one "brown" rode away on a yellow motorcycle. The other "brown" stayed behind and threw an ax at him, clipped his fingers off, and told him, *Vamos.*

There was so much in this to disbelieve. Hardly any of it made sense. It played like some weird dream Ivy Kafka might have had. He was a ruined man, and she worried that like ruined men before him, he had discovered meth. When she put that nasty drug into the mix, a horrific kind of sense became possible. Did *he* rob and kill Mr. Pfaff? Then chop off his own fingers to support the story he was telling? That made meth-sense, almost.

She would come back to Ivy later, ask him everything all over again. It was handy that meth users could never keep their stories straight. In her experience, a man on meth devoured himself on the half hour and shat out a different person.

She accelerated onto the highway and moved her mind. On the topic of looking around, step two was to get a forensic team into the burn site as soon as the embers had cooled. Overnight, anticipating, Denise had called the neighboring counties. La Crosse County, two counties north and much larger, could do it. The hit to the sheriff's budget would be about fifteen grand, money she didn't have. But based on what Ivy had told her, she didn't have a choice. She also needed a separate arson investigation. In the past she had used Crawford County's specially trained deputy for this, at $275 per hour. She touched CRUISE and called in.

"Book them both, Denise."

"Ten-four, my queen."

"I'm headed back out to Pinch Hollow to poke around if things have cooled off enough."

"Be careful."

"You know me."

"I do know you," Denise said. "That's why I'm reminding you to be careful. Chief Deputy Morales has not gone home yet. Can I send him out to meet you?"

"Sure."

"Hon . . . ," Denise began, and sighed.

"What?"

"I want to help you. I mean, to not get too down about it. Just ask me if you ever need to know the difference between a girlfriend and wife."

She and Denise had perfected a gag where they inoculated each other against sexual harassment in the workplace by timely application of small, customized doses of that same poison. Denise was offering a treatment for personal use.

"Sure, why not," the sheriff said. "What *is* the difference between a girlfriend and a wife?"

"About thirty pounds."

"You make me stronger, Denise."

She touched END and glanced in her mirror. A small old car paced itself a hundred yards behind. Was it faded silver? Was it crammed with junk? Was this Harley's blond girlfriend? Stalking her?

Stronger, she told herself. The world was full of shitty little silver cars.

———

Morales was already parked behind the Roads truck that blocked the top of Pfaff's driveway.

Step three? Well, she couldn't be clear about step three yet, except she felt compelled to search for a nexus between the Nelson Flores assault, Carlos Castillo's mauling at a fight club, Kenny Kick's flagging of Main Street with the Southern Cross, and Ivy Kafka's bizarre report of brown men conducting mayhem and murder.

It was hard to see how it could all be connected. It was just as hard to believe that it was all coincidental.

She got sick to her stomach heading down Pfaff's driveway. Her gum shot out first, then stomach acid, coffee, and finally what felt like a chunk of her love for the Bad Axe.

"Fuck."

Morales looked only mildly startled.

"*No chingues*," he said.

"Is that 'No shit'?"

"Street Spanish. You said you wanted to learn some."

"OK. No fucking *chingues*," she said.

"Don't say that to strangers. Want some gum?" he offered.

"Ha. I have some."

The charred remains of Pfaff's house still smoldered and steamed in a familiar way. Rural house fires, and barn fires, were not uncommon.

She had seen dozens. The causes ran to old wiring, faulty heating or fuel storage, drunkenness and drug abuse, insurance fraud, and to the occasional malicious act of arson, likely what they were looking at now.

"*¿De que enteraste en el hospital grande?*"

There were times when she was tired enough that she never noticed that Morales had spoken Spanish. She told him Ivy's story.

"Two Hispanic men?" His tone was dry.

"According to Ivy," she confirmed.

He turned away. He had found a garden rake somewhere. Now he lifted it, reached over a foundation of cinder blocks where the porch had collapsed, and snagged out Pfaff's tuba. The valves and tubes had melted. The big silver bell was warped and scorched. He said, "So, sure, of course the bad guys were Latino . . . because?"

"Skin color. And association."

"Lots of us around."

"Yes. And he said one of them spoke Spanish."

Morales said, "Hmm." He raked the tuba out onto grass that was still soggy with water pulled from the river. Pfaff's crop of dandelions was back to business as usual, blooming in the hot wet earth, asserting yellow life around the ash-black trauma.

"So Ivy Kafka knows Spanish?" Morales sounded skeptical. "I mean, from French or Russian? Or Norwegian?"

"He told me the guy said, '*Vamos, Señor Ivy, vamos.*'"

"I see. Junior high school Spanish."

She felt stupid for a minute. "But it can mean *Go away*, right? *Get out of here?*"

"Maybe. It'd be kind of sarcastic. Literally it's *Let's go*. I'd say *¡Largate!*"

Morales bent and touched the tuba bell. It had cooled enough that he could smudge away the scorch and expose the silver beneath. He looked up at her.

"Ivy Kafka said he was here delivering mail around seven p.m.? Isn't that unusual?"

"I'll be right back," she said.

Her breathing didn't feel right as she climbed back to the top of the driveway. Her blood pressure felt high. Up all night on nicotine, only six days off this year, she thought, why should she be surprised?

The bullet hole through the mailbox looked neither old nor new. Kids shot holes through mailboxes all the time. Strangely, the item inside the box, postmarked two days ago, was both *from* Augustus Pfaff and *to* Augustus Pfaff. She carried the envelope back down the driveway by a corner, sorely tempted to open it. Then she opened it.

It contained a single sheet of paper. The centered type said:

A ROUND US
Once Upon a Time in the Bad Axe
Copyright 2018, Augustus Pfaff

This was his book title, she guessed. Why send it to himself?

When she arrived again on Pfaff's yard, Morales had waded into the embers. He was poking around with the rake in the area where the kitchen used to be, beside a toppled old round-shouldered refrigerator. She was about to yell at him to get out of there when he snagged and rolled what looked like a roasted body. He jumped out on his own.

She was throwing up again, emptily, when her phone buzzed beneath her badge.

"We now have a clear-cut person of interest," Denise told her.

"Go ahead."

"Jon Detweiler, the dad of Serenity, the Syttende Mai queen, called to report what his daughter just told him. She was out late and she just now heard about the fire at Pfaff's."

"Yes?"

"Last evening, a young man, a stranger acting nervous or upset, came to the festival gate and asked Serenity for directions to Pfaff's house. He told her someone else had misdirected him. She told him how to get there."

The sheriff waited.

"Ivy told it straight, Heidi. Brown skin, white coat, yellow motorbike."

The Syttende Mai queen hid her face in the flank of the fat white goat she was milking.

"No!"

The sheriff said, "So this guy *wasn't* asking you about Mr. Pfaff?"

"No! Jeez!"

Her father had said that she had been out late raising hell after her queen duties and didn't learn about Mr. Pfaff until she got up for chores an hour ago. Now she looked a little hungover and flustered. Was she changing her story?

The sheriff couldn't quite read Serenity Detweiler, not yet, except to know that she was a certain kind of girl. Queens were big in coulee country. Dairy Queen, Rodeo Queen, Snow Festival Queen, River Days Queen, Morel Mushroom Queen, Apple Queen, Harvest Queen. Every major theme or event had a queen, an alternate queen, a junior queen, and generations of past queens, with retinues of princesses at every level, as if the daughters of farmers needed a wide range of institutional opportunities to declare feminine beauty. This scenario seemed to fit Serenity Detweiler. She was a robust blond girl, six feet tall, with big hands and feet, wide hips and shoulders, a shallow bust, nice teeth, and a pale, almost featureless face. She was probably a straight-A student, played basketball and a wind instrument, and was on the student council. No doubt she had always wanted to be pretty. Now her prettiness was official and could never be taken away, even as she slumped in dirty barn clothes, sullenly milking a goat.

"But you did talk to this person? He asked you directions?"

"Yes!"

"To Mr. Pfaff's?"

"No! Jeez! He twists things around!"

By *he* Serenity meant her dad. A queen and her dad—that was probably always complex. It had been for her. Sixteen years ago, as Heidi White, the only child of a fifth-generation farmer sinking into irreversible debt, the sheriff had competed for and become the Crawford County Dairy Queen—one county south—and from there, without intending to, she had swept to the state title and spent her senior year of high school in a gown, sash, and tiara, getting carted around the state to shill for the Wisconsin Milk Marketing Board.

She watched Serenity squeeze goat teats expertly. Syttende Mai queen was a much easier gig, mostly a one-off. As Wisconsin Dairy Queen, the sheriff-to-be had made her busy parents proud, but her yearlong queenship had added another thing for them to do, and it didn't fix her dad's depression. It had also been hell on her grades, her softball, and her rodeo, and it had cost her a boyfriend and several girlfriends. Then, yeah, she was not at home to stop it when her mom and dad were senselessly killed by a meth-head trying to cover up his dumb-ass theft of a pressure washer. No. Instead of being there to truly save her struggling parents, Dairy Queen Heidi White had been across the state selling cheese.

For a few moments, Sheriff Kick couldn't shake a resurgence of the darkness that had consumed her after the loss. She had nearly died. The day she finally stopped drinking and smoking and using drugs was the day her counting habit had begun: 4,165 days ago.

"That's not what I said! He makes things up!"

Serenity's protest brought her back.

"But that's what your dad told my dispatcher," the sheriff said.

"That this guy said he was looking for Mr. Pfaff and asked you where his house was."

"No. He didn't. He only asked me how to get to an address on Pinch Hollow Road. How do I know who all lives on Pinch Hollow Road? I only figured out about Mr. Pfaff this morning. I was just doing my job, greeting people at the gate." She threw a glare toward her father, watching from inside the barn. "He acts like we were making out or something. He's all freaked out because—"

She stopped herself. Overnight, a county board member had sent Jon Detweiler a cell phone photo of his daughter talking to a handsome, well-dressed, dark-skinned young man with fashionably wild hair. Serenity's dad had forwarded it to the sheriff just as she was pulling into his driveway. Was he a "brown," as Ivy said? In the photo, the sheriff's person of interest looked more African American than Hispanic. No—she meant Latino.

"Can you describe him for me?"

"A little taller than me. Kind of Rasta hair. I'd say about twenty. Dressed nice."

"What does that mean, dressed nice?"

"White puffer coat, jeans, boots."

This was the guy in the photograph. But Serenity was leaving something out.

"What color was his skin?"

"Oh my God!" she wailed, startling the goat. She shot another hot look toward her father. "Really? Does it matter?"

The sheriff's forehead hurt. Discreetly she used an old tissue to pinch the dead wad of gum off her tongue.

"Yes," she told the girl. "Yes, it matters."

————————

Minutes later the sheriff sat in her Charger at the end of the Detweilers' driveway, on her cell phone with Rhino, waiting while she deliberated. This kid was "brown" to Ivy. He was no doubt "black" to the queen's father. Probably black people looked at him and saw "white." He could be anything. He could be an Inuit or an indigenous New

Zealander. But this was a BOLO—be on the lookout—and she had to speak to the beholder, and the beholder in the Bad Axe was going to be a man on a tractor, a woman driving a school bus, a drinker on a stool in a bar . . .

"OK," she said tensely to Rhino. "Put it out there. Be on the lookout for a light-skinned black male, twenty to twenty-five years old, on a yellow motorcycle. He's our person of interest in the incident at Pfaff's."

"Wait," said Rhino. "Ivy said Hispanic. Not Hispanic?"

"Latino. No. And also, Rhino?"

"Yes, ma'am?"

She glanced at the Charger's clock. It was quarter to eight. She was supposed to brief her dayshift crew in fifteen minutes. She was thirty minutes away. She was closer to home than to Farmstead. On her phone were at least two unread texts from Harley.

"Can you have Morales do my briefing for me, please?"

"Ten-four."

She had just climbed her Charger out of Plum Hollow to the central spine of Bad Axe County and was pushing it along U.S. Highway 14, almost nodding off, when the trash-packed silver Civic with yellow license plates passed in the other direction. Groggy as she was, she thought she might have imagined it. But now she was awake, taking on more Nicorette to stay that way. A mile later several bikers on choppers rip-snorted past, heading toward Farmstead. She counted seven bikes. What did you call that? A convoy? A gang? A mob? Why were they here?

Shit. Nothing felt right.

Halfway down the Kick family driveway she spat the spent gum out her window. Harley and Opie were in the front yard. When she got closer, she could see her husband and oldest child were red-faced and rigid.

"I'm glad you're here," Harley greeted her, his tone cheerfully accusing. "I texted you for help. This is how your daughter wants to go to her 4-H meeting."

Opie corrected him. "No, Daddy, this is how I *am* going to my 4-H meeting."

The sheriff assessed them warily. Maybe it was the contrast with the serious shit she was dealing with, but Harley seemed too exasperated for the essentially gravity-free situation of what his daughter wore to a Saturday morning club meeting. Opie, for her part, seemed too dug-in and defiant.

To give Harley credit, though, Opie had chosen to wear baggy, unclean sweatpants, leather work boots caked with dirt, and a sloppy T-shirt with the Green Bay Packers logo. Her curly red hair had disappeared up inside one of her dad's John Deere ball caps. She looked like a typical Bad Axe male on a morning-after, shrunk down by his bad behavior to seventy pounds and four-and-a-half feet tall.

"Sweetie," the sheriff intervened with a shortage of foresight that was fatigue-and-nicotine inspired, "Kelly's mom will be picking you up, and you'll be with all your friends. Do you really think you look good?"

Opie stamped a boot. "What is *good*?" she demanded.

Fair enough. The sheriff exchanged glances with her husband, sparks traveling both directions. The twins, Taylor and Dylan, emerged from the house ready for the same meeting—it was an annual all-club breakfast—dressed like average little boys.

"And do I look good to *who*?" Then Opie corrected herself, possibly the only seven-year-old in the world who knew and cared about the difference. "To *whom*?"

"You look good to me," Taylor answered his big sister.

Dylan said, "Who's whom?"

Opie continued, "Why can't I wear whatever I want? Like Daddy does?" She shifted gears and stuck her little chin out, the way she did when she had discovered some new way to challenge her parents. "By the way, to *whom* it may concern, I, Ophelia Kick, did not ask for my vagina."

At the magic word, her little brothers went ape. Harley winced and turned away. The sheriff tried to hug her daughter—"Come here, sweetie"—but Opie twisted away. She had seen her friend's mother's minivan coming along the wide curve of Pederson Road, its bright-red paint job flitting in and out of view across bold green alfalfa. Opie took off down the driveway at a clodhopperish sprint, her little brothers trying to catch up.

And that was that.

As Sheriff Kick sat down on the porch step beside her husband, the agonizing question crept from her heart.

What if one of ours is different? And what if different isn't safe?

Then another terrible question.

Your blond girlfriend, who is she?

But she decided not to speak right away. She took Harley's large, warm hand. Their assorted barn cats must have scattered from the father-daughter conflict because now they rematerialized. The tiny one-eared male the kids called Blackie came trotting around the corner of the house, showboating with a female warbler in his teeth.

She tried to clear her throat. It was raw, and it stung. A cramp pinched her hard between her hips. She probably needed to eat. Or crap. She really couldn't tell. A weird spasm crossed her face, her eyes trying to shut, the nicotine flaring them open. Blackie looked up at her with feathers in his mouth.

"We need to talk," she said to Harley.

"Yup."

"You might be right that I'm pushing myself too hard."

"Yeah, maybe."

"I can't deny it's affecting the family."

"Good. We agree, then."

"But I don't think it's right to blame me for what's going on with Opie."

On that he was silent.

"I think," she continued, fearing she was too tired to handle this but going on anyway, "that putting Opie's feelings in the context of my job, my stress, actually might be disrespectful to her, as if this is just some game she's playing for attention. Imagine what that might be like, someone assigning a false cause to the way you feel about yourself, telling you you're not serious. 'Just stop it.' 'She'll get over it.' When 'it' is being herself. Imagine the damage that could do."

Harley remained silent.

"That is the opposite of love," she said.

She gritted her teeth. Past their mailbox rolled that old silver Civic. She bit her bottom lip. *Is this bitch really stalking me?*

"And we promised to love each other," she said.

Shut up now, Heidi. Your wires are crossing. This is not the time for a fight.

But she moved closer and touched her chin to her husband's shoulder and whispered raw against his neck, "Goddamn it, Harley. Goddamn you."

17

The seven bikers, from the leader to the tail gunner, spaced themselves to occupy a hundred yards of highway as they rumbled through the sour air of soybeans under early-morning herbicide application. Cut by low sun, their seven shadows tracked across the ditches into the fields, leaping the dips and lunging over the swales. The leader flicked his right boot to warn of an eviscerated possum over the fog line, and the signal relayed back. The tail gunner, on a surge of throttle, thundered through the re-gathering blowflies.

In his vivid REM sleep, Neon Shivers begins to hear them as they growl past the Bad Axe County Public Safety Building, then past the TOWN OF FARMSTEAD, POP. 2,259 sign. In proximity now of the still-sleepy Bad Axe County fairgrounds, they make their pipes explode like howitzers. The leader touches his brake and swings his left arm. They follow him into the lot of the Red Barn Motel. Neon dreams their thunderclaps, then startles awake.

His long, weird night in a strange place is over. His new life begins now. At least that was the theme of his dreams, which still feel so deeply real. He fingers back the heavy curtain and watches seven bikers surround the Valkyrie, fencing it with their choppers. He lets the curtain close and waits. He queues a text to his stepfather, Dan, who owns the bike—*may need help here*—but doesn't send it. As his nerves surge, he wonders why rich, white Dan is the one he would turn to. But then he knows why. Because Dan calmly solves problems.

In a minute more, a heavy fist pounds on the motel room door. Neon double-checks that it is chained. He double-checks how he feels, what he wants, what his granny might have meant when she told him that her cousin Vernice Freeman was hoping that "her jar fly" would come along. Last night on his phone he looked up "jar fly." Now he knows it is a term used mostly in the South for the cicada, the insect that lives as a larva underground for years before emerging as an adult, his research has told him, *to sing at a pitch that cannot be ignored, inspiring the human imagination at least since Homer's* Iliad *and the Chinese Shang dynasty.*

That sounds good to him. Sounds like purpose. He opens the door to the chain, just to get a sense of history at the moment when he begins to live.

A bearded man in gang gear says, "Folks looking for you, boy."

18

"What?" Harley said, surprised. "Goddamn me why?"

"Who is she?"

He jerked his head back to regard her through a squint.

"She?" he said with his voice rising. "Who is who?"

"This woman you're seeing."

"What?"

She turned her head and stared beyond the yard into the acres of dew-glistening alfalfa. His response, she felt, told her all she needed to know. Her own chain of emotional logic wrenched her heart and made her angrily discard her husband's hand. She had to protect Opie, who stood for anyone in danger; therefore, she had to work until there was no danger; therefore, because she wasn't available enough, her husband was screwing another woman, who now was stalking her. Them. Whatever stalkers did.

He tried to retake her hand. She jerked it away.

"Heidi, what—"

"What the fuck, Harley?"

"I don't know."

"Unbelievable."

"Heidi," he said, and followed with a deep breath like he used before stepping up to hit a baseball, "I'm not seeing anybody."

Un-fucking-believable.

She watched a crow coast down to the barn roof and call its others. This was baby-bird season, and the nests in the barn eaves were flush with easy prey. Harley reached for her, and she smacked his arm away.

"If you're going to leave me," she said, "just do it."

"What are you talking about?"

"Who's the blond chick you've been meeting out at Ring Hollow Dam?"

The idiot went stiff. "Oh," he said. "Oh, right. Her."

The cheater crossed his arms, uncrossed them, wiped his palms on his jeans and leaned back fake-casually against the steps. She could have said it with him. "It's not what you think."

Her phone buzzed twice beneath her badge.

"Go ahead and take that," he said hopefully.

"You wish," she said, and let it ring.

"No," he said, "what I wish is you were off for the weekend and we could really talk about it. It's not what you think, Heidi. I don't know what you're hearing. People make assumptions. But I'm afraid to start a serious conversation with you."

"So it's serious," she concluded.

Her phone buzzed again. He pounced.

"See what I mean? You're only half here. I'm not even going to start the conversation if you're going to just disappear in the middle of it."

"Who is she? Give me a name."

A third double-buzz. Harley puffed his chest and let the air out through his lips. "OK, sure. Her name is Sylvia. Who is she? She's someone I knew in school."

"Sylvia what?"

"Crayne. Sylvia Crayne."

"Spell it."

"With a *y* and an *e*. It's not what you think."

"Just keep saying that," she suggested.

Then she gave in and looked at the first text. Morales had told her: *POI at RB Motel.*

Her person of interest was at the Red Barn Motel.

His second text said: *Citizens arrest!*

That was never good.

His third: *I'm now arresting citizens as well.* A photo was attached: the back of a biker jacket with a skull and the slogan *One Percenter.*

"Jesus," she muttered.

She texted back: *On my way.* She dropped the phone into her pocket. Harley closed his eyes and began to shake his head.

"Gotta go," she said through gritted teeth. "Time to deal. What time does your tournament start?"

"Four."

"We're going to need Mom's help today."

"I'll set it up."

"The kids will get dropped back home in an hour or so. You'll get the boys and their rabbits to the festival contest?"

"Yes."

"I'll try to make it to Opie's pig wrestle."

"OK."

"Please feed my geese."

"I will."

She owned sixteen white geese, and she vented feelings to them, called them her "practice cows," stand-ins until she felt she could manage a dairy farm again. The creatures had a taste for Denise's double-dirty jokes. She thought of one now. It was used, but it had just the right edge.

"And ask them why you don't mess with a woman who has both PMS and ESP."

She stood and glared down at her husband. She said, "Because she's a bitch and she will find you."

His head was in his hands.

"They love that one."

"Heidi, please . . . She's not . . . Please believe me . . . I know I should tell you what's going on. I will, I promise. But I need to talk to Sylvia first. I have an obligation to her. . . ."

He stood and tried for a hug. She stepped back. He reached. She slapped.

"Don't touch me."

"It's OK, Heidi. I love you. I mean, only you."

"Don't you dare fucking touch me."

Going out the driveway, she watched him in the Charger's mirror. He sat back down on the porch step. His head sagged between his broad slumped shoulders.

She reached the road and mashed the gas.

19

A half mile down Pederson Road, over Clock Creek and just beyond where the nine Glick children, out hoeing their potato field, no longer had a view of the road, she came upon the silver Civic pulled onto the shoulder with its flashers blinking.

Driving on the spare tire . . . that's what you get. She imagined writing an unsafe vehicle ticket and calling a tow truck to drag her out of the county.

She stopped behind. The yellow plate read Arizona but didn't look quite right. Still, Arizona made sense. Before she and Harley met, he had played baseball at a junior college in the Phoenix area. Apparently while she was self-destructing after the murder of her parents, Harley was dating a future hoarder and stalker.

But when she climbed from her Charger, she saw that the Civic's spare tire still held air. The next surprise was when a bloated youngish man pried himself out of the driver's seat, managing a thermos and a cigarette in his right hand and putting up a left-handed salute.

"Good day, comrade! Pray tell, does fuzzy logic tickle?"

What the hell? "Is there something I can help with?"

The way he dressed like her Grampa Heinz was disarming: cuffed jeans held up by suspenders, white tube socks and black orthopedic shoes, a cheap plaid sport shirt.

"Do you have," he said with mock excitement, "a *pamphlet* for me?"

He seemed too young for the wardrobe. His thermos didn't have its plug in. Likely it had booze inside, and likely he was drunk.

"Sir, are you having car trouble?"

"How sensitive of you to ask!"

His voice was deep, snide and artificial, like it came from a radio. His head seemed way too big, a ponderous cylinder atop his narrow shoulders, shagged with pale eyebrows and unshaved pale whiskers and topped with an incongruously black mat of bristles.

"Stand back!" he warned. "My vehicle is allergic to nuts!"

The Civic's cargo was a compacted potpourri of trash and personal items. She brought her hands to the weapons on her belt, Taser and firearm.

"Sir, is there a problem?"

"Aha!" He looked aside, like someone else was listening. He kept the thermos in his right hand and dragged on the cigarette with his left. "Rope," he pronounced, "has many historical uses." He swirled whatever was inside the thermos. "But I'm terrible with knots." He had yet to look at her squarely, was looking at her chest, her throat, her forehead. He put his left hand to his ear, appearing to listen.

"What's that you say? The global village called? They want their idiot back?"

"Sir," she repeated, spreading her feet for a wider base, "are you having car trouble?"

"No, ma'am. You are so sensitive to ask, but this baby runs like a nigger with a chicken."

"Get back in the car," she snapped. "Show me your license and your registration."

"Ho-ho! That mouth! Visualize duct tape!"

She popped the snap on her Taser holster.

"You're just like I thought," he said. "Only mouthier. Just like my new friends say. And even more full of yourself." He dropped his cigarette and stepped on it. "And prettier. But bad news, Snowflake. You have no legal authority over me."

"Get in. Now."

"As a matter of fact, you're too pretty." He swirled his thermos. "See, that's the thing. That's the trouble I'm having, why I had to declare the bounty and come all this way to reward myself. You're too hot. That pretty head of yours warrants action. You just do not have the face of a traitor."

"I'm sorry?"

"This is not what a traitor's face looks like." He drew back the thermos and swirled it. "Patriots of the jury . . . a traitor's face looks like *this*!"

He jerked the thermos forward and flung a liquid at her. Even in midair she knew it was acid. She smelled it as she threw her arms up to shield her face. She felt it strike her wrists and hands and splatter her left eyebrow, temple, and ear.

Her next sensation was a chill. Then her knees and palms hit gravel. He was laughing weirdly. Her mind raced. She had to get water. Her skin began to scald. Her left ear fizzed. She had to keep her eyes shut and get water. His car door knocked her over. His engine coughed and started. She drew and blindly emptied a clip a foot above the ground where she thought his tires should be. The car screeched and thumped and was gone from her awareness.

The smell of dissolving skin sickened her as she groped along the hood of the Charger. She found the door, opened it, found the trunk release. She could feel acid running down beneath her uniform, searing her ribs and then her hips. Last week she had forgotten she was snack mom for Opie's soccer team. She groped inside the trunk. The case of Powerade was still there. In hard jerks, she emptied the first bottle into her face. Then another. She dumped the third over her head, the fourth down her shirt behind her stiff vest, a fifth and sixth bottle over each hand and wrist, and then another to her face.

At last she dared to open her eyes. The Civic hadn't made the curve ahead. It was in the ditch against a tree. He was running awkwardly across Glick's sprouting sweet corn. He held a phone to the side of his head. He was making a call.

She gripped another Powerade in her blazing fist. She closed her eyes, screwed the top off, tipped her head back, and emptied it. When she looked again, he was staggering along the edge of Glick's field. Then her eyes spasmed shut. One at a time, she pried them open— her hands tight with pain, barely working—and flushed her eyeballs. Through the blur he had reached the scrubby woods that went up a hillside, over a low ridge, and down the other side to a goat farm along Erickson Road.

She touched her radio handset and gasped toward the mic on her shoulder.

"Ten-twenty-four, Pederson Road at Clock Creek! Ten-twenty-four!"

She flushed her eyes one more time. She dumped one more bottle down her shirt.

Then she fit a new clip into her pistol and started after him.

20

The moment Ivy had been left alone, he had opened cabinets in the recovery room until he found his blood-crusted clothing, stored in a plastic bag on top of his boots.

He had dressed himself one-handed, leaving things unzipped and unbuttoned. He had sneaked down a back stairwell and emerged outside the hospital building. His heartbeat had pounded out his missing fingertips, but he had felt no pain. There would be a prescription for him at the pharmacy downstairs, a nurse had told him. But he had felt fine.

He had located the bloody Sportage in the parking lot. He was not supposed to operate a motor vehicle except for work. If he broke that rule again he could go to jail. For this reason he had driven back to Farmstead very slowly with his eyes squinted and his head hunched down between his shoulders, thinking that way no one could see him. He had felt no pain at all.

His subsidized apartment was in a four-efficiency at the edge of town beside a thousand acres of GMO soybeans. Inside was his secret from Emily Swiggum and Uncle Sam. The several thousand pieces of undelivered mail that spilled out of Ivy's only closet normally made him cringe and limp about, feeling damaged and ashamed. But this time he had felt no pain at all. It was junk anyway. The dude from Chicago had enough cigars. Kristi-Jo could do downward dog without a magazine. He had chugged three beers and changed into an outfit with no zippers or buttons or shoelaces: an old pair of sweatpants, moccasin-style slippers, and a green-and-gold Packers jersey that read *FAVRE 4*.

On his wall phone, paid for by the Lutheran church his family had belonged to, he had dialed Kenny Kick. Kenny hadn't answered. Well, Kenny had shit to do. Whatshisname was coming. He had left a message.

"The browns got me. With an ax," he had said.

"I'm in. I'm coming," he had told Kenny. "I'm gonna make a difference."

He had explained, "I'm not supposed to drive, so I'll be coming in by bike. Tell your man Stang."

Stang Jr. still operated his dad's canoe rental down where the Bad Axe River dumped into the Mississippi. It was a long ride, but Ivy had kept his head down and he had kept on chugging. Each time he pushed a pedal, a lump had squeezed up through his heart and gone out his raised and trapped left arm. Then the lump had bifurcated into his severed fingers, where it had landed—*Wham wham!*—so hard it made him dizzy. But it wasn't pain.

Then had come the steep and curvy downhill, three miles to the river, and he had quickly reached a point of no return—just beyond the sign that read 11 PERCENT GRADE—where gravity had taken over and wiped his mind of all but the understanding that with one slip he would be a streak of flesh and bones on the road.

He had lifted his slippers off the pedals and spread them, skimmed them on the asphalt like outriggers. This had quickly burned the soles of his feet. With his right fist, he had mashed the brake lever to the handlebar. The brake pad had shrieked for about a hundred yards before it went soft and silent. After that he just went down, just down, and down, out-of-control, the lavish coulee springtime a hot green blur through his wide-open soul.

He had arrived at the bottom white-faced, blue-lipped, and shaking. He had turned south along the river and begun pedaling again. He had crossed a bridge and turned up Cave Hollow Road at the far downstream end of the Lower Bad Axe River, where it fattened out and ran sluggishly through mud-scented bottomland.

Now he pedaled pain-free and in bright sunshine—*Wham wham! Wham wham!*—through a fecund, tangled swamp-scape. Distantly ahead was the ridgetop he had come from. There was no going back.

At last he reached Cave Hollow Canoes. Stang's chain-link fence displayed a sign made with black paint on parched plywood: BOATERS DO NOT EVEN THINK OF PARKING HERE.

That sounded like a Stang. Ivy still remembered all the big talk, all the stupid angry bluster, from that one winter years ago when Stang Sr. had milked for Ivy's dad.

The gate was wrapped in chain and locked. COME BACK AFTER MEMORIAL DAY. But there were people inside. About a hundred yards in, beyond the ranks of dented aluminum canoes, stood an old blue metal barn. In front of the barn, Ivy counted seven pickups and three motorcycles, big hogs, chopper-style. One of the pickups was new, blue and silver like the one the internet had bought for Kenny Kick.

Ivy used his good fist to rattle the chain.

"Hey!"

He grabbed the gate and shook it. Three strings of barbed wire wagged along the top.

"Hey! Hey, Kenny!"

He paced in unsteady strides to one corner of the fence, away from the Bad Axe River.

"Hey, Stang! Kenny sent me!"

He paced to the opposite post. The fence along this side was hung with snarls of flotsam from recent high water. Gripping chain link, he tight-roped a hundred yards along the caving riverbank. He cornered and arrived at the back of the barn.

"Hey, Kenny! Hey, Stang! It's Ivy! It's Ivy Kafka! The browns got me!"

He rested, not sure what to do. *Wham wham! Wham wham!* His own heartbeat almost knocked him off-balance. Back here was where the float trips ended, the boaters got out, and Stang dragged his canoes up from the river and through another locked gate. The watery scenario made the farmer in Ivy queasy. The Bad Axe still flowed strongly here. He imagined if a fellah messed up and drifted past this takeout, then the river swept him quickly into Mississippi backwater. There it spun him through a doldrums of black tree stumps before it sucked him under the highway bridge and under the railroad bridge and dumped him out into the big water, headed for the Gulf of Mexico. Ivy looked away. He avoided all water bigger than a creek and boats of any kind. He would always be a farmer that way.

Wham wham! He refocused. Just beyond the takeout gate, an old box elder had gone to rot and fallen on Stang's fence.

Could he climb the tilted trunk?

He guessed that with just one hand he wouldn't have the balance or the strength. He stood there rocked by his heartbeat.

Then he heard Kenny's voice in his head.

Man, oh, man. What's it going to take?

He climbed the fallen trunk like a sick raccoon, sinking his one claw into the spongy bark, wobbling and wheezing, making weird little squeaks with his mouth. About ten feet along its length, right where the tree mashed the barbed wire, its trunk narrowed and forked. He shinnied out the small branch. He drooled and gasped and made raccoon noises. He heard an engine and looked up. He thought he saw Kenny's truck busting uphill out of Cave Coulee. He hoped not. At last the branch bowed, lowering him into the realm of Stang's property. He was about to dangle and drop when it broke.

He came down hard on his side with his injured hand beneath him. He heard a rabbit's death scream rip up through his lungs and out his mouth.

A door slammed.

Boots crunched gravel.

A cold gun barrel touched his skull.

A voice snarled, "What the fuck?"

He couldn't speak.

"What the motherfuck?"

The same voice bellowed, "Security breach! Security breach!"

Ivy took a kick to the gut. Then one to the head. A boot planted squarely on his bandage and seemed to pop his heart. A knee crashed down in the center of his back.

"Stang! Some asshole got inside the perimeter!"

Maybe time passed. Maybe he passed out. Grenades kept exploding in his hand, tossing him about in slippery blackness.

"Who sent this motherfucking cuck?"

Kenny, he was unable to say. *Kenny Kick. Kenny said I could make a difference.*

21

By the time Sheriff Kick started after her attacker, he was already well gone into the woods on the far hillside. She followed deer trails up the steep slope.

From the ridgetop, she saw him a quarter mile below in a green meadow full of goats, tottering for a pasture gate along Erikson Road where a shiny blue-and-silver pickup that sure looked like Kenny's honked and pulled over.

———

Back in Glick's field, she angled across corn seedlings toward where Clock Creek went under Pederson Road. Her skin blazed with a weirdly crisp kind of pain, wrists and hands, one side of her face, her ear. She had to get to water. But she wasn't thinking right. Clean clothes first. She bent her course to the road and returned to the Charger. The trunk was still open, drink bottles strewn. She lifted out the duffel bag that held her spare uniform and headed back toward Clock Creek.

Where was her help?

Just as well now. Under the bridge, she stripped to her underwear and lay on limestone cobble, letting the cold water rush over. *You're too pretty. You're too hot.* Harley used to tell her that, letting her know how lucky he felt to be with her.

It was when she went to transfer her radio handset to the dry uniform shirt that she noticed that acid had eaten through the pigtail connector. Her call for help had gone nowhere.

In the stiff, clean uniform, she drove forward to the Civic and saw that she had shot out both left tires and put holes in the rear door. She photographed his Arizona plate and his VIN number. A phone charger trailed from his dash. His pack of Kent cigarettes was on the passenger seat with his lighter. On the floor she found his one-liter jug of muriatic acid.

"I'm coming in with chemical burns," she told ER reception at the Bad Axe hospital.

"Send a deputy and a wrecker," she told Rhino. "Impound it. BOLO on the driver." She described her grandpa Heinz, plus a weird horse head, minus forty years and a soul. "But internal lookout only. No more citizens' arrests. Withhold all details. Nobody, Rhino. I control the narrative on this. Internal BOLO for Kenny Kick too."

She took his jug of acid to show the ER what was eating her skin.

She reached back inside the Civic, took his cigarettes, and lit one.

OK, then. This was her thought. *Fucking game on.*

22

"Crawford Toyle is coming," the voice fumed.

Ivy hadn't heard Rolf Stang Jr. speak in twenty years, not since the winter when his dad milked for Ivy's dad, but the voice had to be his, tight and simmery, brimming with hot resentment, like the few times the kid had spoken back then, hissing foul language at Ivy's mother for asking him did he want any more sausages or should she turn the stove off.

"Crawford fucking Toyle is coming," Stang Jr. ranted, "and we have people climbing the goddamn fence, like we're a fucking bag of assholes."

Ivy recalled this as something Stang's dad had said often. A cow that moved too slowly was a bag of assholes. Stang Sr.'s world was littered with bags and bags of assholes.

Ivy understood that he was sitting, his spine propped against something hard and cold. His eyes opened stickily: blood and vomit down his shirt, his injured hand naked in his lap. His bandage was gone. His first and second fingers were half as long as before, inflamed like newborn mice, prickling with stiff black stitches. And he noticed he felt seasick, like he'd been spinning, bobbing, drowning in the kind of high brown water that was his farmer's nightmare. He wondered where the pain was. He couldn't feel it, but he sensed it. The pain was catching up to him. It was a vast hidden force, moving toward his fingers like a coal barge out of a fog.

"Where's Kenny?" someone said.

"Fuck Kenny," Stang said. "Imagine I'm Toyle. Imagine I'm here when this happens. I'm looking at this shit. I'm thinking, What a bag of dicks. I've been to goddamn ground zero on the Champs-Élysées with the Yellow Vests. I marched at fucking Charlottesville. How many times have I been the featured guest on *Bubba the Love Sponge*? What am I doing here with these fucking bags of sperm?"

"He's crying," someone said.

Ivy stared through a blur at his naked hand. It was a red helpless thing marooned on a sharp rock. The coal barge was going to hit the rock.

"Who is he?"

"He keeps saying 'Kenny.' "

"He's crying."

"Here's his wallet."

He closed his eyes. His hand seemed to hop in his lap. The barge was inches away.

"Well hot damn," someone said. "Slap my ass and call me Snow-flake. *This* is Ivy Kafka? Hey, Stang, it's just Ivy Kafka."

"I know who the fuck it is," Stang snapped back. "But Toyle wouldn't."

The barge hit. Ivy dissolved into a red-hot blackness. Inside that space he was in junior high school again, 1995, and there were the Stangs, the senior and the junior. Stang's dad had showed up hungover after that Labor Day, after canoe season, looking for work because Ivy's family was known as good people who would throw a man a rope. From there Stang Sr. had bitched and slacked and bragged all the way around the calendar until Memorial Day, canoe season again, when he had asked for advance pay and walked away. One predawn in January, Ivy, going outside for chores, had discovered a little boy shivering under a blanket on the floor of Stang Sr.'s truck. Stang said his wife had run off. Every morning after that, Rolf Jr. came inside the house and sat at the kitchen table gobbling sausage, eggs, and biscuits, all runty and sniffly, all bruised-up and ringwormy, refusing to converse with Ivy's mom, unless to cuss her out now and then, silently watching under his brow as Ivy ate and got his books, kissed his mom and headed off to school.

Someone shook him.

"Looks bad, man. I guess it hurts, huh?"

Stang Jr.'s shoulders were wide with muscle now. His head was shaved around a glossy, russet-colored topknot. His neck and wrists and hands were a helter-skelter of multi-colored tattoos. He wore a pistol strapped under each arm. His flat, freckled face lunged into focus as if Ivy had just straggled home half-dead from some long misadventure and opened his front door and here inside his own house was that same little river rat, but fattened up, thick-lipped, deep-eyed, all decorated, owning the place now, deciding whether to let Ivy in.

Stang said, "You're in a lot of pain. It'll get worse. But maybe at some point we can fix that. Maybe we can work something out. You think about it."

Engines rumbled. A metal door slammed. Stang stood.

"I'm Crawford Toyle!" he hollered. "I walk into this place, what do I see? I see a bag of empty scrotums! I see the once-mighty white man laying down to die! Get this place ready!"

"Look at me," Stang said a while later. "Yo, Mailman Ivy."

Ivy couldn't find him in a blur of red, white, and black. He heard shouts and grunts. Men punched each other. One of the barn doors had been rolled open. Painful sunlight streamed in.

"Someone did this to you. Look at me. Who did this to you?"

He could hardly whisper. "The browns."

"The fucking browns?"

Ivy had to wait for his breath to come back. He watched Kenny's truck pull up and swing around to back up and park by the fence.

"Yeah."

"You tell someone?"

Ivy waited, watching. It wasn't Kenny who got out from behind the wheel. "Yeah."

"You told who?"

Men barked and snarled. They kicked each other.

"I told the sheriff."

That looked like Kenny's shirt, but it didn't look like Kenny. Kenny always wore a hat. No, that was Waylon "Taz" Kramer. He was more staggering than walking, carrying a paper sack by the neck.

"Look at me. You told Sheriff Snowflake the browns did this to you?"

Ivy tipped his gaze down. Stang's shirt was off. He wore small, fingerless, blood-stained boxing gloves. His heavy shoulders glistened black and green.

"I told her. Yeah."

"What'd she say?"

"Talk. All talk."

Ivy recognized that the blurry colors came from banners, red-white-black banners, hung around the canoe barn. He saw a boxing ring and a fight cage. He saw iron plates and bars and dumbbells, shirtless men toiling. Beyond that, his eyes could only skim the blaring sunshine. Off Kenny's passenger seat wobbled some heavy-headed guy in a checkered shirt. So two morning drunks get out of Kenny's truck, Ivy thought, and neither one is Kenny. It all began to spin.

"Kenny . . . Kenny said . . . I could make a difference."

"Damn right you can make a difference."

"But I never shoulda . . . I'm gonna need . . ."

"It hurts, huh?"

"Yeah."

"Here you go."

Stang reached, tipped Ivy's chin, shoved tobacco-bitter fingers through his dry lips, leaving something even more bitter and seedlike on his tongue.

"That'll hit you faster if you chew it. We'll get you a new bandage too. Hey. Mailman. I'm talking to you. Look at me."

Cracking the pill with his molars, Ivy watched Taz Kramer toss Kenny's key to Stang.

Taz slurred, "Ize on my wayda get tequila like you said and Oklahoma calls goin' like help me I've fallen and I can't get up." He thought he'd made a joke. Ivy saw he was wearing Kenny's shirt. Or one just like it. "Anyhooz, we got the tequila."

"OK, yo, listen up," Stang interrupted himself, taking the sack and pocketing Kenny's key. "This here is Mailman Ivy. Mailman Ivy, you know Fuckhead Taz, came on board recently, and this here is another new guy, showed up last night, Oklahoma Terry. Since you're all in the same bag of assholes, maybe you can make brother together."

Dizzy already, Ivy looked away from Taz, at the other guy. That stunted body, that huge whiskery skull with the stiff black poll on top, those wide, watery eyes, shifty-sad, giving a fellah the sense that he wanted to get around behind his back and knock him down—Ivy recalled he had a steer once that looked like Oklahoma Terry.

"Never reason with treason," he announced in a strange, boomy voice, seemingly to Ivy, followed by a snort and a snicker. "I melted the snowflake. But now ZOG's got my chariot. I'm gonna need safe passage back home."

"Get the fuck out of here," Stang told him. "I'm talking."

Stang lifted a tequila bottle from the sack to inspect it. It was half-empty.

"We celebrated hydrochloric justice," explained Oklahoma Terry, his eyes sneaking around.

"You two jigs get out of my face," Stang snarled. "I got a good man here."

"Where is Kenny?" Ivy said when they had moved on.

"Mailman Ivy, look at me."

He didn't. He watched Taz and Oklahoma Terry stagger past the fight cage.

"I just don't understand where Kenny's at."

A slap stung his face. He kept watching. A squeeze of his fingers made him gasp.

"Fuck Kenny. *Look. At. Me.*"

Stang rattled pills inside a tiny bottle.

"You don't need no Kenny." He shook the pills again. "I got you right here."

23

"I'm fine," she snapped at Rhino before he could ask.

"No payoff," she reminded him. "No news. No reward. My story to tell."

"Got it. But, Sheriff, maybe you should take a little time . . ."

"I hit a bump holding hot coffee. I'm fine. That's official."

She couldn't blame him for his skeptical face. She wore clear latex gloves over gooey ointment. White gauze disappeared up her uniform sleeves. The left side of her face appeared to be stamped by a new birthmark that glistened pink beneath the same ointment. The ER doctor had cited potential complications, including septic shock, and urged her to rest at home for at least forty-eight hours. In the hospital parking lot, pain medication had clashed with the impact of another cigarette. Now she felt a swooping, lunging energy as she headed for her office.

Parade comarshal Bob Check was waiting for her.

"What the heck happened to you?"

"Hot coffee meets pothole."

He had written notes on a parade application. His gaze lingered on her face.

"I'm fine, Bob," she insisted. "Go ahead. What have you got?"

"The Sons of Tyr," he began, putting on reading glasses, "call themselves a 'heritage organization.' Under 'Organizational Purpose,' they 'seek to illuminate, honor, and defend the contributions, traditions, and sacrifices of our great forefathers . . .'"

She tapped her computer to life. She opened her phone gallery and scrolled to find her attacker's plate number and VIN. "Go ahead. I'm listening."

"'Of our great forefathers,'" he continued, taking a moment to refind his place, "'upon whom the greatest civilization in world history is founded.'"

The Civic's plate was phony, retired two decades ago and registered as antique-collectable. She opened the VIN lookup site.

"The greatest civilization ever? That's us? Really, Bob? Right now?"

She looked up and saw the old man frowning. She forced herself to soften up.

"I forgot. Tyr is a Viking?"

"Tyr is a Norse god of war."

"Right," she recalled. "Who got his arm ripped off by a wolf."

"In defense of justice."

"Of course."

Feeling scattered, she left the VIN tab unclicked. While Bob kept reading, she searched for the texts Morales had sent with his photograph documenting the citizens' arrest at the Red Barn Motel. She had never made it to the scene.

She enlarged the photo with her fingertips. The citizens had trapped her person of interest in his motel room, harassed him verbally, and tipped his motorcycle over. Their jacket patches read: *One Percenters— Midwest Chapter*. In two seconds, Wikipedia had an explanation. Ninety-nine percent of bikers respected the law. That left one percent, the outlaws, who proudly resisted tyranny and called themselves the One Percenters. Sure, so laws were tyranny until a "black man" broke one. Then outlaws like the One Percenters became citizens.

Rhino stuck his head in. "He's waiting in the interview room."

She nodded. But she owed Bob Check a few more moments. After all, she had asked him to look into the group.

"So, Bob"—she paused to finish typing in the Civic's VIN—"whose name is on the Sons of Tyr's parade application?"

"Jacob Vig," he seemed pleased to report, because, in general, the Vig family was solid Bad Axe stock. But Jake Vig she knew was a creepy hacker type who owned Coulee Compu-Shack. Last summer she had issued Vig a warning for flying a drone with a camera that happened to stray over the boys' outdoor showers at Sugar Creek Bible Camp. Now that same guy claimed to be representing "the greatest civilization ever."

"Can you just talk to him, Bob? Just pick his brain a bit? Find out who the wolf is that ate his arm?"

Bob blinked at her. Her ear felt red-hot. Her own voice felt muted. She tapped her pocket to feel the Kents. How crazy was this going to get?

"Tyr's arm," she reminded him.

"Ah."

The VIN search hit. The Civic belonged to a man from Chapel Hill, Oklahoma, named Terry James Lord. She dumped the name into CrimeNet and let it run.

"What I mean, Bob, is see if you can find out who it is that guys like Jake Vig"—*and Terry James Lord*—"are defending us against."

She knew on sight that Neon Michael Shivers, twenty-two, from Fox Point, a ritzy north-side suburb of Milwaukee, was not one of the "browns" who robbed and killed Augustus Pfaff and torched his house. She knew this because he was dressed exactly as he was in the photo with Serenity yesterday, and not one speck of carnage or soot upon him. But who was Neon Michael Shivers? Why was he at Pfaff's place at all?

"Thank you for waiting," she began as she sat down opposite him at the interview table. "This has been a busy morning for us."

He took his earbuds out and placed them into a case that fit into the pocket of his coat, a down-filled, cream-colored Tumi. Yes, he looked like a rich kid, richer than her anyway, but he didn't seem like a happy one.

His pale green eyes coasted over her gloves and gauze sleeves and the shiny burn on her face. "Not a problem," he said.

He was bi- or multiracial, like Serenity Detweiler had noted. He was strikingly handsome with his freckled brown skin, his shapely nose and lips, his hip hairstyle, his wary gaze above half-moons of depression or deep fatigue.

"I'm sorry you were harassed. We're charging one of those men for kicking over your bike. Is the bike OK?"

"It's mostly OK."

"Good to hear. At least my deputies treated you well?"

She asked because Czappa had arrived first, from across the highway where he was just starting festival duty.

Neon Shivers shrugged. "Whatever."

"Actually, Mr. Shivers, I'd like a specific answer to that."

"One of them was plenty rude. But it's not the first time. Won't be the last."

"I see." Her pulse was slowing. She exhaled. "Thank you."

He used drugs, she thought. But not exactly for fun. Neon Shivers had a certain feel to her, a vibe that touched her core as a mother, one of those gifted kids who puzzles you, frustrates you, saddens you with his inexplicable dysfunction, his insoluble loneliness and unfocused anger. Her fear arose again: *What if one of ours is different?* For starters, she thought, his parents had named him Neon. Where did a kid go from there? Maybe *Neon* was hard to live up to. Maybe it was like naming a daughter *Madonna*. Or Ophelia? His last name, Shivers, rang a distant bell for her that quickly faded.

"So, what brings you to the Bad Axe?"

"This."

He scrolled through photos, then handed her the phone. She was looking at Arn Solverson's round barn, a minor tourist attraction in the Bad Axe. Her department was sometimes called to chase off trespassers. Once or twice the barn had been vandalized. The usual.

"Flip left," he said, telling her to see the next picture. "And that."

The next photo was something she could not recall having seen before, a historical marker. She knew she had seen one like it, northeast of Bad Axe County in Hillsboro, commemorating runaway slaves who had settled in that area. This read *Lyric Valley*. The Bad Axe had a Lyric Valley Road. She could picture the feedlot on the high end of it, then a hardwood forest webbed with blue plastic hosing for maple syrup collection, then an Amish sawmill. But she had never heard about any special history in that area. In his photograph, the marker was faded and off-level, mostly occluded by a thriving buckthorn shrub that seemed to be uprooting it.

"What is your—"

She needed to gather herself for a moment under the sudden heavy resonance of Neon Shivers's attention to the round barns, connecting them to race, to slaves, to ancestry, to forgotten Bad Axe County history—like Mr. Pfaff.

"What is your interest in this?"

He took the phone back. With his thumb and forefinger, he blew up the photo of the marker until his own last name stood out: ALGA SHIVERS, SON OF THOMAS SHIVERS, A TENNESSEE SLAVE. She had heard of Alga Shivers. He had designed and built the round barns in the region.

"You're related?"

"Way, way back," he said, "and around a couple corners. My grandmother's father's uncle's grandfather . . ." He gave up the tangled genealogy and shrugged. "Something like that. I have the name, anyway. My dad's side, Shivers. My granny had a cousin who lived around here into the 'nineties. Somebody up here is writing a book and he interviewed my granny about her cousin. He sent my granny a copy of the book to review. I guess he sent it a while ago and she never looked at it. She's almost blind. But she wanted me to give it back, a bunch of pages in a box."

She touched the gum blisters in her pocket. What she craved now was another cigarette.

"Augustus Pfaff? Was that the author's name?"

"Yes."

"Have you met Mr. Pfaff?"

"I have not."

"Have you ever had any contact at all with Mr. Pfaff?"

"No."

"Were you at his house last night?"

"Yes."

"Why? Why not mail the box of pages back?"

"OK, well." He looked uncomfortable and maybe annoyed as he put his phone back into his coat pocket. "I was going through some shit. People were telling me I should talk to my granny. So." He shrugged. But she could see he felt anything but indifferent. He glowed like a sky before there might be a storm. "I mean, a therapist suggested it."

She waited.

"Going through some shit due to my race," he said. "Or lack of it. Or excess of it. I don't know. Anyway, yeah, so I kinda took an interest in all this."

The phone appeared again, then was restowed. By *all this* he seemed to mean the history captured by his photographs.

"My granny said I should check this stuff out and she gave me the book to give back to the dude. So after I found the barn, and the sign, last night, I took the book to his place."

There was so much to unpack out of this. But she had to focus on the last hours and death of Mr. Pfaff.

"What time was this?"

"It had just got dark."

"Was Mr. Pfaff there?"

He shrugged. "I don't know. It felt weird. There was a big musical horn on the porch and the door was open. It smelled like a gas station. I heard some noises. I couldn't tell if somebody was in there. I left."

"Do you have the book?"

"I left it on the porch."

So that manuscript had gone up in smoke along with however many copies of the published book Mr. Pfaff had planned to sell at the festival and beyond.

"Did you read it?"

"I never even opened the box." Neon Shivers stiffened and sat forward. "So what happened? Why am I here?"

"We'll get to that. But, Mr. Shivers, first let's back up an hour or so. Last evening at the festival, you asked a girl for directions—"

"The queen."

"Yes, this year's Syttende Mai queen, Serenity Detweiler. You told her, she said, that first somebody had directed you the wrong way."

"Yeah. I followed this dude's directions and ended up here, in this town."

"Can you describe him? What he was driving?"

He withdrew his phone once more and swiped it several times. He handed her a photo of a dust cloud caught in twilight on a gravel road.

"I wasn't sure I should trust him. He offered to deliver the book for me. I didn't bite. I tried to get the license plate as he was pulling away. I guess it didn't turn out. He was driving a pickup and pulling some kind of trailer."

She couldn't see much behind the cloud of amber dust. But she could zoom on the number that told her where the bridge was. The sunset was in the right-hand corner of the sky, which gave her direction. So the man Neon Shivers had met was heading south at the time, downstream along the Little Bad Axe River, just about to cross the township line. He could have been on his way to Pfaff's place.

"You were only a couple hundred yards from where you wanted to go," she told Neon Shivers. "It was just ahead of you."

"Yeah. That's pretty much what the queen told me. She sent me right back there."

"Can you describe the man?"

"Uh." He shrugged again and made an uncomfortable face. "White?"

She waited.

"Asshole 'cause I looked black to him?"

"Mr. Shivers—"

"Yeah. Yeah, OK. He was a middle-aged white guy, I guess somewhere around forty. Hat. He had a little chin beard with tobacco spit in it. There was a lot of hair down the back of his neck, right into his shirt."

For the second time today she was hearing a description of her brother-in-law, the free-speech hero, Kenny Kick, he of the spanky new blue-and-silver GoFundMe truck. Well, she would protect her community, no matter who was involved. Harley could be mad and fuck it out with his friend. She swallowed a bolt of dismay and suddenly she felt toxic with worry and fatigue.

"How would you describe his truck?"

"It was red and all beat-up."

Right. Like the Amish kid had told her. So the driver seemed like Kenny, but not driving Kenny's new truck.

"And pulling a trailer?"

"Almost like it had shelves."

"For canoes?"

"Yeah, maybe."

She looked at the dust-cloud photo again and constructed a map in her head. The Little Bad Axe meandered through the meadow east of the road, left in the picture, flowing forward, the direction the pickup was going, south. Yes, she had that right.

So Kenny, and she was betting it was Kenny, was heading toward Pfaff's place. Then, when asked about Pfaff's place, he had sent Neon Shivers in the opposite direction. That made Kenny a suspect, for sure. Arson and murder. And because it had looked like Kenny's truck picking up Terry James Lord, she would also treat him as a suspect in her assault. Bad news for her marriage. Good news for Sylvia Crayne.

She pulled her focus back. As for the idea that the red truck might have been pulling a canoe trailer . . . and why Kenny would be driving that truck instead of his own . . . that stumped her . . . as did the idea of canoes in general. Within a forty-mile radius of that spot in the photograph she knew of maybe a dozen outfitters who rented canoes on the Bad Axe, Kickapoo, Wisconsin, and Mississippi Rivers. But it was still pre–Memorial Day, not canoe season. And even if it were canoe season, nobody in their right mind floated the Little Bad Axe. It was too small, too crooked, had no access, was replete with mudholes and jammed with beaver dams. Did she need to canvass the canoe rental places? If Kenny was pulling a canoe trailer, whose trailer, and why there? She took a mental snapshot and moved on. She had to clarify the stakes.

"Mr. Shivers, Augustus Pfaff was the victim of a homicide last night. Shortly after you were there, we think. Or possibly somewhat before."

She watched the features of his face startle out of their sullenly handsome alignment and regroup into an anxious scowl that said, *What?*

"He was robbed and shot, we think. Then his house was burned to the ground."

The kid narrowed his eyes.

"I knew something wasn't right. . . ."

She rubbed her forehead. Gently, unconsciously, she touched the damaged skin across the top of her cheek. She winced and squeezed her teeth together. By now, she felt sure that CrimeNet was ready to tell her about Lord.

"Mr. Shivers," she said quietly, watching him begin to nod distantly, like he was gone already as she said it, "I think, for now, that you ought to go home."

24

But Terry James Lord was a cipher. He had never been charged with a crime. A browser search hit nothing she could use. Hoarded catalogs inside his vehicle showed he got mail at the address of a home owned by Thomas and Marie Lord. These were his parents, she presumed, but she could not find a phone number. A deputy from McClain County in Oklahoma had been sent to see what the Lords had to say. But she wasn't going to wait.

The impounded Civic was visible from her office, and the sickness of his mind was crammed against his dirty windows for anyone to see. Rhino had been scouring chat rooms and showed her a fresh post, only an hour old, that illustrated what a hero he thought he was now.

Snowflake melted. You are now free to move about the Constitution.

She walked down the corridor to Dispatch. *Don't,* a voice told her. She resolutely ignored it. He would come to her, if she pushed the right buttons. She just had to be ready.

"Rhino, how would I talk back to him?"

"What do you want to say?" he asked her.

"*Fake news. He missed me. I spilled coffee on myself, and I'm fine.*"

Halfway to her office, she came back.

"Add *I'm still pretty*,'" she said.

She came back one more time.

"*Too pretty.*"

By noon, the La Crosse County forensic team was on Pfaff's property, and the remains of the house were cool enough that they could begin. Sheriff Kick was getting updates from Deputy Schwem, assigned to duty there. The team had already recovered a shotgun with shells in both chambers, probably Mr. Pfaff's, and what probably was Ivy Kafka's handgun, an old .38 Colt six-shooter. If it had been fully loaded, Ivy had fired four shots, exactly as he said. The ballistics, the connection between Ivy's gun and any bullets found in Pfaff's body, or casings found in the ashes, could take weeks to develop. She couldn't wait for that.

"Rhino, any progress on the Crime Busters warrant?"

"We just got it. It was a tip from a cell phone call. I'll have a name as soon as they get back to me with the number."

Around one, Schwem called her, sounding both short of breath and grim. He said, "They just carried out his body."

"Go ahead."

"Well." She had to wait for her deputy to swallow several times. Schwem was a local, an ex-student of Mr. Pfaff's, grieving with the rest of them. "Well, he's, you know, like, cooked. You'd expect that. But the thing is, they're telling me it looks like somebody might have chopped his arm off with an ax."

She was quiet. That explained why there was ax on the scene in the first place. But why cut off his arm? "And is the arm there?"

"They haven't found it."

She hung up, knowing that forensic analysis of a severed body part could take weeks. Same for a meaningful autopsy of a brain and other organs. As for the arson investigator she had hired, he was just now on his way from Prairie du Chien. The way those guys worked, she could wait a month for his results. She tapped the pack of Kents but went with gum and felt the dry, astringent tingling in her blood. All this backward movement . . . while it felt like something else was moving *forward*.

"Sheriff?"

Rhino was in her doorway.

"Go ahead."

"About Crime Busters. The mushroom hunter who called in the tip about the bloody boat anchor is Sy Vang. He's related to that Hmong gal who bought Mudcat's, the new owner."

"Find him."

"No need," Rhino said. "He's here. Part of the Crime Busters system is they give the tipster an immediate heads-up if there's been a law enforcement warrant to find out who they are."

Her dispatcher stepped aside. Into her office tentatively shuffled a stocky man about her age and her height wearing a Brewers hat, a Badgers shirt, jeans, and tall rubber boots. His knees were muddy, and he carried a paper grocery sack. Same as seeing Neon Shivers in person, she knew on sight that Sy Vang had not manufactured a phony tip.

"Hi. I'm Sheriff Heidi Kick. You're in Julie's family?"

"I'm her brother."

"You find any morels?"

"Not that day, when I found the anchor. I was too early. But . . ." He held the grocery sack forward. "These are for you. If you like them."

"I love them," she said. She reached for a notebook. "But I can't take them. I just need to get a more detailed statement."

————

So Deputy Larry Czappa lied. Czappa had destroyed evidence. Sy Vang's statement left her with no doubt: there had been a bloody boat anchor near the scene of the Nelson Flores beating, right up until Czappa got there and declared the tip a hoax.

She paced to her office window, gnawing Nicorette and hearing festival sounds wafted across the soybean field. Lord had made some connection in the Bad Axe. Someone he could call for help after his attack on her had shanked. She doubted it was Kenny—least not Kenny primarily, or Kenny alone. No matter how many times she busted him, Kenny wouldn't knowingly help a guy throw acid in her face. She paced back to her desk. More forensic photos had popped up in her email. She stared at one that seemed to be of an old-school tower CPU like hers. This was Pfaff's computer, melted and charred, with its side panel pried open.

"Knock knock."

It was her buddy Bob Check.

"Come in, Bob."

His weather-whipped face seemed redder than usual.

"Sons of Tyr?" he said.

"Yes?"

"They're all right. Good guys." He sounded a little too vehement. "OK, sure. They plan to carry weapons, but, you know, just historical stuff, pikes and clubs and whatnot." He sounded almost defiant. "For fun."

She stopped her gum, held it smashed between her molars. Her injured ear rang as if her head might explode.

"Weapons?"

"Just Viking stuff. Part of the costume. Like on the heritage float. Heck, I hear the colored kid carries a pitchfork."

"Jake Vig told you they plan to carry weapons?"

"Yup. He said he talked to Deputy Czappa, who said if the colored kid carries a pitchfork then it was obviously OK. It's just historical."

She turned to her window and said a few bad words silently. *Czappa the evidence destroyer told Vig the drone perv that because the "colored kid carries a pitchfork" it was OK for adults to carry weapons in the parade.* She turned back and challenged him.

"But, Bob, you look upset."

"Well," he said, "I talked to Jake inside his store. When I stepped outside, there was this out-of-town girl, this tourist, with blue hair and a goddamn ring in her nose, all up in my face and calling me a Nazi, because I talked to Jake."

The sheriff felt herself go speechless.

"So I get on my phone and I call you guys, and Rhino tells me he's not going to send a deputy just because some girl from out of town called me a name I didn't like. Did she touch me? No. Did she threaten to hurt me? No. Am I in some protected group? No. Then that is not a crime, Rhino says. We have the First Amendment. She can say what she wants. But, then, Kenny Kick—Sheriff, help me out here—you think Kenny ought to be arrested, for what he did with that flag? Even when they dropped the charge?"

Her silence was a yes. The county board chairperson collapsed into her guest chair.

"God bless America," he said.

She sat too. Nothing felt right. Absolutely nothing. And all the wrong things felt connected. How did she undo this?

Rhino stuck his head in. He calmly took a savage glare from Bob Check.

"Sheriff, the hospital called."

"Go ahead."

"Carlos Castillo can talk."

25

Her chief deputy had gone home to bed hours ago. But David Morales never looked rumpled or sleepy, even when a task like this one yanked him back out of bed at noon. Still, he hadn't seen her injuries yet, and the sight startled him into an awkward, wincing silence.

"I'm fine."

"You're not fine."

"I will be. Let's get started."

"I can take over today."

"I said I'm fine." She almost snarled it. His eyes widened and he stiffened. Then, redirecting himself, her chief deputy seemed to tell the injured kid a joke. Castillo smiled through sewn-up lips. Morales nodded at her: *Go ahead.*

"Mr. Castillo," she began, "tell me how you got involved with a fight club."

Morales listened and translated, "He wants to know if he's in trouble with ICE."

"Tell him not yet. That depends on his story."

Morales passed that along. Castillo needed help to reach his plastic cup of water. Morales took it to the sink and refilled it for him. The kid sipped gingerly. Then he talked to Morales.

"I wanted to make extra money," Morales relayed when he paused. "Back in Honduras I was a boxer and a wrestler. I heard rumors about amateur fights for good money, with gambling stakes. I started asking around. So then I met a guy."

Morales stopped there. "Met a guy where?" she followed up. "And describe the guy, please." Castillo understood and looked at her. "Mudcat's," he said. "Guy is—"

He continued in Spanish to Morales, who passed along, "Short, hairy, and drunk. The guy told him to show up at Mudcat's at ten p.m. on Thursday night, sit outside behind the party porch—"

Morales leaned in as the kid sped up. His translation became a layer under Castillo's agitated voice.

"I was just sitting there, and somebody hooded me. I was totally surprised and frightened. They drove me somewhere. Then I was at the fight club. I sat in the vehicle for a long time. Then they took me out and stripped me and taped my hands and put gloves on me and took the hood off and shoved me inside a cage with this old white guy who was slow. He was out of shape. All this guy had was a big mouth. A dirty mouth. He was a crazy-bad fighter. There was no reason anybody would put money on him, against me, but that's what some of the crowd were doing. And they were cheering for him, not me. It made no sense to put money on this man against me. Honestly, I was just trying to win without killing him. I just wanted to get out of that place."

She put a hand up and stopped them both.

"What place? What kind of place?"

Castillo shrugged. "It was outside. They parked trucks on a hill and shined lights on us."

In other words, anywhere. "OK. Go on."

"Then, between rounds, suddenly my water bottle tastes funny. Then he's hitting me, his gloves are all over my face, and where he hits me it stings. See, they doped my water, and they put mace on the guy's gloves, and my eyes are closing up. I couldn't see. I felt weak. I blacked out, and then he really started hitting me."

He stopped for a sip of water and rested with his eyes closed.

"This is not a normal fight club," Morales said to the sheriff.

"I guess not."

"To me," Morales said, "it sounds like white-man fantasy camp."

She had only heard of baseball fantasy camp, Harley talked about it, and she wasn't in the mood to be called cute. She waited with a scowl for her chief deputy's explanation.

"The 'I'm a race-war hero' fantasy," he said. "Paramilitary training for the race war. Guns. Martial arts. Throw in gambling and cheating, alcohol and probably drugs, women as chattel for breeding, it's heaven on earth for some guys."

He watched her react. Castillo's story so far had shocked her to the point of disbelief, and Morales had just placed the story in a context even harder to fathom. He continued, "I've only been here a couple of months, Sheriff. How am I the first one to see this in the Bad Axe? It's here like everywhere else. The twist here"—he nodded at Castillo—"seems to be bringing in a kid like this as a special attraction, then rigging the fight. He's got more to say. I promise you."

Sure enough, when Castillo was rested, he continued.

"After the fight they drove me somewhere else. I remember it was two guys who almost looked the same, and they tried to put me in this dog kennel, keep me there, like I was somebody's property now, but I got away and swam across this river into a forest. I came out on a highway and then this weird silver bus that I saw at the fight club, it stopped for me."

Sheriff Kick and Morales exchanged glances. They knew what bus he was describing. The "Missus Sippy" was a repurposed school bus painted beer-can silver, windows and everything, and jacked up on monster truck wheels. Revelers paid to ride the Missus Sippy between the taverns up and down the river. His first week on the job, Morales had responded to an on-board brawl.

"The nice old-lady driver took me home," Castillo finished. "From there I don't remember, but I guess she dropped me off here. She saved me."

The sheriff parked her Charger at the fairgrounds and began to work her way through the festival crowd, using her all-business body language to make space and discourage curiosity and sympathy. Hot coffee. Not a big deal. No glory for Lord. She kept her eye out for him. Passing the music stage, she saw that each member wore a black arm band as the Principals of Polka defiantly belted out "The Beer Barrel Polka." It was past noon, which made it beer o'clock. The suds were flowing, and the dancers sang full-throatedly along.

> Roll out the barrel, we'll have a barrel of fun
> Roll out the barrel, we've got the blues on the run
>
> Hey! Hey! Hey!
>
> Zing, boom, tararrel, we'll sing a song of good cheer
> Now's the time to roll out the barrel,
> 'Cause the gang's all here!

She suddenly felt sad and gulpy. The gusto seemed a perfect way to honor Augustus Pfaff. A time came back to her when he had explained that *zing, boom, tararrel!* was not a nonsense rhyme. The lyric, he said, referred to the sound of bullets flying outside Czech beer halls during the 1939 Nazi invasion. "Roll Out the Barrel" was an anthem of defiance, Mr. Pfaff had told her, for a people who refused to be broken by violence and hate.

Well.

She stopped at the entrance to the beer tent, where a volunteer checked ID's and counted heads with a clicker. Only one hundred people could occupy the beer tent at one time.

"Ninety-seven, Sheriff. All legal."

"Good deal, Colton. Is my mom-in-law in here?"

"She was." He couldn't help his eyes from sliding off hers to the gleaming red skin around her left ear, then glancing down at her goo-filled gloves. "But she came back out a few minutes ago. I think she said that your daughter is gonna be in the pig wrestle soon."

Damn it. She had forgotten. Now her legs felt weak. As she hurried on, she saw that the parade floats for tomorrow had been lined up on the harness-racing track for display and judging. The float Opie would ride on, the library-sponsored heritage float, was missing its bearded Amish elder—Opie had to pig-wrestle—though the other actors were on board for review by the judges: the kid dressed as Blackhawk, the Hmong kid in ceremonial dress, the black kid dressed as an ex–African slave and now a farmer—yes, the kid had a pitchfork—and the Mercado Chavez kid in his sombrero. It all felt off-key now, inappropriate in a perfectly Bad Axe kind of way. While the intent was inclusion, the float now seemed ancient and naïve, up for flame-throwing, mockery, and nastiness, putting innocent kids in harm's way. She wasn't the only one looking. A man in biker gear took pictures with his phone. When he saw her watching him, he pocketed the phone and walked away. She popped two Nicorette blisters—when could she smoke again?—and continued across the fairground.

This weird silver bus stopped for me . . . The nice old-lady driver . . . she saved me.

And here she came now, riding piggyback down the midway on the back of some huge drunk dude, hollering and spurring the guy like a horse.

Her husband's mother.

Kenny's mother.

The kids' grandma.

Driver of the Missus Sippy party bus on the river, Belle Kick.

She saw the sheriff and dismounted. "Whee!"

"We need to talk, Belle."

"Talk away."

26

"Yeah," he says into his phone. "Who am I? Her grandson. Neon Shivers. Yeah, I can wait."

After his interview with the sheriff—*Mr. Shivers, I think, for now, that you ought to go home*—he had steered the Valkyrie back out into the countryside, becoming more aware that it was beautiful, seeing how it was alternately groomed by farmers and too steep and wild to farm. He had refound the historical marker making claims about Lyric Valley.

One more time he had read:

THE ADVENT OF THE AUTOMOBILE, AND OTHER ELE-MENTS OF CHANGE, LED TO THE GRADUAL DECLINE OF THE RURAL AFRICAN AMERICAN POPULATION.

What?

Black people had to leave here because cars were invented?

The ancestors of an architect, an engineer, a builder of round barns, had to tuck tail and limp off to the cities, where they could be red-lined into ghettos, *because of cars*?

Yet the Amish were fine?

Decline . . . to zero?

Sure, things change. Maybe there were fewer German, or Polish, or Norwegian people out here now than a hundred years ago. But entire populations of white immigrants did not wholesale up and vanish. They mingled and remained.

And other elements of change?

Which?

What did this mean?

From the historical marker, he had ridden the bike to a ridgetop where his phone had some reception. He had found a little cemetery beside an abandoned church. He had stood the bike there and climbed higher behind the cemetery, reading faded gravestones as he went.

Lots of Nordegaards and Oestertags. Hansons. Hansens. Johansens. But no Shivers.

He sits beneath a lone oak that is just now fully leafing, waiting for the switchboard at the nursing home to locate his granny and put her on the line.

He likes the long view and the clean breeze. And it's weird for him to notice things like this, to bother or to care, but he sees that now he is actually on a prairie. He feels proud of this observation, this deduction. This high ground that he climbed a mile to reach is not a mountaintop but a prairie, just now erupting with grass and wildflowers and a few massive ancient trees like the one above his head. This terrain is inverted. It is the opposite of mountains. The flatland is on the top. The rugged stuff is down. He likes it.

At last he hears a different ringtone. Then she answers.

"It's Neon, Granny. How you doing?"

"Neon?"

"Neon, your grandson."

"My grandson?"

"Wayne and Laura's kid. I came to see you."

"Laura?"

"The white woman, Granny. My mom, Laura."

"Oh, yes. Yes. Laura. Now, who is this?"

"It's Neon. Your grandson. You gave me a book to take back to a man . . . and you told me all about the round barns that one of us designed."

"Alga Shivers designed those round barns."

"Yes. Right. I saw one. I took a picture for you."

Her memory has compartments—like boxes or drawers, or maybe like scrapbooks. He understood this the last time he saw her. Some compartments are well stocked and organized. But they are separate. Connecting them is difficult.

"A man who was writing a book about the barns interviewed you about your cousin who lived here. Then he sent you the book, to make sure that he got it right. You couldn't read it, but you told me about the round barns and the ancestors . . . and you sent me out here to take the book back. Do you remember?"

"I remember."

"Do you?"

"Is this Neon?"

"Yes."

"Did you take the book back to the man?"

"Yes. I mean, no."

He stumbles, not sure what to tell her. Should he give a very old and somewhat demented woman terrible news? If so, why?

"I mean, there was a problem."

"He was a nice man," she says. "He played a tuba for me and danced and made me laugh." Then she mumbles something. Someone is with her, probably an aide. The phone clatters. A young woman's voice, sounding Southern, tells Neon, "Y'all hang on just a sec."

As he waits, he hears the rumble of bike engines. The sound expands, then bristles and pops. Below the cemetery passes a string of five Harley-Davidsons, badass hogs, every rider bearded, wearing mirrored sunglasses, black leather, one rider with a lady in a side car, one bike pulling a trailer. It's a different group from the one that harassed him at the motel. But the same too. Neon stiffens as a beard bends and sunglasses glint, one head turning his way.

"She had to use the toilet," the aide informs him. "Here she is."

"Granny?"

"Is this still Neon?"

"Yes, it is. I wanted to ask you something."

"Well, go ahead and ask, child. You worried I'm too busy?"

She sounds sharper now.

"OK, see, there was a bit of a problem returning the book to the man. Something bad happened, actually. I don't want to explain right now. I'm fine, don't worry. But I wasn't able to give the book back, and it's kind of not going to happen now. So I wondered. I remembered you said that your cousin lived out here, by herself, forever, like way up to nineteen ninety."

"My cousin Vernice Freeman, yes. She was Alga's sister-in-law's grandniece. Never married. Kept to herself. She had a bitty little house in Bad Axe County."

Neon drifts a bit, listening to the bike noise trail away. He is trying to picture a black woman living out here alone. How? Why? Doing what?

As if his granny understands that he can't quite make sense of what she just told him, she says, "Mm-hm. It's a rare truth, for sure. Vernice lived there on her own until she died in the fire. She was about seventy by then. I was out there two times. I told the book writer about my visits and what went on. He said he would put it in the book."

"Can you tell me?" Neon asks.

He hears nothing on the line. A bird sings loudly over his head. He sees it dart away: bright orange.

"When was the first time?"

"Well, that was with my granddaddy and my uncle Hiram, yes, because Vernice lived all alone and somebody was terrorizing the black folks."

Neon wonders, *Other elements of change?*

"There wasn't many of us by then, but a few of us is always too many for some. This was in the 1960s. Black folks were all over the TV for the civil rights, looking mad and scary and smart. Black Panthers, Dr. King, Malcolm. I was a grown woman. Me and Grand-daddy Harold and Uncle Hiram drove out from Milwaukee to try to bring Vernice back with us. She wouldn't come. She wanted to keep on living in her little house out nowhere like some old witch, eating garden greens and fishes out of that crick. She didn't even want to talk much to us. So my daddy left her with a big silver gun. Later on, we heard she was suspected to have shot a man with it. I told that to the book writer. Shot a man who bothered her. After that, the family sent me out to stay with her a month on account of she was ill. That was summer of 1966. I never saw her after that."

Neon's skin prickles.

"She died in a fire?"

"That was another thirty years later. Her house caught fire. She died in that. That man asked me all of it. I told him, 'As far as I knew, she was real careful about fire.' Vernice was real careful about all manner of things. How else could a single old black lady survive out there? I told him, 'Now you put that in your book. My cousin Vernice was real careful not to burn herself down.' I gave him that to think about and write in his book if he dared."

The choppers have thundered off the ridge. Now they descend. The hollows gradually swallow their racket.

"Granny," Neon says, "can you think of anyone at all who might have known her, anyone who maybe is still alive and I could talk to? Do you remember anything about your cousin's neighbors or friends?"

He waits through a pause. He does like this sweet air, this long, green view.

"There was a neighbor a few miles down the road."

Neon thinks she sounds wary now. Not forgetful or confused. More unsure of what she wants to say.

"Do you know the neighbor's name?"

"It was real pretty out there."

"I know," he says, "and you told me how pretty it was. It sure is. You were right."

"But I told that man my skin crawled the whole time."

"You said your cousin was sick. How was she sick?"

His granny shuts him down. "Lady business." Some things she won't talk about.

That orange bird darts back into the tree overhead and starts to sing again.

"Did she have any friends?"

"Well . . ." His granny answers him after another silence.

Neon wonders what still bothers her.

"At the neighbor farm there was some kind of large young white person . . ."

This is a strange expression. *Large young white person.* Meaning what? But he keeps listening.

"Come by to look in on her just about every day, always bringing fresh eggs. They were speckled eggs."

Neon is excited now and plunges on while his granny is still making sense.

"Do you know where your cousin's house was? An address? The name of the road?"

"Vernice's house? I haven't the faintest anymore. I couldn't tell you beyond it was Bad Axe County and somewhere near where the black folks used to live."

He needs more. He feels urgency, an emotion both unfamiliar and relieving. If he doesn't know where the cousin's house was, how can he find the *large young white person* who was a neighbor?

"Granny," he presses on, "you just remembered speckled eggs. Any chance you can recall the neighbor's name?"

"Why, yes."

She surprises him. She surprises him so much that he forgets to ask about the "jar fly"—if by that she means a cicada, buried and coming back to "sing."

"Yes, I do recall their name," Neon's granny says. "Because I had just started a job in the typing pool at Miller Beer. Their name was like my typewriter. Their name was Royal."

27

"I'm fine, Belle. Leave it alone. I'm fine."

The sheriff steered her mother-in-law toward the rodeo bleachers, a few minutes ahead of Opie's pig-wrestling event.

"Some people got a screw loose."

She scanned for Lord. She guessed by now he had seen her reply, daring him to try again.

"I spilled coffee, Mom."

"Like hell you did."

"Nothing happened, and I'm perfectly fine. But speaking of screw loose, when is the last time you saw Kenny?"

"Ha. He cleaned my gutters last weekend like a good boy."

"Are you sure that's the last time? Not Thursday night, Friday morning?"

"Not that I recall."

She guided Belle up into the bleachers.

"I'm going to sit right here next to you," she said with her voice low and tight, "like I would anyway, looking like your daughter-in-law, which I am, but this is a law enforcement officer speaking with a person of interest in a crime. And you need to tell me the truth. If you do that, this could turn out OK."

The kids' grandmother smelled like metabolizing booze and stale tobacco. She coughed and growled, "Unless you can't handle the truth."

"Let's not do that."

"Do what?"

"Let's not quote people quoting movies in a bar."

Belle was feeling nervous and defiant or she never would have tried to sneak a Skoal tin open down between her legs.

"And no, don't dip. There is no tobacco use permitted anywhere on the fairgrounds."

Harley's mother snapped the tin closed. She twisted to see who was watching them. The sheriff continued.

"You were involved in a crime. More like several crimes. But you kinda-sorta did the right thing. You behave now, and we can probably work this out."

Belle made a show of ignoring her. "Oh, look. There's the piggy. So cute."

In tense silence, they watched the piglet brought out in the arms of the Bad Axe County 4-H president, Dick Bratz, who displayed the greased-up little fellow, pink-skinned with black spots, his hooves wheeling.

"You were driving the Missus Sippy early yesterday morning," she said to Belle. "Is that correct?"

Harley's mother whistled and clapped. Dick Bratz set the piglet inside a barrel. The rodeo ring had been shrunk to a thousand square feet by a double stack of hay bales. Pigs were fast, especially young ones, and they could jump. The dirt inside the hay bales had been soaked and turned into mud. A dozen excited little girls waited to give chase.

"Let's go, Opie!" Belle roared with her leather lungs.

"This is a criminal investigation, Mom. You need to answer me. You dropped an injured young man off at the hospital early yesterday morning. Am I right?"

Belle harrumphed. The PA announcer began to introduce the contestants. Each little girl trotted out of a rodeo gate, vaulted the hay bales, and raised a wave.

"I just talked to the young man at the hospital," the sheriff said. "His name is Carlos Castillo. He's still alive, he said, by the kindness of an old-lady bus driver."

Belle's head snapped around.

"Old?"

"You took him home, then put him on your off-road buggy. You rode in across the field behind the hospital with your headlights pointed at the security camera. You wanted to help him, but you didn't want anyone to know it was you."

"The bastard called me 'old'?"

"Mom—"

"I didn't commit any crime."

"He told us about a fight club. You were part of that. What happened?"

"For Christ's sake, shush up. Here she comes."

The PA speakers crackled.

"And our final contestant . . . Miss Ophelia Kick!"

The sheriff leaned away from the fierce old woman and watched her daughter line up with the other girls inside the hay-bale perimeter. Opie waved to her mom with an anxious frown, and the sheriff sent back a smile, pure face muscle, with an *I'm fine* thumbs-up. Then Opie waved to someone else out of view from the bleachers. After a moment, there came Opie's cheating daddy in his Bad Axe Rattlers baseball uniform, herding her twin little brothers with their caged 4-H rabbits.

She looked back at her daughter then. It came as no surprise that Opie would dress herself in an outfit that was more sensibly masculine than what her little girlfriends wore. Today, where the other girls wore things like pastel shorts or junior yoga tights, Opie wore her barn overalls under her long-sleeved flannel pajama shirt, which she had buttoned to her wrists and chin. Where the other girls took a chilled-out attitude toward mud by wearing sneakers or flip-flops, Opie wore her tall rubber muck boots. The other girls were bare-handed. Opie wore a pair of rawhide fencing gloves, dry and stiff and nicked up by barbed wire.

"Mommy's fine," she told the twins before they could ask. She glared at Harley. "I hit a bump with hot coffee in my hand." His look told exactly where the trust was between them. Just as he sat down strategically on the other side of his mother, the sheriff noticed something pinned to Opie's right sleeve.

She asked anybody, "Is that black arm band for Mr. Pfaff?"

"Nope," Harley answered. He kept his gaze ahead.

"Then?"

"She really wants to pig-wrestle." He kept his voice flat. The boys rattled the bleachers with their rabbit cages. "She doesn't want to miss out. Especially since there's a prize. But she also thinks it's cruel to the pig. So she's participating under protest."

"When was this discussed?"

"You were busy," Belle said.

"By the way, thanks, Ma," Harley said then. "Thanks for agreeing to take the kids this afternoon."

The sheriff jumped when the referee fired his gun and tipped the barrel.

Out bolted the little pig, every bit as quick as a dog. From all angles charged nine of the ten little girls, all knobby knees and bouncing ponytails, kicking up tracers of mud and leaving their ill-considered footwear stuck behind.

Suddenly everyone around the sheriff was hooting and hollering. Harley, Grammy Belle, Taylor and Dylan, all were in distress because while the other girls chased the pig, Opie seemed to stand there doing nothing.

"Daddy," wailed Taylor, "she's just standing there!"

Except Opie never stood anywhere just doing nothing. God love her, the girl was extracting something from her bib pocket. She was putting on ski goggles, eye protection.

And now, like the amazing little creature that she was, an amazing little athlete too, Opie "trailed the play" the way her soccer coach had taught her. She "saw the field." Soon, displaying her father's grace at shortstop or on the mound for the Bad Axe Rattlers, she made a smoothly decisive lateral move. Her anticipation was perfect, and she plucked up the pig on a short hop.

From there, because of her decision to wear old dry gloves that were roughened by wire cuts, she maintained a solid grip on the frantic piglet through his greasy skin.

Grammy Belle whistled and shrieked. "Atta girl! You got the little shit!"

The sheriff's daughter carried the piglet kicking and squirming back to the barrel in the center of the mud pit and gently lowered him in. She turned and faced the referee, staring steadily through her goggles.

"Ladies and gentlemen," boomed the PA guy, "Miss Ophelia Kick!"

"Stay here, boys," Sheriff Kick told Taylor and Dylan after Harley had left to start his Hollows Hardball tournament. She took another look around for Terry James Lord. He would try to get her alone again, she believed. "Stay right beside your rabbits. Opie will come up and be with you. Grammy Belle and I are coming right back."

She guided her mother-in-law firmly by the elbow to a private place behind the stock barns.

"Mom," she began, triggered by the smell but otherwise ignoring the start of a Marlboro, "did you see that?"

Belle gushed smoke. "See what?"

"What Opie just did. She tried to do the right thing. She felt trapped inside some bigger thing that she felt was wrong. But she tried."

"If you say so."

"I think that's what you did too, yesterday. Something happened that was wrong. That kid got himself nearly killed in an illegal prize fight. You tried to help him. What happened? Mom, talk to me."

She took a drag. She turned her head and shot smoke from her nose. Her eyes darted to the sheriff's and away. "You just said what happened," she rasped finally. "He got beat up in a fight. A cage fight. I didn't know they took him somewhere else or tried to stop him from leaving. I just found him on the road."

"They? Who?"

"I don't know who runs the fights. I don't wanna know."

"Where was the fight?"

"It doesn't matter."

She coughed for a while and seemed weakened. "OK, whatever. This time it was at Steinbeck Auto. Out on the property behind their back building. It was a nice night, so they did it outside. None of my passengers knew where they were."

She paused to catch her breath. Her glance seemed resentful.

"But don't bother Steinbeck because he ain't got nothing to do with it. And it's never in the same place twice. That's how they do it. The fight moves around. It doesn't take much to set up a cage and a betting window. Nobody cares where the fights are as long as they get there. They're all good and drunk by the time I deliver."

"But you—"

"I drive the party bus. That's it. I go where my boss tells me. Once or twice a week I pick a group up at Mudcat's, fifty bucks to get on board. We hit a half dozen bars and then about midnight I take 'em to the fight, wherever that is. I sit around and wait and then I take 'em back to Mudcat's when it's over."

"But why—" the sheriff began again.

"It's called making a living. Some people don't work for the government."

"But you found this injured kid. Why not call 911?"

"Because then I'd have to tell about the fights. If I do that, I'm out of a damn job."

Belle looked away in the direction of the temporary RV camp where the festival workers stayed. She sucked hard and exhaled.

"I never get out of the bus. Those are my orders. I don't know who's running that show. After I picked up this kid, I called my boss. I said, I got this Spanish kid, he's hurt bad, what do I do? He said, 'Dump him off at the fairgrounds. Lots of Spanish there. Somebody there is gonna help him.' "

"But you didn't do that."

Abruptly Belle began to tremble, fighting tears. A chill went up the sheriff's spine. She had never seen Belle look remorseful or scared.

"No. No, I didn't. That wasn't good enough for me. But I didn't dare let anybody know that I didn't do as I was told. It didn't used to be like this. There's been some new people involved."

Belle adjusted her grip on her shortening smoke.

"Mom, they didn't find that kid until fourteen hours later."

"Yeah. Well, I thought they'd do a lot better than that."

The sheriff watched her mother-in-law tremble and fumble the cigarette stub to her lips. Music drifted over the roof of the stock barn. The band had just struck up the "Pretty Paula Polka." Royal Strander was busting out the oompahs. She touched her phone and waited for Rhino to answer. She asked him, "Any word on Kenny Kick?"

"Negative. His truck's not at home, and he's not either."

She ended the call. "Let's back up. When is the last time you saw Kenny? I need the truth now."

Belle gave a wet little cough that sounded like it squirted from her heart. "OK," she said. "OK. I saw him at the fight Thursday night. I'm sure he wasn't supposed to associate with the driver, but he came around the nose of the bus to see me. He brought me a cup of beer. He sat on the step and we talked about youse all and how much we love you."

She shook so hard she dropped the cigarette. The sheriff took a deep, slow breath. Then she made the crime-to-crime leap over the Kenny bridge that she'd been constructing all day.

"The next night, Mom, someone killed Augustus Pfaff. Shot him and burned his house down. Kenny was seen nearby in someone else's truck at the wrong time to be innocent. Now we can't find Kenny."

The sheriff let that sink in.

"We all know Kenny," she said. "He wants to be part of stuff. He wants to be a man. He'll never stop looking for his dad. He'll never stop wishing he was like his little brother. But he's not bad. He doesn't want to hurt people."

Belle sniffled. She stepped on the dropped butt and stared down at the black smear.

"I'm thinking this all might be the work of some people Kenny got mixed up with. I'm thinking they're dangerous, to Kenny and to you too. I think you're afraid of them."

Belle shook out another Marlboro, but she only held it.

"You can't watch the kids, Belle. I can't let you do that."

"No."

"But tell you what, Mom."

"What?"

"Good news, basically."

"What?"

The sheriff wrapped her mother-in-law's thin shoulders in a one-armed hug.

"You're under arrest. Kind of. More like house arrest. Harley won't ever forgive me, but you'll be safe in my office until I get this sorted out. I'll call Gabby Grimes and have her take the kids to Harley's baseball tournament. She can watch them there, with their dad to help if needed. And I'll tell Rhino and Denise to let you outside to smoke."

"You're arresting me?"

"Yeah, Mom. Kind of."

But Belle went easily, and they looked like family, walking arm in arm across the fairground to the sheriff's Charger as the kids trailed. Dylan and Taylor lugged their caged rabbits. Opie proudly bore her pig-wrestling prize: a $25 Culver's gift card.

But what little relief she felt faded quickly. Dylan's rabbit got scared and shot piss that hit a stranger. Next they passed Augustus Pfaff's empty meet-and-greet booth, a reminder of his gruesome death. As they packed into the sheriff's Charger, Opie pointed out it was illegal unless they all had booster seats. "I'll write myself a ticket," the sheriff promised. She put the windows down and began to roll. She would deliver Belle into the care of Rhino; then she would pick up the baby-sitter and head to the baseball field. Halfway across the parking lot Opie aimed her finger toward a small crowd of people and shouted, "Nazi!"

Belle coughed. "Where?"

"Nazi! Nazi!"

"Sweetheart, please."

"Mother," Opie scolded her back, "I do, by now, know the correct Nazi sign. I just saw it on a man's shoulder."

Sheriff Kick put up the windows. They rolled another twenty yards.

"And by the way, 'Please,' what?" Opie asked. "Please ignore Nazis?"

"Sweetheart . . ."

She couldn't finish. As the Charger waited to exit the fairgrounds onto the highway, she saw the yellow Valkyrie coming north out of Farmstead. Neon Shivers had ignored her advice. He had not gone home. As the sheriff turned toward the Bad Axe County Public Safety Building, she watched in her mirror as the kid turned his bike into the fairgrounds.

28

"Hey! Nice bike!"

Neon Shivers can't see which one yells it from the group of men drinking at a picnic table on the edge of the parking area.

That's OK. He digs the friction now, the menace. A man is dead, his house and body torched. This is what Neon has been missing. The shit inside him is real. It is both undead and deadly. He has known it all along. Why go home and let it kill him from the inside?

"Nice yellow Jap bike!"

So lame. He raises an all-purpose middle finger and heads for the bandstand. Polka careens across the fairgrounds, and he knows he is not supposed to like it, the lumbering tuba and reeling accordion, the toodling clarinet and braying trumpet, the quaint lyrics . . .

Just because you think you're so pretty,
Just because you think you're so hot,
Just because you think you've got something
that nobody else has got . . .

But when he sees polka in action, somehow it works, the mono-lithic jolliness, the proud innocence, the throwback sentiment, the giddy hopping of the dancers, their touching hands and smiling faces. It is very much as deeply a cultural *thing*, a roots thing, he sees, as what goes on at a Jay-Z or a Drake concert. He just can't like it—right?—because it's old and white.

Tracking down the neighbor of his granny's cousin Vernice has been as simple as asking, except he's been corrected. Not the Royals. *Royal*. One person. But plural. The moment he sees Royal, he gets it.

The tuba player booming out the oompah beat is tall and over-weight, with a wide, straining face inside an unruly frizz of gray hair held back with what looks like a basketball headband. Dangly ear-rings sway, and behind the tuba's mouthpiece jumps a tuft of gray beard. Sausage-size fingers pump the tuba valves, flashing fingernails chewed to red-painted nubs. The other band members are costumed in knee socks, lederhosen, white blouses, and feathered caps, but Royal wears a soiled-blue coverall jumpsuit, like a garage mechanic, and stomps time with fuzz-lined dirty-pink Crocs. So Royal is some of both. More. Less. Neither. Other. Neon doesn't quite know how to understand this—except that he has his piece of *both* and his piece of *other* too.

He listens through the next song. He really digs the friction here—all the eyeballs, the attention hot on his skin—*him*, waiting for *them*. He has been bored, he realizes. He has been trapped inside a hard shell of comfort and boredom and lazy untruth.

No beer today!
No beer today!
You can't buy beer on Sunday!

No beer today!
No beer today!
You gotta come back on Monday!

"Hi, there."
She is at his side, the tall and broad-shouldered queen. She car-

ries a neatly mustard-striped sausage tucked inside a bun, riding in a paper boat.

. "This is for you."

He takes it. "Hey, thanks."

She has pretty eyes, electric-blue, inside a plain face smiling bravely and then losing it. "Back to work!" she blurts, and then she's gone. Maybe a hundred people watch Neon eat.

That polka ends. The dancers wind down, out of breath.

"That was the 'No Beer Today' polka," the accordion player announces into his microphone, "by the great Frankie Yankovic. But there *is* beer today. Tomorrow too. And don't miss the grand parade tomorrow morning on Main Street. But that was a favorite of our beloved friend and leader, Gus Pfaff. . . ."

His voice cracks. He drops his face for several seconds. Neon sees the black armbands on the players.

"May he rest in peace. Gus was into bygones, as you may know, and there was a period after Prohibition when around these parts we continued behaving ourselves anyway, at least on Sundays. Maybe those were better times. At least Gus thought so. Anyway, he would have wanted us to play this next one to close out the set. Cheers, Gus. Thanks for everything. We love you. And heck yeah, old buddy, we *are* drinking all your beer."

The band rebounds into their next tune. Neon has heard it before.

In heaven there is no beer,
That's why we drink it here.
And when we're gone from here,
All our friends will be drinking all our beer.

Neon follows Royal into the mosh of the beer tent, dragging all eyes with them. Royal moves powerfully like a man, but with lady-length strides. Boom, one beer gone, chin beard dripping, boom, beer number two down the hatch with a smack of wet lips still swollen from the tuba, then a wince and a burp.

"And who might you be?"

Into widening blue-gray eyes, Neon explains.

"Halleluiah," Royal says. "At last. But I wasn't just her neighbor. I was close friends with Vernice Freeman. In fact, Vernice and I were best friends, all the way back to when I was just a little one."

A third beer goes down. Then an urgent question.

"Are you in the meat lottery?"

Neon doesn't get it.

"Come on. It's starting. Let's go."

He tags along, trying to time Royal's odd gait into a tent beside the bandstand. This tent is also packed with fairgoers. Deep inside is a tall raffle wheel and a man on a microphone. Neon hangs back, watches Royal produce a mash of dollar bills from an overall pocket and count them out in exchange for red tickets.

The wheel spins, ticks, stops. Royal has pushed to the front. "Eleven!" Groans and cheers. A few winners head to the freezer to pick up their twenty pounds of chuck roast, proceeds to the Bad Axe County Humane Society.

A whisper in Neon's ear: "Or, since we love animals and we're so humane, we could just not kill them and eat them in the first place, right?"

Again he looks into the fiery-blue eyes of the festival queen.

"But do you notice," she continues, "the complete lack of irony?"

He does; he nods.

"This is what it's like to live here."

He smiles.

"I'm on break," she adds. "Just so you know, there's a scholarship for being queen. So what's the deal? Do you know Royal?"

"I do now."

"How was your middagspolser?"

"Um . . ."

"Your sausage."

"How do you say *delicious* in Norwegian?"

She grins. "I have no idea."

The wheel spinner shouts, "Seventy-four! Happy day for seventy-four! Uff-da! Thirty pounds of ground sirloin! Don't eat it all at one time! At least not without my help!"

This goes on, and it's noisy. She gives him a little to tug to say *Let's step outside*. In the shade beside the tent they look toward the group of men Neon flipped off a while ago, when one of them yelled about the Valkyrie.

"I'm Serenity. I know, that's a little too much name, right?"

"Neon. Too much name right back at you."

"OK, anyway, Neon, Serenity is sorry about getting you in trouble and probably messing up your whole day. I was the one who told them you were looking for Mr. Pfaff."

Just as he assures her that she didn't get him into too much trouble, he sees that now she might still. The men at the picnic table have taken note, and one stirs to his feet, aims his gut, scowls, and drops his hands like hooks. Neon imagines his thought: *Mud boy, hitting on the queen.* Then the queen notices Neon looking that way, notices the drunk dude scowling back, and says, "Yeah, it's been weird around here this weekend. It seems like a lot of not-so-nice people from out of town. But I don't mean you. Where are you from?"

Neon's answer is interrupted by a shriek of joy from inside. He is finishing his story about his granny and the book, telling Serenity why he wanted to meet Royal and why he hasn't gone home, when out of the tent rushes Royal clutching a pair of frosty white packages.

"Oh my God. Oh my dear holy God. Not one but two. Fifty pounds of Clausen's best medisterkaker. Oh my dear pork-patty-loving heart. Neon Shivers, we have to go *now*."

Neon feels his whole body say, *Go where?*

"To Vernice's place," Royal answers him. "She knew you'd come eventually. She left something for you. Grab my tuba, will you? My van is right in the middle of the lot, under the light pole."

Neon stalls.

Serenity shrugs and grins, and the gesture seems to mean, *You asked for Royal; this is Royal.* "Maybe see you later?"

"Yeah," he says. "Yeah, maybe, sure."

As he collects the tuba from the bandstand and carries it across the fairgrounds, he feels naked. There is so much friction now that his skin feels peeled off. Does he like this? Can he take it? Maybe. It gets more crazily alive when he bears the tuba past the table of men. The one with the gut who didn't like him talking to the queen says, "Look at you," and he leads two others to follow. Neon has no idea how to carry a tuba. He has no idea how to defend himself here. The moment he is among the parked vehicles, one man grips the instrument and wrenches it away.

"Look at you, boy," he hears again.

The men are swaying drunk. Seen up close, they are not bikers, and they are not much older than Neon is. What they look like to him is something he has seen on YouTube, Proud Boys, cryptic messages on black T-shirts, retro haircuts, a bit of bodybuilding. Probably about fourteen beers ago they had a better, more political, point to make besides, "Look the fuck at you."

He doesn't know how this will go, who starts what, until behind him he hears, "Hold this."

Royal has either waited up or circled back, still holding fifty pounds of lottery winnings.

"Go on, Neon Shivers. Hold my medisterkaker."

Neon accepts the two cold, heavy packages. For several seconds Royal wriggles and contorts like a big woman trying to take her bra off with her shirt still on. Then Royal's hand comes back out the coverall sleeve with a heavy silver revolver.

"What the fuck . . ." mutters the one holding the tuba.

Another says through gritted teeth, "Some kind of sick fucking queer."

Royal points the weapon generally, as if not making a choice yet, thumbs back the hammer, and says to Neon, "Your granny's cousin Vernice gave this to me. She did her business with it. I've been waiting thirty years to do mine."

Just like that, the three Proud Boys are gone. The tuba and the prize meat go into an old gray van mapped with rust spots.

"Let's go," says Royal. "It's a drive. Follow me."

The storefronts cast long, cool shadows as Neon low-gears the Valkyrie along Farmstead's empty Main Street behind Royal's van. The few parking meters are bagged, and the curbs are lined with empty lawn chairs. Parade tomorrow, he remembers.

He follows Royal out into the countryside. In his head, a polka streams along with the greening fields, the red barns and blue silos, the muddy-legged black-and-white Holsteins in their pastures, the weathered crossroads churches . . .

No beer today!
No beer today!
You can't buy beer on Sunday!

The pleasant views repeating on roller-coaster roads . . . everywhere tractors left in fields because today is for dancing . . . and he feels the people and the landscape and the music come together.

No beer today!
No beer today!
You gotta come back on Monday!

Royal drives slowly and distractedly. Neon sees that round barn from a distance. They pass the Lyric Valley historical marker. About a mile beyond it, the van and motorcycle turn onto a pitted gravel road that runs alongside a bright little stream. The stream is small enough to jump across. Small yellow birds dart along its banks.

At last Royal stops. Neon rides up alongside. Royal points across the stream.

"She used to have a driveway across this. It got washed away a long time ago. What's left of the house is over where you see that big hickory. Vernice and I planted that tree. I was thirteen. Nineteen sixty-five. I ran away from my family and stayed with her. The sheriff came and dragged me home. After that, my real troubles started, but

Vernice stood by me. She could have moved away like all the others, but she wouldn't leave me here alone."

Royal stares across the creek through a red-faced grimace. Neon never saw the gun go back inside the coveralls. He wonders if Royal really would have pulled the trigger. He wonders who it was, back then, that Vernice Freeman was suspected to have shot for "bothering her."

Royal says, "She buried a box for whoever came along, which is you. She didn't tell me exactly where. Or maybe I forgot. This was thirty-some years ago. But . . ."

Royal jerks and gulps, overcome by emotion. Neon looks away, hears the distant rumbling of more motorcycles, unless it's thunder out of blue sky. Royal waves at a circling horsefly and forces a smile.

"I'll always miss her. She and I were two real stubborn misfits, kind of fused at the soul. I won't ever leave the Bad Axe alive either. I'm here until they get me, just like Vernice."

This triggers a beery sigh, with tuba lips at the end, and once more Royal tries to adjust back to cheerful.

"But I know what she buried was her story that she couldn't tell while she was alive. She said that in the future, if family ever came around, I should tell them about the box."

"A jar fly . . ." Neon begins. Royal keeps talking.

"Some official history people found me once, the ones who write the historical markers, a bunch of old biddies and fussbudgets who came to ask me about the last old black woman in the Bad Axe. They couldn't look me in the eye, so I said I'd never heard of Vernice Freeman. I never said a word about Vernice until my friend Gus started writing his book. I didn't tell him about the box, but I told Gus what I *thought* happened to Vernice back in the sixties, and who I *thought* killed her later."

Neon waits to hear more. Royal begins to gulp again. "Oh, dear. Poor Gus. He thought history was wonderful. He thought stories were fantastic. When he found out he was something like Alga Shivers's fourteenth cousin three times removed with one-point-six percent African blood in him, he was over the moon. He thought everyone should—"

Royal pops the squeaky van door and with a grunt dismounts heavily. Neon now sees the lump of the revolver in the kidney region.

"I told Gus about your grandmother staying with Vernice once while she was sick. That's how Gus found out about your grandmother, and why he interviewed her and sent the book for her to look at. I mostly stayed away during that time because your grandmother was uncomfortable with me, like most people. Still, a lovely lady. Harriet."

"Yes."

"How is she?"

"OK, I guess. She doesn't see well, her memory comes and goes; she's in a home. It was her idea for me to come here."

"Ah." Royal nods intensely. "Yes."

"Because I haven't been exactly healthy, not OK with myself. Kind of drifting, unhappy."

"Yes," says Royal, still nodding. "Yes, yes, this happens."

"The sheriff told me to go home. Honestly, I feel safer here."

"I see. Yes, safe. We'd like to keep you safe."

They are silent for a bit. Royal flips a stick into the little creek, watches it float out of sight, then extracts a shovel from the back of the van.

"You'll need this."

Neon takes it, worn at the blade, gritty on the handle. Still they stand there. Birds tussle in the brush. Royal sails another stick down the creek. It can't be thunder that Neon keeps hearing.

"Most likely she hid it in the root cellar."

Royal has become agitated. Puffs. Scowls. Launches one more stick.

"Then, Neon Shivers, promise me you'll go home, yes?"

Neon promises sure, yes, but he means no.

"Straight back to Milwaukee. Say hello to your grandmother for me."

"Right."

"Uff-da," Royal then announces. A pouch of Red Man emerges

from the coveralls. In past those loosened tuba lips goes a startling wad, reminiscent of how Royal drank beer. "My medisterkaker's getting warm."

Leaving Neon and the Valkyrie behind, the gray van bumps away down the gravel road and disappears behind dust and birds, into the shimmering, rumbling afternoon heat.

Neon jumps across the creek.

29

Somewhere in the afternoon, after another pill from Rolf Stang Jr. had gone down the hatch, making time slide forward and back, Ivy Kafka had felt so good that he had laughed about something in reference to the visit of the great Crawford Toyle.

"What's funny?

"Nothing."

"What's so fucking funny?"

His reflexes were not normal. He had failed to turn completely out of the way when Stang unleashed a roundhouse punch that hit him in the neck. Ivy's next mistake had been in being too big to go down. Even skin and bones, he still had his gnarly farmer's strength. He hardly felt the punch. Stang had leaned back on one leg and nailed him with a side-body kick. Ivy had just stood there grinning vaguely, saying he was sorry.

"Sorry? Crawford Toyle marched against the Muslims with the DPP in Denmark."

"I know. I'm sorry."

"Really? You knew the Muslims were taking over Denmark?"

"Sorry. I didn't know."

"Right," Stang had snapped. "You didn't know, you sorry sack of dick cheese. You lost your farm. You lost your fingers. Think about it. You want to lose your whole beautiful culture?"

"No."

"What's your problem, then?"

"I just wondered when I was gonna see Kenny, since his nice new truck is outside."

Stang had whistled sharply through his teeth.

"Who's seen Brother Kenny? Mailman Ivy needs to know."

Nobody had.

"There you go. You wanna ever make brother like Kenny did, quit fucking around."

Ivy was still a workhorse even one-handed, and he had not been fucking around. He had stashed about a hundred paddles and life preservers and anchors into side rooms of the barn. He had stacked the iron plates and tidied the bars and dumbbells out of the way. He had swept out the whole barn floor and disposed of all the beer and pop cans and cigarette butts. He had disassembled and stowed the pieces of the boxing ring. Fighting practice still proceeded inside the cage, which he was told to leave assembled for tonight. Somewhere within the slides of time another group of bikers had shown up. As Ivy worked, they had staggered two by two around the cage in sparring gloves and headgear, barefoot and bare-bellied, still in their leather pants, wallet chains slinging, punching and kicking each other, wheezing, calling each other bitches and coons. One had knocked another down, stood over him, and screamed, "Eat my pussy, rag-head!" Maybe this was why he laughed, Ivy had thought. Maybe not about Crawford Toyle. The thing about the pills, he had realized, is that you didn't realize you were on them, except you did realize it, although you didn't, really, and either way it was not so bad to lose a couple fingers.

He had heard stuff as he worked. Stang kept barking at the men, telling them to be warriors. He kept reminding them what Toyle expected to see from the Sons of Tyr. Toyle expected to see a lethal street-fighting force, primed to beat back the blacks and browns and their liberal government lackeys when the shit came down.

"As the shit will come down, gentlemen. As the shit will come down über alles."

Toyle also expected, Stang had said, to see force on display in the parade.

"They need to tremble at our strength, gentlemen. They need to *feel* us."

Ivy had found himself thinking: The parade? The one with the squeaky high school marching band? The clumsy queens and princesses waving from their shabby floats? The parade with Mr. Pfaff's old-man polka band playing on a hay wagon? Where marchers hurled candy to the curb for the kids? *That* parade?

He had been having these thoughts when Stang had pulled him into his cluttered office. With a nod he had indicated that Ivy should look out his grimy, barred window at three women who had come with the last group of bikers but weren't allowed inside. The women sat on overturned canoes in the shade of the barn, drinking beer and smoking.

"See them?"

Ivy had felt slurry but in overall good humor. "I see 'em."

"Those are good white women."

"Yup."

"Those are sacred women."

"OK, sure."

Stang had scowled as if Ivy had disagreed. "They shall take seed." Abruptly seething, he had shoved Ivy. "They shall be bent back and filled with seed and they shall repropagate the race."

Ivy's tongue had suddenly felt dry and disconnected. "Amen," he had managed.

"Every white man and every white woman has a role and a duty."

"Right."

"Every warrior plants his seed."

"Sure. OK."

"Crawford Toyle has twin sons in Norway."

"Really?"

"Toyle plants seed. Toyle has children all over the globe."

"Really?"

"And their mothers don't whore out. They don't get in Cadillacs with niggers. Those kids get taken care of."

"I'm glad," Ivy had said, remembering that Stang's mother had left him, and that was why the Kafkas had fed him breakfast every day that winter while Stang Sr. milked for Ivy's dad.

"You're glad? *Glad?* The fuck does that mean, glad? You're just glad to be here? Is that it? You think that's good enough, the white man oughta just be glad to be here? They took your goddamn farm. Jesus."

"I'm sorry."

"Now they want to take your voice away."

"My voice?"

"They want to silence you."

"I don't say so much."

Stang had stepped to his doorway and whistled. "Oklahoma Terry!" He had turned back to Ivy. "Turns out Oklahoma Terry has some good ideas. You two assholes wanna make brother, work together."

He had dangled a key in front of Ivy.

"Take Kenny's pretty truck."

———

Driving downriver toward the Pronto, Ivy felt his recent pill deplete and his pain return. Time had been easy, slippery and vague—and now it wasn't. Now every second was measured precisely by the pounding of his heartbeat out his missing fingertips.

"So are you married, Mailman Ivy?"

"Nope."

"So you're divorced?"

"Nope."

"Getting some, though, huh?"

"Nope."

"Smart enough to avoid the whole species, huh?"

Oklahoma Terry had a kind of laugh that Ivy didn't care for. Laugh, or don't laugh. That's how Ivy felt about it. Don't half laugh out your nose like *snook snook* and look for other people to laugh with you. Especially when what you said wasn't funny.

"Nope," Ivy told him. "The only species I ever avoided was Brown Swiss because they get too big. One of them steps on your foot you're walking on a pancake the rest of your life."

"You're a smart man to avoid the whole species," Oklahoma Terry went on. "They take everything. Now they want to give it all to the blacks."

He went *snook snook*, and Ivy felt him watching.

"You hear what happened to your pretty Sheriff Snowflake? Cup of coffee? That's a lie. I did that. Then she taunts me. Isn't that just like the species?"

Snook? he asked. *Snook?*

Pain seemed to bleed out and fill up Ivy's bandage, a fat wad of agony across his lap while he hung on to Kenny's steering wheel.

"Mailman Ivy, huh? Not Brother Ivy? Anybody tell you what you had to do to make brother?"

"Only my mom coulda made me a brother."

"Ah, yes, the sacred species. . . ."

Ivy kept his eyes on the road. His pill was *gone.*

Oklahoma Terry said, "OK, well, as for me, I sure can make a stronger cup of coffee."

"Youse guys gonna grill out?" the clerk at Pronto said when Oklahoma Terry set down a roll of aluminum foil on her counter. He turned and went back down the aisles.

"Yeah," mumbled Ivy. She was a heavy gal with bleached hair, pale skin, and green contact lenses. She wore a lot of rings.

"Yeah. Um, so does Kenny Kick ever come in here?"

"Kenny Kick-Me? He comes in here all the time."

Ivy looked around for Oklahoma Terry. He was somewhere in the back of the store.

"So has he been in here"—Ivy cleared his sticky throat—"as of late?"

She made a saucy face and Ivy knew why. Kenny would tease a

turtle if he knew it was a female. "Oh, you betcha. I just had the pleasure yesterday."

A train horn blew. The Burlington Northern ran right behind the
Pronto building, which now began to tremble.

"Yesterday . . . ?"

"Afternoon."

"Driving his new truck? That one out there?"

"Nope. Yesterday he was driving some old red piece of junk and
hauling a canoe trailer with one canoe on it." She had to raise her voice
over the approaching train. "He had that nasty little shit Rolf Stang
riding shotgun."

It hurt to talk louder, but Ivy did. "He come in for a can of chew,
I guess?"

"Nope. He was filling a can of gasoline. I said to him, 'It ain't floating season yet. What you hauling that canoe for?' It was like he didn't
even hear me. He said, 'I always wanted to try one them cigars—'"

The horn blew at closer range. The whole Pronto felt like it was
cringing, trying to levitate and move away. She was pointing down her
counter.

"—them Backwoods Wild Rums, them right there. 'Now or never,'
he says! He had one of them lit before he even hit the door!"

Ivy put his right hand to his left wrist and felt like he was pulling
his bandage out of the way. But anyway, the speeding train felt like
it hammered right through his fingertips, tore them wide open. He
stared at his bandage, waiting to see it turn red.

"Find everything you need, hon?"

Onto her counter Oklahoma Terry had set down three one-liter
plastic soda bottles and a gallon jug of heavy-duty drain cleaner.

He gave Ivy a nudge.

"This will make a real good cup of coffee," he said. *Snook snook.*
"Won't it?"

30

Neon jumps the creek and lands in a wild place where nature has grown over the past. He knows what an oak looks like, but he can't tell a hickory from any other kind of tree, so he heads off in the general direction where Royal has pointed. For an hour he searches up and down the creek's narrow floodplain among spear-like stumps and surging sapling thickets, finding nothing to suggest a burned-down house.

Something isn't right. Royal might be crazy or a liar. There can't have been a house here. He sits on a shattered log, empty sockets where it once had limbs. Beside him is the desiccated turd of some creature that apparently eats hair. The incident sticks with him, how the drunken Proud Boys had stalked him and cornered him and said, *Look the fuck at you*, like he was all that they had ever wished for. He had been in big trouble before Royal flashed the big silver pistol, handed down from Vernice Freeman.

He stands suddenly and squints toward the narrow gravel road where Royal left him. The Valkyrie is still there. Clammy with relief, he sits back down. He can still leave any time he wants. But he doesn't want to want to leave—because he knows he won't.

He won't be home tonight either. His stepdad, Dan, taught him to ride the Valkyrie, and he is welcome to use it as long as Dan knows where and when. Dan Jansen is as white as angel food cake. He is mellow, intelligent, and he laughs a lot. He has a shit-pile of money. Neon knows he's not supposed to, but he likes Dan, the only one who doesn't seem to judge him. Dan and Neon's dad, Wayne Shivers, get along. One time about a month ago the three of them had played Hustle at the hoop in the driveway of Dan and Mom's house. Neon had won easily, and the two older men had slapped him on the back. Then they all moved inside for gin and tonics with Neon's mom and the honey-haired bombshell his dad is dating, Cheryl, daughter of some bigwig who, like Dan, is a money-tree shaker for the Wayne Shivers for State Senate campaign.

Sitting on the log, Neon rewinds that evening. In the middle of the second gin and tonic, when he was across the living room changing a jazz CD, the conversation behind him had paused, and his mom and dad—and even Cheryl—had looked at him with puzzlement and pity. He was just out of treatment—he had overdosed on oxazepam—and he had sensed acutely what they were thinking: Plenty of kids are bi-racial. What's the big deal? Why can't it be an asset? Why is this kid always dragging his feet? Why is he beating himself up? What's the story here? Sensing this, Dan had praised Neon's CD choice and broken the spell.

Now he notices the log's polished surface. There never was a house here. There couldn't be. Floods. That was why a log was here. She had to live on higher ground. He has to be smarter.

————

Shadows lengthen. The air softens. For a while he worries again that Royal might be crazy, or just mistaken. But at last, on a shelf of forest hardly bigger than that driveway basketball court, beside a trickling spring, he finds what he thinks is a remnant of Vernice Freeman's house, the outline of a foundation.

He aligns himself, and beneath the thick mat of leaf litter and tiny pink wildflowers he sees a rectangular shape. A hummock of soft soil, when he kicks into it, turns out to be the stump of a chimney, stream-bed rocks still mortared together and scorched black. Yes, this is her house, buried under thirty years of forgetting. When Neon kicks through the duff, what looks like a rotting log becomes the remains of a hand-hewn beam, gnawed narrow by flames. What started the fire? *Believe me*, his granny had said, *she was real careful.*

He kicks out more charred wood fragments, more scorched chimney stones, then a rusted bucket, then pale-blue shards of stoneware dishes. A hundred feet from the foundation, a clogged little hillside grotto must have been her root cellar with its hobbit-size door.

Most likely, Royal had said, *she hid it in the root cellar.*

The door's timbered archway has collapsed, the hillside has slid, and if the box is in there, Neon thinks, he won't find it easily. But he raises the shovel and drives its blade into the slump of dirt and stones that blocks the rotten door.

Maybe he won't ever find a box. But he feels astonished and excited. An old black woman lived here, alone in nature, a century and a quarter after the first slaves arrived and decades after their last descendants had left for the cities.

He stabs and twists with the shovel. He wasn't born yet. But he knows some things about the time period toward the end of her life. Michael Jordan was a new superstar. AIDS was new too, and so was Nintendo. President Reagan was protecting white America from black welfare queens, while Steven Spielberg made *The Color Purple* from the Alice Walker book. The Rodney King riots were just ahead. Right here, a seventy-year-old black woman, the last pioneer in Lyric Valley, awoke with her house on fire, everything in flames, fight or die, and Vernice Freeman had fought *and* died.

Part of the root-cellar doorframe breaks loose, and Neon twists free a rusted iron spar with dangling bolts. In his new stillness, he hears a grinding, droning noise in the distance. He remembers, with a spike of nerves, the Proud Boys again, and the posse at his motel door, and the convoy of bikers below the cemetery. The sheriff thinks he should go home. So does Royal. He knows he should trust them. But he wants to trust himself.

The sound grinds closer, closer. Then distinctly the rumbling turns off the paved road and works its way on gravel up the ravine toward

Neon. He feels her then, his great-great-whatever, Vernice Freeman, a sitting duck, nowhere to go.

Armed with the rusted iron spar, Neon comes with his heart banging to the rim of the flat ground. He looks out across the rocky floodplain and the tiny stream to the gravel road that brought him here, in the center of which the Valkyrie is still parked. He is relieved to see not a marauding gang of bikers but one large man in an orange vest, driving a heavy green tractor that dangles a crane mower. As the tractor creeps along the road, the mower hacks down weeds and brush along the shoulder. It's just a worker doing maintenance.

But the Valkyrie is in the way. The tractor approaches. Neon hollers—"Hey! Hey, sorry, hold on, I'll move it!"—but he can't be heard. The tractor-mower bears down, and Neon understands that his *nice yellow Jap bike* will be crushed, and he will be trapped in Bad Axe County.

But the driver shuts down the mower. He ladders from the cab to the road—a giant, sun-scorched white man, shirtless under his reflective vest—puts his fists to his hips, his puzzlement and frustration clear from a distance. Neon remembers he has locked the bike. It won't roll. The tractor-mower fills the whole road, and there is no place for it—except down the bank and into the rocky little creek.

This huge guy makes a decision then. He picks the Valkyrie up—six hundred pounds!—as if to throw it in the creek.

"No! Shit! Wait!"

Hollering, Neon mashes through hillside forest toward the creek. Soon he is among willow saplings and can't see the road. He listens for the crash.

Instead, he hears the mower restart. When he can see again, the Valkyrie is reparked thirty feet down the road. The big man has carried it out of the way. There is no other explanation. The tractor-mower has moved on up the road.

Neon stops with his pulse in his throat.

Astonished, he looks at the sky, then at his phone. He still has time before sunset.

31

Sheriff Kick hit her husband with a text that felt careless and cold.

Your mom can't watch the kids. They are in the left field bleachers with Gabby.

Back at the Public Safety Building, she checked on Belle in her office, then took her laptop to the deputies' break room, poured herself coffee, and scowled her way through more forensic photos of the crime scene. One of the La Crosse County investigators had walked downstream on the Little Bad Axe River and taken pictures of what looked like boot prints and a canoe keel dragged across a muddy shallow. She would ask Denise to call canoe rental outfits.

Her attention had just swung back to Terry James Lord when Denise stuck her head into the squad room.

"It's McClain County, Oklahoma."

Back in Dispatch, she put LINE 1 on speaker.

"This is Sheriff Heidi Kick."

"Well," began an older man's reedy voice on the other end, "I'm glad to hear that. I'm glad to hear your voice."

"I'm sorry?"

"This is McClain County sheriff Mike Overbay. I'm glad you're OK. We've been out to visit Terry Lord's parents. We found out that just his mother is still alive. She said he was living with her after a divorce until she threw him out. We visited his ex-wife in the next county over, and, Sheriff, let me tell you, that woman came to the door with a can of bear spray, and we do not have bears in Oklahoma."

He paused. "What would be my point?" He then answered himself uncomfortably, "Sheriff, now don't go hashtagging a dumb old man, but would you happen to be kind of what they call a strawberry blond?"

She glanced at Denise, who was rolling her eyes. "Kind of. Yes."

"Freckles?"

"I've got freckles, yes."

"Pretty green eyes?"

"Green eyes. Yes."

"Uh, do you . . . would you mind . . . I guess I'm trying to ask about your body type."

Denise was flipping the bird at the dispatch phone console. The sheriff touched her arm to calm her.

"Would you like me to send you a picture?"

"Tell you what instead," Sheriff Overbay said. They waited ten seconds, hearing keyboard clicks. "I just sent you folks the picture I came up with."

Denise sat down in front of her monitors. She opened email. The sheriff moved to see over her shoulder.

"That's his ex," Overbay was saying, "Lila Rogers-Lord, you see her now? She said Lord was into all kind of big-talking, don't-tread-on-me, sovereign-citizen baloney, thought he was the next Ammon Bundy. She pointed us to a friend of his. The friend told us, no, Terry Lord had no friends, but he had been talking nonstop about you, Sheriff, for a month."

Denise opened the photo file. Lila Rogers-Lord looked dully angry, but beneath that she was pretty enough, or had been once, a compact strawberry blond with green eyes and freckles. Denise shot the sheriff a look. She felt a chill. She and Lord's ex-wife could have been sisters.

"My guess?" Sheriff Overbay said. "About a skunk of his stripe? This fella'd really like to hurt her, but he can't."

She sent Bob Check an email he wasn't going to like. In the restroom, she looked at her face. Her skin was starting to welt up into long gray bubbles. Her ear looked like it came from a Halloween costume. She washed her gloved hands and dabbed more ointment on the injured skin. She washed the gloves again and fumbled with the paper towel.

Then she heard a voice outside the door. She stopped crumpling paper towel.

Or voices. . . .

She took two soft steps toward the door, thinking, *Anyone can walk into this building. Anyone, anytime.* Thinking, *Lord has support here in the Bad Axe.*

The voice—or voices—went quiet.

There are security cameras everywhere—but maybe that's how he becomes a hero. That's how he gets on internet and TV.

She forced a deep, slow breath. She had asked for this. He had come for her again.

Her pistol felt weird with gloves on. She peeled them off and quickly wiped herself. She took another two soft steps. One silent millimeter at a time, she turned the door bolt. She returned both hands to the pistol, cocked it and held it body-mass high.

She squinted her eyes nearly shut to protect them. She raised her boot, kicked the door open, thrust the pistol with both fists.

"Get on the ground!"

Poor Bob Check stopped reading her email out loud. He sank slowly to his knees.

32

In the hour before darkness, oaring with the shovel through heaps of fallen root-cellar wall, Neon finally finds the buried box.

It is a metal toolbox, rusty blue, three feet long and shallow, a handle on top, latched and wrapped in rotten rope.

He carries it out beneath the sky, tentative and excited. Vernice Freeman has left behind three items: on top, a small book with a decomposing leather cover, tied shut with a string. This book is laid over a rusty ax with its wooden handle sawed short to fit into the box. Beneath the ax on the toolbox bottom—Neon stares, his nerves thrumming—are the skeletal bones of a severed human arm.

He doesn't know what he should do next—except open the book.

He needs to sit first, catch his breath, cool off and calm down, savor the unfamiliar keenness of his mind. *I told Gus what I thought happened to Vernice back in the sixties, and who I thought killed her later . . .* For so long, Neon thinks, he was dead and buried too. He and this box together are the jar fly, the buried voice, the forgotten story, coming back.

Inside the leather cover he finds dried flowers pressed among the brittle pages. Beneath each pressed flower is a pen-sketch of the flower when it was new and alive, and in careful cursive she has written its name.

Blue spiderwort.
Trout lily.
Mayapple.
Milk thistle.

There are many, many more pages like this. At first, he is disappointed. Then he understands this is her story: for a while, Vernice Freeman was at peace.

English aster.
Black-eyed Susan.
Forget-me-not.

Then, after that last flower, placed perfectly, he comes upon folded, yellowed newspaper clippings. Beneath these on the pages, in that same fine handwriting, his granny's cousin begins to talk about change.

August 13, 1966
I will tell now before I go. I know who did all the violence to what few of us black people were left, and it was not what folks said. It was not a ghost . . .

A ghost? Neon looks away into the gathering shadows, then back into the past. The first clipping is from 1963 and has this headline: FIRES, LIVESTOCK DEATHS PLAGUE REMAINING NEGRO FARMS. He uses the light from his phone as he skims it. Some unknown and unseen person is terrorizing the "Negro families," shooting livestock, burning barns and houses and places of business. The Bad Axe County Sheriff's Department has no suspects.

He looks back at a phrase: *what few of us black people were left . . .*

She has sketched a picture there—a building that seems to be a bank—and an arrow off that page to the next page. He turns it over.

First this was not so much hate as the farming changed. There was refrigeration, there was trucks and highways, there was seed patents, there was big new machines. The black farms couldn't get the loans to keep up. Around here and everywhere else black folks could not borrow money.

She has sketched a line of power poles and wires leading off the page.

And the white towns got rural electric twenty years before it came to Lyric Valley. So there was only a few us left, and HE took care of that.

Neon turns forward. Here is another clipping, folded inward so that what he sees is an advertisement for farm equipment and another for TV dinners and frozen orange juice on sale. He reads beneath it:

Yes, I know who did all the violence to what black people were left, and HE was not a ghost. No one saw HIM, no one could guess where HE came from, no one could explain HIM, as this was a good place and we folks had done nothing wrong. So all those crimes had to be a ghost. This is what they said.

He unfolds the article. It's a feature from the *Wisconsin State Journal*, a state-wide newspaper: COULEE DWELLERS FEAR THEIR FARMS ARE HAUNTED. He doesn't feel the need to read it.

No HE was not a ghost, HE was a hateful man, and as I did not have live-stock nor barn nor place of business and since I was just a lone Negro woman who would not leave my house to let him come and burn it, HE came and took my body. That is how I seen HIM . . .

What? Neon reads it back.

HE came and took my body. That is how I seen HIM and how I knew who HE was.
    After that, when I had the chance I caught HIM coming over the Lyric Valley bridge and I killed HIM and HE disappeared.

All it stopped.
THEN you can talk about a ghost. Not before. Then.
Hollow Billy.

Neon unfolds the next clipping. WILHELM SKAARGAARD PRESUMED DEAD. There is a photograph: a sullen man's unshaved face. The ancient clipping makes it hard to tell, but his skin might be a shade darker than you might expect on a Norwegian, and his nose looks like Neon's. The article reports that Wilhelm Skaargaard's boots and clothing had been collected from a dike along the Mississippi. No other trace of him was found. This little piece of the story finishes on a mournful note. *He was known to all as "Billy," and had assorted occupations.*

On the next page, Vernice Freeman gives more explanation.

Some of my Milwaukee people had come the year before and gave me a big silver gun. I practiced it. Then I got HIM coming back my way over the Lyric Hollow bridge, drunk as a skunk, to take me again, HE thought. I shot him and I buried him there.

Here is the piece of HIM that I kept, to show what I did, to prove what I did so the story will be told true—NOT A GHOST, A MAN—and the ax that I took it with.

Neon swallows a sickly surge of excitement. He looks at the severed arm in the toolbox, gray bones from the elbow to the hand. He looks back at the photograph of Wilhelm Skaargaard. Vernice Freeman killed him, and the terror stopped.

That big silver gun I used I gave away to another one who needs it for protection, Royal Strander, my good close friend, as I will never kill again.
I pray to God to forgive me.

Neon turns the page.

When she was born, I gave the baby to Colliers—

This takes Neon's breath away. *HE took my body*. She was raped and made pregnant.

He doesn't feel ready for this. He calculates how old she was then. At least forty. Alone. Pregnant. His granny said she had come from Milwaukee to help with "female business" and that her "skin crawled for a month."

> When she was born, I gave the baby to Colliers because I could not keep her and they couldn't have their own and the baby looked white enough. Marinette Collier she was called. I was sorry because Colliers turned out to be drinking people and she had a hard life. My baby grew up and went with many men who never knew she was my child but then she married HIM, the one who found out (I would guess her drunk brother, mean Bud Collier, told HIM), and this is what happened.

Neon unfolds a clipping from the local paper: CAVE HOLLOW WOMAN DISAPPEARS. The article begins: *According to the Bad Axe County Sheriff's Department, Cave Hollow Canoe owner Rolf Stang Sr. reports his wife missing. Marinette (Collier) Stang, 29, was last seen by her husband on November 6 outside a tavern on the Great River Road at Blackhawk Locks getting into a Cadillac with Illinois plates.*

To which Vernice Freeman answers:

> She did not disappear but HE killed her, even they had a boychild. This I know, HE was another hateful man and this "missing woman," my child, was thrown in the River. HE told a lie to the world and his boy, who but unwilling is my poor blood grandson and will have my eternal love.
> HE knows I know.
> Now HE will come after me.
> I am ready. I have lived.
> I ask the Lord forgiveness.
> Let all things be known.

33

Hatred?

Old as dirt.

Hate crimes and hate groups?

Ancient too, deeply woven into the fabric of the nation, of all nations. Heck, the Ho-Chunk hated the Illini, who hated the French, who hated the British, who hated the Americans, and Americans all hated one another in the Civil War, did they not? Blood and bones everywhere. Hatred was human. Get over it.

These were the first arguments made by Bob Check, one of the sheriff's favorite people, comarshal with his wife for Sunday's Syttende Mai parade, chairperson of the Bad Axe County Board of Supervisors, and the county's most powerful decision maker. They were both still shaky from the scare at the restroom door, which she had not explained yet.

She offered him a cup from the Mr. Coffee in the squad room. He raised his three-fingered right hand—two were severed by a combine, she had heard—telling her *No*, or more like *Hell no*. Bob had a few festival beers in him, she guessed, and of course it annoyed him to get her difficult email and have to leave his wife and grandkids at the fairgrounds, to have to meet with her and think about this ugly stuff right now, with "Baby Doll Polka" booming across the soybean field and the final round of the tractor pull due to start any minute.

"I hear you, Bob."

"If what you think is true, then this ain't anything new or different."

"You're right."

"People just want attention. Don't give it to them."

His points aligned thematically with those made two months ago by several on his board of supervisors, questioning the sheriff's fitness for the job after she had "made a mountain out of a molehill" and "embarrassed the community" and "dragged in the media" in the case of Kenny Kick. Bob had played the middle ground on that one, thereby supporting her. He was honest enough to understand that Kenny's act was some kind of provocation, intended to inflict something on someone. Bob had been wise enough, yesterday, to share her curiosity and concern about the Sons of Tyr. But her email had suggested major acts of sacrilege, and Bob Check had his limits.

"Ignore them. They'll give up and go away."

"But what if it's more serious than that, Bob? What if people get hurt? More people."

"For Chrissake, young lady," he fumed, "you don't throw the baby out with the bathwater!"

"Well, Bob, what if that baby is a monster?"

"Aw!" He threw both arms up, his weathered face gone crimson. "For cry-eye!"

Knowing she would have to make her case, she had brought her laptop to the table where her deputies ate lunch. Harley's mom was in her office on makeshift house arrest, with Rhino leaving the dispatch desk and walking Belle outside on the half hour to smoke. As the sheriff worked the laptop keyboard to bring up a photograph, her raw fingers looked alien. The skin from her knuckles to her wrists had drawn together into strange ridges and wrinkles. Her subtle pink fingernail paint had dissolved. Her hands looked a hundred years old.

"This is Nelson Flores, Bob. This happened just a couple of days after the flag thing."

He squinted at the laptop screen with his ferociously blue eyes. The photo documented Flores's gruesome facial injury.

"Hit with a boat anchor, my guess, while waiting for the coulee bus on the Great River Road. The anchor was found by a mushroom hunter, who marked where it was. But when Deputy Czappa went to find it, it had somehow disappeared. No suspects yet. And just Thursday night, this kid here—"

She showed him Carlos Castillo.

"—got beat up at a fight club. Did you know we had a fight club in the Bad Axe? He got drugged and beaten by a much older white man with mace on his gloves. Other men made money on it. He says they tried to imprison him in a dog kennel. He escaped."

Movement at the window drew her eyes from the screen. There was Belle now, lighting up in the jail's exercise yard, Rhino standing by with his arms folded on top of his big belly, wearing his remote earpiece to the dispatch phone and moving gently to "You are my baby doll. . . ."

"My mom-in-law took Castillo to the hospital," she told Bob. "She's worried for her safety. That's why she's here. She feels threatened by whoever runs the fight club. My brother-in-law, Kenny, is involved in this—and Kenny's gone missing."

She brought a different screen forward, the newspaper's new online edition.

"This is the article on Augustus Pfaff in the *Broadcaster*. I'm sure you saw it. 'Local Author Looks Back on Bad Axe History.' He was going to self-publish a book about the history of the round barns, and that includes . . ."

She leaned in closer and read aloud.

"'The story of the fugitive slaves who settled in the Bad Axe and lived here for several generations, integrating with the settlers and the immigrants from Europe. Mr. Pfaff's book will detail lost family trees and document interracial relations going back four generations. It will include a ghost story, a murder mystery, and other surprises.'" She looked up. "Did you read the article?"

Bob Check grunted suspiciously. "I read every word in the paper."

"I have to show you something else."

But first she stalled, understanding a kindhearted old man's reluctance to believe.

"We have to face this, Bob. Augustus Pfaff planned to tell the truth about the racial history of the Bad Axe. Some of us are related to slaves and don't know that, or have been hiding it. His book was supposed to go on sale at the fairgrounds today."

She opened a photo file sent by the forensics team.

"And this is Mr. Pfaff's house as of this morning, burned to the ground, with all the copies of his book, his research, everything."

She opened another photo. Bob Check winced and looked away. She closed it.

"That was his body, Bob. Burned. Missing an arm."

She gave him a few moments.

"And I don't think he was the only one in danger. The crime was interrupted by Neon Shivers, the kid from Milwaukee, and then by Ivy Kafka. And by the way, Bob, we can't find Ivy now either. He walked out of the hospital this morning. I have a deputy checking on the hour. His car is home, but Ivy is not. He's not in any tavern that we know of. And we have to worry about the Shivers kid too, don't we? I advised him to go home. But this afternoon he was seen leaving the fairgrounds, following Royal Strander's van on his motorcycle. Royal and Mr. Pfaff were good friends. I'm sure Royal contributed to Mr. Pfaff's book. I'm sure Royal knows what's in it. And the Shivers kid is here because of the book. He was bringing a copy of the manuscript back to Mr. Pfaff. Whoever killed Mr. Pfaff probably thinks that Neon Shivers read the book."

She let that sink in, watching Bob grip and ungrip his fists. Then she shared a close-up of Pfaff's charred arm stump.

"According to the forensics people, Mr. Pfaff's right arm was very likely cut off with an ax. A very sharp ax."

Bob Check jerked his head away and glowered out the window where Harley's mom was smoking. His hands shook. He grabbed one with the other.

She repeated it. "An ax." It felt primal, vengeful and savage. An ax struck fear to the bone.

"But the investigators haven't found an ax head in the fire. I'm going to proceed on the assumption that the killer brought his own, a personal throwing ax, given what happened to Ivy. In other words, he planned to cut up Mr. Pfaff, who was about to reveal to the world who in the Bad Axe is the decedent of black slaves and doesn't know it. Or who knows it—and hides it."

She opened one last file.

"This photo is safe to look at. This is Mr. Pfaff's computer."

It was the charred and melted CPU with its side panel pried out.

"The killer took his hard drive," she said. "Why could that be? My guess is he was afraid it would survive the fire. And why be afraid of that? Because if the drive survived the fire, I would be reading Mr. Pfaff's book right now, making a list of names. I would be using that to figure out who killed him. Now we don't even know where he had the book published. Everything's gone."

Bob Check looked at her ferociously.

"You'll find out who killed Gus anyway. That's what we pay you for. You'll figure it out."

"Yes," she said. "I will."

"But one bad apple don't spoil the whole barrel."

She tried not to jump on this. She tried to speak gently.

"Bob, but the proverb says that one bad apple *does* spoil the whole barrel. It's a pop song, Donny Osmond, Michael Jackson, that says it doesn't."

He burst from his chair—"Doggone it!"—and began to pace with a limp.

Craving one of Lord's cigarettes, she slipped two tabs of Nicorette between her lips and crunched. Instantly the buzz climbed up her neck. Her eyes seemed to crinkle, and her heart darkened.

"Bob, this is privileged information, withheld while we investigate. My hands, my face . . . I didn't spill coffee on myself. A man threw hydrochloric acid on me. Remember the bounty on my head for being a traitor? As this guy threw the acid, he said, *This is what a traitor looks like.* I'm a traitor because I charged Kenny with intimidation because he flew that flag intending to intimidate. In the context, I considered it hate speech and I still do. Bob, the man who threw acid on me has friends in the Bad Axe. I thought you were him outside the restroom."

He exploded again. "Doggone it to hell, Sheriff! We don't hate people here! That's not who we are! Does every ding-dang thing have to do with the color of somebody's skin? We don't care! Heck, I'm pink. Poor me. I got all these brown polka dots. Poor pink-brown-polka-dot Bob Check! Next thing you know . . ."

She closed her ears to the soundtrack of her beloved dad going off the rails years ago. Next thing you know there's fifty naked Kenyans living in the White House. Next thing you know people are going to marry goats, and the government'll put you in jail if you don't like it. Next thing you know . . .

She had two more things to show Bob Check, if and when he calmed down. Then he would convene his board of supervisors to act on her advice, or not. Her point was not that the Bad Axe was spoiled, that the whole community had gone bad. Her point was to keep everyone safe until she could find the few bad apples. At the start of this conversation, way back before Bob told her *hate is old as dirt*, her email had laid out three things that she, as sheriff, did not have the authority to do. The county board had to formally approve. First, she wanted to close the fairground gate, designate a No Weapon Zone, and inspect incoming guests. Second, she wanted to pay overtime for at least three extra deputies through Sunday night. Finally, she wanted to cancel the parade. The board would convene a special meeting at seven, just minutes ahead.

"Bob?"

He still paced, but he had stopped yelling. She turned the laptop toward him.

"This is from Denise. She and Rhino are kind of my social media eyes and ears. Look at this picture from the internet. It's Kenny Kick, still flagging Main Street, all day every day."

The sheriff changed screens.

"Just this week, Bob, that picture of Kenny and his flag on Main Street popped up on a website called Stormfront. And this"—she made sure he was looking—"is Stormfront. White Pride, World Wide. The voice of the embattled white minority. Here's a link to Stormfront's radio channel. At this very moment, David Duke is on the air. And why are we, little Farmstead, Wisconsin, our own Kenny Kick and his flag, on Stormfront's website?"

Her stomach turned. It felt just like in her first weeks as interim sheriff when she had been forced by events to click her way into the cesspool of pornography and organized sex crime. She opened the article and read the post aloud.

" 'Calling all brothers to join the Sons of Tyr and special guest international white civil rights leader Crawford Toyle to march on Farmstead against oppression of the white voice—' "

"Goddamn it!" roared Bob Check. "Goddamn Mickey Mouse internet!"

He didn't have anything to say next. He slammed the squad room door on his way out.

She finished reading the call to march.

" 'While hopefully fucking up some antifa,' " she read, " 'and shoving the Bill of Rights up the ass of race-traitor Sheriff Heidi Kick, a.k.a. Sheriff Snowflake.' "

———

Ten minutes later the special board meeting to consider her requests had begun. She had closed the laptop but was still sitting there in the squad room, in a weird state of agitated paralysis, both hyper and exhausted, when Denise appeared.

"Heidi, there's a fight at the fairgrounds."

34

Back in high school when she was the statewide Dairy Queen, Sheriff Kick had been a target for all types, for well-wishers and backstabbers, for starry-eyed little girls and sweetly wistful old men, and especially for horndogs, ass-grabbers, and creeps. Her patience was constantly challenged, and there had been some tense moments.

But she had never gotten into a fistfight.

She would have performed just fine, though, if she had, and Serenity Detweiler was of similar farm-girl stock. The 2018 Syttende Mai queen looked no more than superficially injured.

In fact, the sheen of lusty rage on Serenity's face implied that she was hungry for more. The fight had gone to the ground. The queen's gown told that story in grass stains and dust. She was barefoot. A mortified member of the Lady Lions Club stood by holding a pair of sparkly blue heels. Serenity's tiara was snarled in her waist-deep buttermilk hair, hanging upside down between her broad, heaving shoulders. She had a welt on her neck, one eye was closing fast, and both her elbows were scraped and bleeding. Her perfect teeth showed in a wrathful smile, and through them, producing gasps and probably resigning her queenship, she seethed, "Motherfucker."

"Oh, dear," a Lady Lion murmured.

Serenity used the word again. "Let the motherfucker up. I'm gonna kick his face in."

For a moment the sheriff thought that she had finally found either Terry James Lord or Kenny Kick. But a closer look spoiled that hope. The county ag agent, Howie Herfel, had his big knee planted matter-of-factly between the shoulder blades of Waylon Kramer, a petty criminal, tavern brawler, and all-purpose meth-dervish whom people called "Taz," after the Tasmanian Devil. Not Kenny, then, and not Terry James Lord either, but definitely a man of that caliber.

"Binch!" Taz raged at the Syttende Mai queen as Herfie muffled his face into the dirt. He didn't have a shirt on. His back was scratched and bleeding.

Sheriff Kick had jogged from her Charger. She was breathing strangely fast, recalling the ER doctor's warning about complications as she made a wider assessment of the conflict. Among maybe two dozen observers, mostly strangers, there was aggressive pushing and shoving that Deputy Czappa strove to contain, with the drunken help of a few men from the beer tent.

Who were these people? The skirmish looked like the ad hoc jousting at the outskirts of a hockey fight. There were clearly uniforms and teams. It was sinewy outsiders in bandannas, dreadlocks, and cargo shorts, including persons of color, including women, including talky accusations and name-calling . . . versus obscenity-and-death-threat-spewing white men who were on average fifty pounds heavier, dressed in black, covered in tattoos, and sporting flattops or shaved-and-top-knotted skulls.

Out of all these combatants, Deputy Czappa restrained a tiny hectoring white woman with blue hair and a nose ring. Czappa spun her and pushed her away so hard she nearly took flight.

"Go back where you belong."

She caught her balance. "Tool," she spat back. "You're a tool. This is how it starts. All cops are tools."

The sheriff watched for a few more moments, unsure of her course of action. One of Czappa's drunken helpers, Bjarne Eide, attempted to mediate a push-fight between two young men, one from either team. Eide was saying, "If you say *he's* a fashish, and he says *you're* a fashish, then heck I guess I'm a fashish too, we're all fashish. So let's get along."

A screech—"Pig!"—turned her. Czappa had pursued the blue-haired woman. He twisted her arm behind her back, her fingers up behind her neck. He was shoving her ahead as if taking her into custody.

"You can't say that," he was seething. "You can't talk that trash. That ain't how it works around here."

"Czappa!" the sheriff barked. "Let go of her! Now!"

She wasn't ready for this. Farmstead wasn't ready for this. Nobody was. She wished Bob Check and his board of supervisors could see it.

Then ominously the conflict dissolved. While her attention was on Czappa, the two sides disengaged, backed away, as if they all knew this was not the main event. *Shit.*

The sheriff drew Deputy Czappa off behind the smoky brat stand. The fairground lights had come on and the sky was a rich black blue. Still, for a dizzy moment she had to look at her watch to see what part of the day it was.

"It's past seven," she told him. "You're done soon anyway. Go home. Call in sick tomorrow. If I so much as see your face in town, I'll suspend you."

"Good," he sneered. "I got shit to do."

She shut Waylon "Taz" Kramer into her Charger and came back to talk to witnesses. Taz had gone on a bit of a streak, she learned. Already drunk when he arrived, he had tried mooching beer tickets and gotten himself escorted out of the tent. After that, he had invited himself to dance with a woman who did not want to dance with him. The Coulee Cats, five local guys playing country-western covers, had stopped in the middle of a song. Over the PA system their lead singer had told Taz to leave the woman alone.

As a protest to this "political correctness," Taz had stripped off his shirt, jammed it down in a garbage can, and begun to march bare-bellied about the festival with his arm stuck out in front of him, saying, "Stop the extermination of the white man." To the sheriff, this felt like Kenny flying the Confederate flag—Taz getting a big idea from elsewhere.

As if following the advice of Bob Check—*they just want attention, don't give it to them*—local festivalgoers had looked the other way. But witnesses told her that Taz's performance had gotten him invited over to a picnic table near the rodeo ring where some men from out of town were drinking outside the beer tent. Apparently Czappa, on duty to prevent exactly that kind of thing, had left them alone.

These men had adopted Taz. They had toyed with him a while. Then the story took its turn when they had sent him sneaking over behind Serenity Detweiler to lift up the queen's gown.

Serenity had promptly fucked him up. But not before the men had swarmed over from the picnic table in Taz's defense. And then, "out of nowhere," her witnesses told her, all these hippie-type people showed up, yelling and pointing and pushing, calling names, causing the fight. "Those people are so rude!" one witness told her.

Shit.

She slammed the Charger's door and started the engine. "Have you seen Kenny Kick today?" she demanded of Taz as she turned out of the fairgrounds onto the highway.

"Naw, I ain't see Kenny in what—a month?"

"How about your buddy Terry James Lord?"

Taz was quiet for a quarter mile.

"Uh . . . who's that?"

———

Denise was on the dispatch desk now. That meant she was the jailer too.

"What a douche canoe," she puffed, coming back hot-cheeked with Taz's box of personal possessions in one hand and a Purell wipe in the other, pressed to a scratch on her neck.

"I think I just figured out why men whistle when they sit on the toilet."

The sheriff waited for the punch line, fiddling with Denise's Mr. Coffee.

"That's how they figure out which end to wipe."

The machine was loaded but it needed to be plugged in.

"I'm afraid it's worse than that."

She could feel Denise looking at her injuries. "Do you know the difference between pigs and men, Heidi?"

"I might."

Denise stared at the sheriff fumbling with the plug.

"Heidi, you need to go home. You don't need coffee. Put that down. Your hands are shaking. You're all sweaty. Please go home and rest." She paused. "Pigs don't turn into men when they drink."

Mr. Coffee began to sputter. "You know what happens if I go home?" the sheriff answered. "As soon as I get there, right about the time I get this uniform off, you call me. Then the kids cry, I feel terrible, I come back here, and Harley gets laid. Oh—do you know a Sylvia Crayne?"

Denise frowned thoughtfully. The sheriff gave her a clue. "Old flame of Harley's? Maybe from high school?"

"Hmm. There were a lot of those, hon. We had a Steve Crayne in our class. I recall he had a pretty younger sister."

"That's her, then. Pretty."

Denise sighed. She set Taz's box of personals on the dispatch desk.

"Heidi, we can handle things without you. Morales knows what he's doing. You hired him for exactly this reason, someone from the outside you could trust, so you could let things go. That's why Morales is on night shift. Right? So you don't have to be?"

She couldn't argue. But leaving Morales in charge felt wrong at the moment. Turn this race-baited mess over to *Morales*, her new Hispanic deputy from Texas? Really? Ask *Morales* to guide her stubbornly white community through the dark night ahead? Did she honestly expect that even the well-intentioned people, the Bob Checks, would go along if Morales determined that the darkness was the whiteness? That didn't seem wise or fair. *She* was the elected official. Not one person in the Bad Axe had voted for Morales.

She poured a cup before the machine was done. While its hot plate hissed and spat, she changed the subject. "What was in Waylon Kramer's pockets?"

Denise pushed the box her way. She wasn't surprised to see that Taz had been in possession of three .22 pistol rounds, a whetstone, a twist of foil that probably contained a controlled substance, and a packet of Backwoods Wild Rum cigars with two left. But there was also a hook-less old bass lure in the design of a Budweiser can.

She said, "Kenny carries one just like this. It's the fob on his key chain. He thinks it's super cool. It belonged to his dad . . . who was a complete bum and favored Harley because Harley could play ball. But, you know how it is. . . ."

She sipped the coffee without tasting it. That had to be Kenny's key fob. Had Taz been driving Kenny's truck, picking up Terry James Lord? Denise lifted a damp wad of fabric from her desk.

"Oh, and Howie Herfel fished the asswipe's shirt out of the garbage," she said, making a disgusted face, extending the shirt to arm's length and shaking it out.

The shirt showed Mount Rushmore, but instead of presidents, the heads were race-car drivers.

The sheriff put down her cup. Her stomach rolled. "That's Kenny's too."

Denise said, "Maybe. But they're on sale at Walmart."

"No. No, that's gotta be Kenny's."

———

The lights shone brightly over the baseball stadium. She went to the fence behind first base and finger-whistled at her husband. Waiting, she waved at the kids and Gabby in the bleachers.

Harley emerged scowling from the dugout and jogged to the fence with his head down, shaking it to show everyone this wasn't his idea.

"When is the last time you saw your brother?"

He pushed back his Rattlers hat.

"Really?"

"Really."

He gripped the fence and leaned closer.

"Goddamn it, Heidi. Let up. I heard about Ma. She has to make a living somehow. Kenny is always gonna be Kenny. Just let up. You shouldn't be working anyway. I understand you're not saying what happened, but I know you didn't spill coffee on yourself. You're getting blisters. Go home, please, and rest. Take a nap."

"A nap? Somebody murdered Mr. Pfaff, Harley. I think your brother is mixed up in it. I just broke up a brawl at the fairgrounds. Farmstead is featured on a neo-Nazi website. And you want me to take a nap?"

She watched his fists tighten on the fence.

"Let's all go home," he said. "Somebody else can sheriff and somebody else can player-coach. Let's get the kids and all go home. Let's take care of you, OK?"

"No, thanks." She pressed him. "Did you see Kenny last night when the festival kicked off? When beers in the tent were a buck each until six o'clock?"

"No."

"Has Kenny ever in his life missed beers for a buck?"

"Probably not."

"He's your biggest fan. Doesn't he always come to your games?"

"Almost always."

"Did he ever respond to your message last night?"

"No."

"Is your phone in the dugout? Call your brother again, right now, and say you're worried and you really need to see him."

Harley's face had gone splotchy red. He leaned awkwardly across the fence. She stepped back. As if he had suddenly forgotten where he was, he leaned farther, nakedly straining for some forgiving contact. "Heidi, please trust me. I'm working on it. I'm going to tell you what's going on as soon as I can."

She jerked her arm away.

"Don't even think about touching me," she said.

———

On a hunch she drove Waylon Kramer's mug shot out to the hospital and showed it to Carlos Castillo.

He blanched, his skin fading toward the color of his sheets.

"That's one of the guys," he said in Spanish that she could understand. "That's one of them I escaped."

She used her phone gallery to show him an old photo of Kenny holding a sturgeon. Castillo nodded.

"*Es el otro*," he said.

She could not remember driving back to the Public Safety Building. Her head was too full. Her skin was too sore. Her heart was too heavy. But she had to stay with it. She had to yank herself into the core of this mess and rip the whole thing apart. Whoever murdered Mr. Pfaff was at the center of it all.

Time and space slipped, and she found herself in the squad room talking to Deputy Morales, briefing him on Castillo's ID of Waylon Kramer and Kenny Kick. She was gearing up to interrogate Kramer, she was telling Morales. Then she was going to meet with the forensics team. Her chief deputy was shaking his head and telling her, "*No eres invencible.*"

"What?"

"*No eres Superwoman.*"

"I know I'm not Superwoman. *Pero estoy bien.*"

"*No estas bien. Estas pa la chingada.*"

"Not right now," she said woozily. "I'm fine, but I just can't understand you."

He steered her to the window, pointed past their reflections toward the field beyond the parking lot.

"*Porque tu carro esta en el campo.* Your car is in the field."

Instead of parking it properly, she had left her Charger in gear. It had rolled by itself a hundred yards out across the soybean rows to the edge of coming darkness.

"OK," she said. "OK, I'll take a break."

Everybody just stay put, she begged, heading back to the baseball diamond to get the kids and go home.

Time skipped again—full darkness now—rolling along hilly County Highway M, mostly home—the kids piled together on the back seat whispering. . . .

Headlights winked on behind her, seemed to come from nowhere. She turned on Pederson Road. The headlights turned too. She accelerated, the headlights accelerated. She slowed, they slowed.

She turned into her driveway. The headlights went past.

35

Neon Shivers has reread every word in the little leather-bound book. He has savored the hot energy inside his brain, the itch, the eagerness, and he has decided.

Now he shovels dirt back over the toolbox with Hollow Billy Skaargaard's right arm and the ax Vernice Freeman took it with . . . *so the story will be told true.* For now, the Valkyrie can't carry this load. And he has someplace to go.

As he flings dirt and reburies the box, he thinks of the jar fly, the long-buried voice, how it sings when it comes back alive. Then there is a zombie movie he remembers: an arm plunges upward from the dirt. The dead will not stay buried. Death is not peace. Oxazepam? That is not peace. There is no peace when the truth stays buried.

He stows Vernice Freeman's flower-pressing book under the Valkyrie's seat. He has always read on his own, followed hunches and instincts, tracked bread-crumb trails across the web. He knows the word *quadroon* from the bygone practice of tagging mixed-race children like himself—half and half, a *mulatto*—with the label of the subordinate group. The ugly words have faded, Neon thinks, but for some the shame of otherness remains.

He has to know if the *quadroon*, Rolf Stang Jr., is even aware of why he suffers. He has to know if Stang Jr. ever understood why his mother, the *mulatto*, Marinette Collier, disappeared. He wants Stang Jr. to know that if he needs one, if he wants one, he has a brother.

Neon rides through the exquisite hush of dusk out of Lyric Valley, seeking Cave Hollow Canoe. He understands the landscape now. A ridgeline twists north-south down the center of the Bad Axe. Dump rain on that and the water carves the coulees down to the east and to the west. He has a compass in his mind now. If *HE*, Rolf Stang Sr., threw Vernice Freeman's daughter, Rolf Jr.'s mother, Marinette Collier, *into the River*—River with a capital *R*—then Neon wants west.

I am ready, Vernice Freeman wrote. *I have lived.*

He'd be glad to say that someday.

36

Ivy had suffered in the hours since his last pill had worn off. He had agonized as his pain enlarged and meanwhile the scene around him had become too swollenly surreal to understand.

The Sons of Tyr were training for a war with the blacks and browns and the government . . . and the people of Farmstead? The men around him were psyching up to "show force" . . . at the festival parade, the one with the volunteer firefighters throwing candy to kids at the curb? They believed they were in military training . . . by drinking, lighting fireworks, throwing axes, and racing remote-control toy trucks around Stang's canoe yard?

Meanwhile Oklahoma Terry was rolling aluminum foil into pellets and funneling drain cleaner into pop bottles, calling Sheriff Kick a flag-burning, God-hating, socio-islamo-feminazi . . . because?

Exhausted, fading fast, Ivy had said to himself as he stumbled about the canoe yard seeking a dark place to lie down, *Doing nothing, Mailman Ivy, you are the traitor.*

Somewhere in these hours he had staggered inside the barn and found Rolf Stang Jr. in his office, at his big steel desk, bending into a foggy little mirror. "Um . . ." Stang had turned, small-eyed. He had sniffed twice.

"Mailman Ivy. The fuck you want?"

"I wondered . . . could I get another of them pills?"

Stang had lunged off his desk chair and left it spinning. One side of his thin, rusty beard was hung with red, white, and blue beads. He had grabbed Ivy's shirt, shoved his face in Ivy's face.

"Motherfucker, Crawford Toyle just called me. He's exactly one hour out. Do you not get what's happening here? Crawford Toyle. And you bother me?"

"But I just need a pill—"

"Are you talking back?"

He had shoved Ivy. Ivy had raised his throbbing hand out of the way.

"Are you trying to embarrass me? Is that what it is? I'm not ready! You trying to make a cuck out of me in front of Toyle? You think I'm about to let that happen?"

"Where is Kenny?" Ivy had blurted.

Stang had mocked him in a bitchy female voice.

"Where is Kenny?"

Then he had exploded, "Fuck!"

He had crashed back down onto his chair and snorted white powder off the desktop. Muttering and sniffing, he had pushed his chin toward the mirror and fumbled with a bead.

"I gotta have another of them pills. Please."

"You gotta fuck off is what you gotta do. You gotta fuck off real fast. Fucking *vamos*."

Ivy had flinched.

"Get lost."

Ivy had reeled outside into hollering and laughter. He had drifted away to sit feebly on the ground against a canoe in the dark, shivering, gripping himself by the elbow, digging in his fingers as if he could stop the thumping pulse of pain. *Vamos!* The word had stunned him. He had faded away to the sound of axes thumping their soft wood target. . . .

———

Now he jerked awake. Someone was yelling.

"She took Taz! The bitch took Waylon Kramer! Sheriff Snowflake has a hostage!"

Ivy tried to follow a debate about Taz fighting with the festival queen.

"Fighting a girl! Don't that make him a cuck?"

"Come on! He lifted her dress! He's a hero!"

"But did he win the fight or lose it?"

"She kicked his ass, the little cuck!"

"But what color were her panties?"

The office door slammed, and Ivy looked. Stang wobbled for a moment. Then he said, "Crawford Toyle is coming, you bag of assholes. Think about it. Crawford Toyle. The dude plays golf with David Duke in Reno. He smokes cigars with Drudge and Milo. Those are his brothers. Some government snowflake takes one of them, you think Crawford Toyle stands down?"

Ivy had missed the arrival of Larry Czappa, who used to be a constable for the river towns and somehow was a deputy now. Czappa faced Stang with his hairy arms crossed and his head shaking.

"Taz is not a brother," he said.

"He is now," Stang said.

"That's bullshit."

"Who are you?" Stang said. "Oh, you're just the fight-club guy."

Czappa told him, "You can't just decide who's a brother. There's a protocol. This is an organization." He stepped closer. He had a hundred pounds on Stang. "Who died and made you king? I was there. Getting busted for being a drunken shithead doesn't make you a brother. He started a fight that could have sabotaged the march."

"I'll tell you what's sabotage," Stang said. He spoke to the others. "We lose a brother to the snowflakes, and we just wring our hands and argue. That's self-sabatoge. Hell no. We're going to take a counter-hostage."

The cheers made Ivy shudder. Czappa told Stang, "You're high."

"This aggression will not stand!"

More cheers.

Czappa said, "And you're an idiot."

"Fuck with us," bellowed Stang, "Senorita Snowflake, we will fuck with you!"

Ivy must have closed his eyes again. He must have been unconscious again for a while. The sound of shaking pills brought him back.

Stang's beaded beard and wild stare loomed in Ivy's face. Oklahoma Terry stood very close, dangling a canoe anchor by a short length of yellow rope. Darkness wrapped around them like the walls of a cave.

"Hey," Stang said. He shook the pills. "Hey, Mailman Ivy. You're gonna go with Oklahoma Terry."

He shook the pills again.

"Don't you want to make brother?"

37

Mailman Ivy drove.

Oklahoma Terry rode behind him in the club cab with the anchor, plus an emptied canvas tool bag and zip ties.

On a fresh pill from Stang, Ivy's pain had wandered off, leaving him in a cold fuzz as he navigated twenty miles inland from the canoe barn to the baseball stadium in Farmstead. He parked on the hillside behind the right-field fence, where the lights shined up to Bad Axe Manor and where Kenny's flashy truck could be seen from the diamond. Oklahoma Terry hid down behind the passenger seat. He was excited.

"Here we go, brother."

"If I'da had a brother," Ivy said dully, "I wunta never lost the farm."

Within less than two minutes, the PA announcer informed the audience of a pitching change, *Matt Aspinwall replacing Harley Kick.* In another two or three minutes, the sheriff's husband jogged with his cleats clacking up the access road to his brother's truck and hopped right in.

"Ken, where you been?" he said while he was pulling the door shut. "You OK? Heidi's been looking—"

Oklahoma Terry stunned him with the anchor, then yanked the tool bag over his lolling head. He wrenched one wrist behind the seat, pinned it, then wrenched the other one and zip-tied them together. Ivy put the truck in motion.

Clear of the stadium lights, he looked over. The sheriff's husband bled from under the bag and down his left arm. "Who is this?" he slurred. "Kenny? This can't be you, can it? Kenny?"

"Who's Kenny?" said Oklahoma Terry.

Ivy kept the truck rolling.

"Damn it," slurred Harley Kick, "why you gotta do this shit? You're killing me and Heidi."

"I'm gonna bust his head again." Ivy caught the anchor and pulled it out of Oklahoma Terry's grip. Harley Kick groaned inside the bag, "You shouldn't be listening to Stang, Kenny."

"This ain't Kenny," Ivy said.

"Stang is a loser. He's a bigger jackass than Dad was."

"This ain't Kenny," Ivy said again. Now Kenny's brother thrashed against the seat. "This is Kenny's truck, but this ain't Kenny."

"Then where is Kenny?"

Ivy laughed hollowly. He saw a flash in the mirror as Oklahoma Terry brought down Kenny's lug wrench. Harley Kick made a sound like *pfffff* as his bagged head dropped between his collarbones. "Who's a jackass now, jackass?"

Just like that, Ivy's pill was gone, and every heartbeat hurt like hellfire. He took Norgaard Ridge Road south, and then Wolf Hollow Road west, to stay out of view. The roads were dark and jarring. Oklahoma Terry snickered and snorted in the back. They emerged from the hollows at the Mississippi, just north of the Pronto station, since Stang told them, "And get more tequila." Ivy parked the truck beyond the gas pumps in the dark. He didn't like leaving Harley Kick alone in the truck with Oklahoma Terry.

Inside, he told that same gal, "Stang Jr. said he's got credit here."

She came down off her tiptoes and showed her worry by the stiffness of her body. "Don't nobody got credit here."

"Stang said he does."

"Well, don't nobody."

"He said he does."

Ivy watched her rise back to tiptoes and take another look at Kenny's truck: a front-seat passenger in a baseball uniform with a greasy tool bag over his head, and Oklahoma Terry's shadow looming in the club cab. Her chin trembled.

"OK, just this once."

Ivy watched a large white SUV glide up beside the pumps.

"He wants a fifth of Patrón Silver tequila."

Outside under the plaza lights, once he'd wobbled with the bottle past the extra-long SUV, Ivy wanted to keep going past Kenny's beautiful truck, over the railroad tracks, and right into the deadly river.

Shut this nightmare down for good.

38

Gravity guides Neon to the river. Once there, he retakes his bearings and roars upstream toward bright lights. At a gas station, a shiny blue-and-silver truck accelerates right at him as the driver pulls blindly onto the highway.

Neon swerves, locks his brakes, nearly dumps the Valkyrie.

Still in one piece, with Dan's bike still OK, he coasts shakily under the plaza lights past the gas pumps into a shadowy corner beside the station building. His downhill journey out of the coulees was a dark thrill. His near miss was a chilling twist. He just needs a minute to get his head back, think of what he wants to say.

If you ever need a brother . . .

Something like that. The right words will come.

He stands the Valkyrie and exchanges inhalations with the Mississippi's muddy, fishy breath. He decides to ask the clerk if Cave Hollow Canoe is upriver from here, or down. But he sees her in profile through the window and something about her fierce plump shape, her lank blond hair . . . something feels wrong.

He changes course instead for a burly man in a tracksuit running gas into a white SUV. He is too far committed when this feels wrong too. He stops. The man swells up and glares.

"You want something?"

Too late, Neon notices the sunglasses at night, the radio earpiece, the bodybuilding physique.

"No."

"Yeah, you do. Don't bullshit me. You want something."

"Naw, I'm good."

"You think you're good? You?"

Whoa. He's serious. As the man squares him up, Neon sees he packs a sidearm in a waist holster.

The man demands, "What's so good about you?"

Too late, Neon understands this is not an SUV but an SUV limousine, with Indiana plates, twenty feet long, custom wheels and rims. Now the passenger-side front window hums down and a red-haired woman—cherry-red hair, loose smile—looks him over.

"Cute coat!"

"Put the window up."

"I want a coat like that." She turns and says the same thing in a pouty voice to someone in the limo. "I want a coat like that!"

"Put the goddamn window up," snaps the man outside.

She gives him a face but obeys. As her window goes up, one of the rear windows burps down just an inch, a precise and purposeful movement like an ear tilting to a sound. The armed man seems to take this as a signal and closes on Neon in two bully strides.

"The fuck you want, bro?"

"I'm looking for a place around here that rents canoes."

"You like to canoe?"

"Yeah."

He comes one stride closer. "You like to canoe in the dark?"

"I just wanted to meet a guy. But never mind. Thanks. I'll ask inside."

"What guy?"

"I guess his name is Stang."

He gets a frozen scowl. "Meet him why?"

The truth seems like Neon's quickest escape. This man from Indiana can't possibly care.

"I guess we're distantly related."

But he does care, it seems. He studies Neon for a few long moments. Then he gets a drifty look, like he's hearing something in his earpiece. He almost smiles, almost nods. The rear window glides back up.

"Get in," he says. "I'll take you there."

"Naw, man. Seriously, no, thanks."

"You think I'm asking you?"

Neon sees his own reflection shrunken in the tinted windows of the limo. He hangs there for what seems like an eternity, breathing gasoline and mud, until he understands that he has blundered through the wall of history.

He feels the sidearm jab between his ribs.

"I'm not asking you, black boy. I'm telling you. I'm taking you to Stang's. Give me your phone. Give me your coat too. Get in."

39

A few Sons of Tyr still threw axes at the target under a light at the side of the barn. Others with remote toy controllers raced Jake Vig's monster trucks around the canoe lot.

"Here we go! Watch this!"

At the far fence line something exploded: a hard crack with bright light, then drifting smoke. Vig raised his controller like a trophy.

The explosion seemed to dislodge Stang from inside the canoe barn. He appeared under the yard light all fancied up and looking like a different man, like his old rage had found its shape. His beard was braided and beaded. His skull was shaved and oiled and his topknot was carefully groomed. He wore a tight black T-shirt with the sleeves rolled up over his tatted muscles. His pants were in a new style, suspendered high and tucked into knee-high lumberjack boots. He posed in the light, starting a cigarette. Behind Ivy, Larry Czappa lurked past, singing in raspy whisper that Stang couldn't hear.

> Just because you think you're so pretty
> Just because you think you're so hot
> Just because you think you've got something
> That nobody else has got . . .

Stang blew smoke. He finessed the roll of his shirtsleeves, looking off into darkness.

"Any time now, gentlemen. Any minute."

A toy truck buzzed in front of Stang. Jake Vig trailed with his remote. Ivy's eyes followed. At fifty yards the truck hit the riverside fence and exploded in a brilliant flash bang that rattled chain link all the way to the corner posts. Where the truck had hit, the fence glowed red.

Stang yanked an ax from the target. He backed up ten steps.

"Any minute now, the Sons of Tyr are gonna hit . . ."

With both hands he raised the ax overhead, aimed it, squinting through smoke. With a grunt he let it fly and stuck it dead center.

". . . the big-time."

Ivy reeled away. His fingers pounded freshly. He staggered through the barn and saw Oklahoma Terry shaking one of his soda bottles, talking with Czappa. "The species . . . ," he was saying, *snook snook,* as he dropped the shaken bottle in an oil drum and laid the lid on.

Czappa had a whiskey bottle. He waved it and he said, "Stang makes too many mistakes. I'm always cleaning up his shit."

Ivy stumbled out the back barn door past Stang's empty dog kennel where Harley Kick thrashed and groaned, attached now with real handcuffs to the kennel fence. There he stopped, slump-shouldered, panting through his nose. It hurt. It hurt. He never was a husband or a father. It hurt so bad. He was never even a brother. If he had one he wouldn't be here. From inside the barn he heard a loud pop and a hard spatter, then a long fizz.

"Sorry," he told Harley Kick. His tongue felt thick and bitter. "Really sorry. I'm gonna try to find Kenny."

On the back side of the barn were more canoes, aligned upside down like dull-silver pods in the moonlight.

Ivy shuddered. He felt Kenny somewhere. He gripped the nose of the first canoe and turned it over. Then the next.

40

In a few minutes the limo rolls smoothly alongside the Mississippi. Neon rides in the middle seat, facing backward. A low table is fixed to the floor between him and a small man with a beard who talks on his phone, ignoring Neon.

"That's not a tax shelter," he says. "You call that a tax shelter? The Caymans, that's over, bro. Too much regulation. It's all over in the Caymans."

The windows are up. The dark space smells of the cherry-haired woman's perfume and her boozy breath. She wears Neon's white quilt coat. From the front seat, she calls back, "Whacha name, hon?"

"Neon."

She screeches.

The man opposite Neon has begun to vape from an elaborate steampunk-looking device. "What kind of interest rate can you give me?" He spews vapor, a sour new smell into the mix. "Call me back when you're serious."

In a while, the driver says, "Yo, Neon, my man, you really know Brother Stang?"

"I don't know him."

"Are you jiving with me now?"

"No. I'm not."

"Why you wanna see him when you don't even know him? You said you were related. You better not be jiving with me."

"I'm not jiving with anybody. I don't want to see him anymore."

Opposite Neon, the bearded man takes another call. "No, we're not lost. Keep your pants on, brother. We're there in ten minutes, max."

Now from the front seat sounds the custom ringtone for Neon's stepfather, Dan. The driver pulls over on a bridge.

"Give it," the driver tells the woman.

She hands him Neon's phone. The driver gets out and hurls it. Over the purr of the limo engine and the chorusing of frogs, Neon hears it splash.

Soon the limo swings off the highway and onto rutted gravel. This road twists and turns, goes up and down. The driver gets annoyed, pushy on the gas and brake. Neon watches taillights ignite the swallowing forest.

The man in back finally speaks to him.

"Neon, is it?" He blows vapor. "*Enchanté*. So glad you could join us. We're going to a party." Then he acts perplexed. He asks Neon, "When did I tell the brother that we'd be there? Ten minutes?"

That's what Neon heard, so he nods.

"Dewey!" the man calls to the front. "Find us a tavern."

"A tavern?"

"Anyplace we can get some drinks and chill for an hour or two."

"Drinks!" chimes the woman.

"Look for neon," says the man in back.

The driver laughs and finds a place to turn around.

41

Both calls came while she was in the shower. She heard both messages while she was still naked, red-skinned and wet. The first message, left on her cell phone by the Bad Axe County Board chairperson, cut her loose from what little support she had come to expect.

"I'm sorry, Sheriff." Bob Check sounded squeaky and tense. "The board feels that you should not need extra deputies to keep the peace. And they've decided that the fairgrounds will remain open, without special security procedures. The parade—"

He paused. He was reading a document.

" 'Tomorrow's parade,' " he went on, " 'will not be canceled. Rumors on the internet will not dictate events in Bad Axe County. This fine and friendly community treats everyone the same, and we have suffered enough from the overdramatic interpretation of minor events.' "

She was surprised. She really was. She was surprised enough to hurl a towel that knocked bottles off the shelf beside the sink.

The second message, recorded on the landline answering machine in the upstairs hallway, was delivered through a voice-morph app that the caller had set to *monster* or *demon*. He growled at her like some fiend from a cave.

"This aggression will not stand. This treason will not be tolerated.

You have committed acts of war. Just as you have taken one of ours, we have taken one of yours. . . ."

She withstood the caller's demon-growl insanity to the end, then again, making sure she understood.

He demanded the release of Waylon "Taz" Kramer. As if there were an alternate government in the Bad Axe, at war with hers, he demanded a hostage swap.

"Call me right now," she said to Harley's voice mail. "Call me right now and tell me you're OK."

She waited sixty seconds. She nearly dialed Denise. She stopped herself. She replayed the message. "Act alone. Await further instructions. We are watching you. Mess with us, he dies."

In her bathrobe, numb and trembling, she checked that the kids were asleep. Her service pistol in her fist, she stepped into boots and went outside and walked across the dewy yard and opened the pen. The geese were confounded. Her face looked different, and she had a weapon, not corn. She was confounded too. She had no corn and no joke either. She didn't know why she had come. She sank to the dirt and hung her head between her legs, suddenly gasping to catch her breath.

Don't even think about touching me. . . .

Would those be her last words?

This aggression will not stand. . . .

Doing her job was aggression? Doing her job put her family in danger? She spat hot tears. The geese tried to eat them.

"Fuck!"

Feathers flapped. The geese crowded in, venal and greedy, demanding corn. They never thanked her, and they never cut her a break. This is why she needed them.

"What do you call a woman," she asked abruptly, channeling Denise, "who always knows where her husband is?"

She waited. They waited. This world was so motherfucking cold.

"A widow."

When she could stand again, she let herself out of the pen. She rounded the barn to see headlights creeping along Pederson Road.

The vehicle paused at the mailbox. This time it turned into the driveway.

She slipped out the barn door with her bathrobe drawn across the pistol to conceal it.

Please let him try me now. I am so ready to kill.

But the vehicle came at a feeble pace, haltingly, and it was tagged with Wisconsin plates. When the driver Y-turned within the margins of the driveway—not an attack maneuver, she realized—she thought, *OK, sure, this is my other stalker. This is the girlfriend.*

The headlights went dark. The engine stopped. Sure enough, out stepped a slender, long-haired blonde. She paused to straighten her spine and adjust her clothing. Still, she seemed wobbly and vaguely stooped as she headed for the house.

"Hey! Hey, stop right there!"

The sheriff strode forward into the yard light showing her weapon. She growled, "Who in the hell do you think you are?"

"I'm Sylvia."

"I know that. Who do you think you are, coming here?"

"Harley asked me to."

"What?"

"He asked if I would talk to you."

This had to be a lie. A stalker's lie.

"Why?"

"I knew Harley in high school."

"I know that."

"I'm Steve. I used to be Steve Crayne."

Her breath caught.

"What?"

"Harley's friend in high school. I live in Wausau now. We were pretty good friends. A couple of months ago, when things started changing with your daughter, Harley looked me up."

She felt the pistol go slick in her hand. She crossed in front of Harley's friend to the porch steps, laid the weapon down, and sat. Looking at Sylvia Crayne, her lank blond hair, her rigid body, her loose blouse and sequined jeans, her big feet in strappy sandals, she said, "Oh." She said, "Oh my God. I'm so—"

But why wouldn't Harley just tell her? Sylvia Crayne seemed to hear the unspoken question.

"Very few people know who I am now, and that's the way I want it. Your husband asked if he could just meet with me, privately, because he was trying hard to understand. It was making no sense to him. He asked if he could just talk to me about my life. He was in the dark about your child, he said, and he was scared, and he was worried he could never understand."

"Oh," she said again. "Oh. You were Steve, and now you're Sylvia."

"Yes."

"And Harley's still your friend?"

"It's funny. Once we started hanging out again, it really didn't seem any different. Yes. Harley's still my friend."

"And he understands now?"

"That part he does, I think."

"What part?"

"I'm still me. He's still him. We're still friends. It wasn't about gender or sex when we were both boys, and it's still not."

The silent minute was an eternity. She could have picked the pistol back up from the step and popped herself.

At last Sylvia Crayne said, "That's all. My parents, my grandparents, my cousins, my teachers—the Bad Axe doesn't know about me yet. I'm not ready for that. Just tonight, Harley said there was trouble and asked my permission to tell you. I said I would tell you myself. Your dispatcher said you'd gone home. I'm sorry. I hope I didn't come too late."

She re-dressed herself in jeans, boots, and her Carhartt jacket with its pocket big enough for her pistol. She replayed the message.

Act alone. Await further instructions. . . . Mess with us, he dies.

She took Terry James Lord's cigarettes from the console in the Charger and lit one.

By the time the smoke was done, she knew what she had to do. She extracted one sleeping little boy at a time, bundled him in a blanket, and laid him on the back seat of the family's aging silver Dodge Caravan. Then she picked up Ophelia and felt strong little legs clinch around her waist. Coming down the front porch steps she felt hot tears against her burned ear.

"What happened, Mommy?"

"I just have to take care of something, that's all."

"That's not all. What really happened?"

"It's going to be OK, sweetie."

"Your gun is in your pocket."

"Shhh."

"Help me, Denise."

"What's wrong?"

"Just help me."

Together they carried the children into the sheriff's office. Grammy Belle startled awake on the old leather sofa. The sheriff whispered in her ear: her second boy, her golden one, the perfect athlete, the only Kick ever who could stay out of trouble, was in trouble now.

"I need you to promise me, Belle, that you're going to tell the truth about the party bus."

"Damn right I will," Belle rasped, and got up to help.

Using jail blankets and pillows, they made beds for the kids on the floor. She kissed foreheads and hugged Belle and locked them all in her office. When that was done, thinking she might throw up, she entered the restroom and found Denise upset and dabbing at her makeup.

"Send someone to pick up Randall Stone," she commanded.

"Why Randall Stone?"

"Owner of the Missus Sippy party bus. I'd guess he'd be at the festival in the beer tent."

Denise blinked. She looked frightened. Her eyes were full.

"Heidi, please. What happened?"

"Nothing."

"This is not nothing."

"I just need the kids to be safe."

"Where is Harley?"

At his name, she turned away, bent over a sink, and began to splash her face with water, pausing once to retch. She dried her face with paper towels and turned back to her dispatcher. "Hostage."

"Oh my God," Denise said. "Oh, Heidi. Oh no. Oh my God."

"In exchange for 'Brother Taz.'"

"Oh, for fuck's sake. That shit-whistle? Then let's just do it."

"Never. We can't do that."

"Heidi, it's your husband."

"All the more reason we don't negotiate. Who do they take next time?"

Denise closed her eyes and nodded.

"Only you are going to know this, Denise. Have someone pick up Randall Stone. And put Taz Kramer in the interview room."

She left the recorder off. She drew down the blinds so she couldn't be seen from the hallway. She kicked the chair from under Taz's bony ass and watched him crack his mouth on the table as he dropped. He stared wide-eyed from the floor, sucking blood from his lips.

"I hear you're somebody's brother."

"Huh? I don't know what you're talking about."

"I hear you're Tyr's son."

"Who?"

"Your daddy, Tyr. The Norse war god. Apparently Bad Axe County is in a war with the ancient Vikings." The words tore out of her. "That makes you a prisoner of war. A mythological war. What do you think? I'd say a prisoner in a mythological war is not a good thing to be."

She paused, watching his eyes pop and roll, hoping her pulse would slow. She felt dangerous. Her mouth was dry. Her ears rang. She was truly seeing red, through the throbbing capillaries of her blurry eyes. Her burned skin seemed to sizzle.

"Not a good thing to be, because I'm going to say that a mythological war means that I can follow mythological guidelines. I can leave you in here with a wolf that eats your arm off."

"Shit." He twitched hard. "What?"

"I'm going to say it means I can bring in a dragon to chew your heart out."

She could see the panic in his eyes, his substance-altered brain contorting with cross-whipping realities. He yanked against the wrist that was cuffed to the table. He dangled in a one-armed fetal position.

"Look at me," she commanded.

He struggled up to a squat and watched her wildly over the tabletop. She felt wild too.

"I can impale you on Odin's spear. I can hit you with a thousand-ton hammer. If you're a son of Tyr, then I believe the rules say that I have access to a giant eagle that will gobble up your dick like a grub worm, right before it pecks your eyes out."

"Ah, man. Please don't say that shit to me. Please. I ain't even made brother yet. I don't even know how. I don't know what they want from me. I ain't hardly even one of them guys."

"One of what guys?"

"Sons of Tyr."

Good. That was out of the way. She was right. *They* were the Sons of Tyr.

"But I just heard that you did 'make brother.' And they want you back."

He shifted on his haunches, darting his eyes and licking blood from his lips. "Really?"

She felt herself slow down and inspect the emotional landscape she had just created.

"Really," she assured him. "I just heard they want Brother Taz back. That's you."

"Shit, man. Really?"

"They really want you back."

"Cool. Yeah, cool."

"Get up and sit on the chair."

He did. She kicked it out. Again his face smacked the table going down.

"But I really want to chain you to a rock and let my eagle have at it."

"Come on, man. Please."

"Or you could tell me something."

She could see him calculating now. If he *was* Brother Taz, a Son of Tyr, what would they do to him if he talked to her? But what would *she* do to him if he didn't? She watched him itch and sweat and bat his eyes. If she were him, she'd split the difference with a half-lie/half-truth. What Brother Taz needed now was a tightrope he could try to walk, tell a lie or two, balanced by a truth or two, fantasize that he was safe from both sides. She helped him get started.

"Where is Terry James Lord?"

"Uh . . ."

"You picked him up in Kenny's truck after he threw acid in my face."

"Um. I did? What? Uh . . ."

"That was you, right? Because you had Kenny's key fob."

"Kenny's what?"

So that was his balance on the bullshit side, lies about Terry James Lord and Kenny Kick. He could have it. She would take the truth about Harley.

"OK. I guessed wrong."

She watched his relief.

"Come on up and sit down."

He did. He hung on to the corners of the table. She let him stay.

"Why were you chasing Carlos Castillo?"

"Who?"

"The Latino kid who got beat up at the fight club Thursday night."

"Oh. Oh! That guy. Oh, yeah."

"You chased him, but he got away."

"Yeah. Yeah, see, they weren't gonna hurt him. Um. They just wanted to keep him. They wanted us to put him in this . . . Well, it was a pretty nice place, really."

"Why did they want to keep him?"

"They wanted him to fight again. They. Sons of Tyr. I mean we. Us guys. There was . . . I mean somebody . . . One of us guys wanted to fight that beaner kid again tonight."

Tonight. She glanced at her watch. It was nearly ten o'clock.

"There's another fight tonight? When?"

"Shit." He began to scratch the top of his head, too hard and too fast, as if he knew he might have chosen the wrong thing to lie about. "Uh, I guess midnight?"

"Where?"

"Unless you're a brother, you don't ever know where that shit happens until it happens. You gotta pay and ride the bus like everybody else. I wasn't a brother yet, so . . ."

She rounded the table. She poured him a plastic cup of water. When he had it in his hand, she swiped it out.

"Why did you lie about Kenny's stuff? That was dumb. Denise took that Budweiser fob out of your pocket. You had Kenny's shirt too."

"He gave 'em to me."

"When?"

"Uh, yesterday."

"Where is Kenny now?"

She watched him try to climb back on his tightrope. Time to lie again.

"He's shacked up with a lady friend over in Zion. I think."

"I see. Ride what bus?"

"The Missus Sippy."

"Where do they get on it?"

"I don't know. It changes."

"Who runs the Missus Sippy? Who would I talk to?"

"I don't know."

She kicked his chair out one more time. Then she opened the blinds so he could raise his bloody face and see Denise outside waiting with the Missus Sippy's owner, Randall Stone.

"Everybody knows that, Mr. Kramer. So now you're going to tell me who run the Sons of Tyr."

"My mom-in-law told me everything," she began with Stone. "She's in custody right now. She faces charges unless she testifies against you, and she's eager to do that."

Once more she left the recording system off. Randall Stone was beered-up and his eyes were wet. A big, soft-boiled man in a baggy white suit, he sold himself as an old-time riverboat wheeler-dealer, a colorful character from a Mark Twain adventure. Her predecessor as the Bad Axe County sheriff, Ray Gibbs, had died aboard the *Mississippi Queen*, on top of one of Stone's ladies for hire. Not even three years later, Stone's paddle-wheel nightclub boat was sinking in debt, undercut by nearby Ho-Chunk mega casinos.

"And given what Belle told me," she said, "you're on the hook for half a dozen different crimes, including off-river gambling, assault, money laundering, and, of course, since you're getting income from Wisconsin, tax fraud."

"God Almighty."

"No, Mr. Stone. I'm not God. I'm just not Ray Gibbs. I'm an actual sheriff. And I will call the feds on you. *Tonight.*"

He slumped and sighed.

"But here's the thing," she said. "I really don't want that much from you. You give me what I want, I'm willing to give you another chance to be a good citizen. What do you say?"

"What do you want?"

"Mr. Stone, is there an illegal prize fight tonight?"

"Yes."

"Are you providing a bus?"

"Yes." He had begun to look hot. "But tonight . . ." In keeping with his riverboat gambler schtick, he mopped his face with a breast-pocket handkerchief. "Tonight the bus is only from a small private party to the venue."

"From where to where?"

"At this point"—he jumped as if he had just seen her surrounding him in the dozens of mirrored windows—"at this point I don't know. Last minute, someone calls my driver."

"Who calls your driver?"

"Gibbs set that up, back in the day. It's never the same number. Lately they distort the voice. I never know."

"Is it Rolf Stang Jr.? Is it my deputy Larry Czappa?"

Because Stang Jr. had founded the Sons of Tyr, Taz had told her, while the fight club had always been Czappa's, since back when he was a constable for Gibbs. The merger, two groups into one, was going like cats and dogs, Taz said.

Those names made Stone jump. "I don't know who calls me. I don't want to know."

"Who's your driver tonight? Not Belle."

"I don't know yet. Possibly myself."

"Who pays you?"

"No one pays me. The driver deducts my fee from the cash the riders pay to get on board. It's a headcount times fifty, divided by two. The take is normally three or four hundred bucks."

"What's the ante tonight?"

"I . . . I . . . Tonight? I'm going to cancel tonight."

"No," she said.

"I'm going to say the bus broke down. I'm going to say sorry, no can do."

"No," she said, "you're not. You're going to run your bus. What's the ante tonight?"

"Two hundred. But for tonight it's going to be collected by someone else at the pickup site. It's some kind of fundraiser."

She let her thoughts catch up, her plan settle in.

Yes.

Wherever that bus went tonight, she was going to find the Sons of Tyr, and the Sons of Tyr had Harley. She would start there. Maybe find him. Maybe put a gun to someone's hate-infested skull and make Harley appear. She would figure it out. Wherever it was held, she had to get to the fight.

"Tonight," she informed Randall Stone, "I'm your driver."

42

Kenny's shirtless body seemed so small, kinked there on the ground, so almost alien with its short legs and its hairy ball for a belly, its bald skull and furry neck, its short thick fingers.

Ivy let the canoe he had lifted drop back to the earth with a soft boom. He sank to his knees beside his friend.

Maybe Kenny had just gone on a rip-snort and lost his shirt and was sleeping it off under a canoe with his face in the dirt. These things happened.

But when Ivy nudged a leg it was rigid. Ivy rolled him slightly and saw a neat black hole in the back of Kenny's head.

I have manned up, he heard Kenny telling him. *I am making a difference.*

Ivy's head hung, and his eyes closed. His damaged hand pounded enormously in his lap while the other still touched Kenny. *You gonna get with us and make a difference?*

Was it too late?

In the gloom ahead of Ivy, two dozen more canoes aligned like iron filings between the barn and the gate to the Lower Bad Axe River. Behind Ivy, Kenny's younger brother grunted and rattled the fence of Stang's dog kennel. Beyond, from the front side of the barn, the period of anxious waiting for Crawford Toyle had emptied the beer keg. Now the bourbon had run out. A collective garbled snarl echoed around Cave Hollow. A bottle rocket screamed and exploded. In the reflection under moving clouds, Ivy saw an old red pickup with a canoe trailer attached, one canoe strapped across the lowest struts. He could see that the truck had rounded the barn and parked strategically, bringing that one canoe back to fill an outer gap in the formation. But the job had not been finished. The canoe was still on the trailer.

Ivy worked his hand between Kenny's stiff hip and the gravelly dirt, then into Kenny's pocket. He fished out Kenny's lighter. Then there was a set of keys. But these did not include the key to Kenny's own truck. Ivy had that now. Was the key to the red truck on this ring? Had Kenny had been driving that truck, bringing back that canoe? And then . . . ?

Ivy sat behind the wheel of the red pickup. One key fit the ignition. He turned it halfway and switched on the dome light. He saw mud and sand on the pedals, more on the passenger-side floor. He switched the light off.

He sat a minute and remembered the game cameras watching Mr. Pfaff's driveway. He remembered the shotgun against the porch rail, beside the tuba. Mr. Pfaff had been on guard. Had someone threatened him? Had Mr. Pfaff been ready to defend himself against someone . . . who came instead down the Little Bad Axe River? In this canoe? Which then got trailered back to Stang's place by Kenny?

Yesterday he was driving some old red piece of junk and hauling a canoe trailer. . . .

The gal at the Pronto had told Ivy that. Stang was riding shotgun. Kenny had filled a can of gasoline and bought Backwoods Wild Rum cigars. So this had happened on the front end of the canoe run, Ivy decided, before Kenny had dropped off Stang upriver of Mr. Pfaff's with an ax and a full can of gas.

Ivy stepped from the pickup and eased the door shut. He crawled across the trailer base and squatted under the upside-down canoe. He sparked Kenny's lighter and panned it along the ribbed floor and inner hull. He saw dried gore. Maybe some of it was his own, mingled with

Mr. Pfaff's. But it seemed like something much bloodier than an ax blade had left its mark on the canoe floor. Mr. Pfaff's arm, he had to guess.

He toppled from the trailer and lay on his back, watching fireworks paint the bottoms of the clouds. Kenny had been part of all of this. Kenny was an accomplice and a witness. It had earned him a bullet through the head.

As Ivy put this together, powerful headlights swooped above the barn roof and lit the clouds. A vehicle banged across the bridge, sounding its horn. Stang sounded ferociously ripped as he bellowed, "Here we go, people!"

Ivy struggled to his feet. As he hobbled around the barn, Stang bellowed again.

"Brother Terry! Where is my new brother, Brother Terry!"

Oklahoma Terry didn't seem to be around.

"Brother Ivy! Get over here! Do the honors! Hold this!"

Just like that, on Ivy's flat right palm, with his throbbing bandage for balance, he held a shaky tavern tray under two shot glasses and the heavy bottle of Patrón tequila.

The vehicle pulled off the road and rolled in slowly through the gate, parting the Sons of Tyr as they murmured *fuck* and *damn, bro* and *never seen one of them before.* Ivy hadn't either. He had never seen a vehicle like it, white, with Indiana plates, designed like an SUV but with six wheels and at least an extra ton of girth and height.

He glanced aside at Stang. Stang rerolled the sleeves of his T-shirt. He touched his beard, grooming his beaded braids downward. Then he put his fingers in his teeth and whistled sharply.

"Company! Receive!"

A bottle rocket screamed, banged, drizzled. Several Sons of Tyr stepped forward with automatics. Like soldiers, except hammered, they took rifle-stand positions.

The vehicle stopped and shut down. For a full minute, its engine ticked but nothing else happened. It became so quiet Ivy could hear the Bad Axe flowing past a hundred yards away. He could hear Harley Kick thrashing his handcuffs against the fence of the kennel. He could hear his own heartbeat rattling the shot glasses on the tavern tray.

The silence didn't break until the front passenger door opened and a woman tumbled out, saying, "No, *you* fuck off!"

She slammed the door. She stood there giving everyone an eyeful. She had bloodred hair and long bare legs jacked up on tall heels. But the main attraction was her goofy-huge breasts, squeezed by a top that read *This Shirt Can Say Nigger Because It's Black*—except the top was pink. Over her shoulders she draped a puffy white coat that to Ivy seemed familiar. She looked around.

"What kind of skeezy shithole is this?"

Beside Ivy, Stang jerked and became rigid.

She said, "We drove nine hours!"

A man emerged from the driver's side, sunglasses up on his head. He strode scowling around the grill of the massive vehicle. He was as tall as Ivy, well-groomed and tough-looking, in a snug black athletic suit. He wore an automatic pistol on his hip.

He paused to look around, same way the woman had.

"Nine hours!" she repeated. "And then we sat around for another hour in this stupid, skeezy bar!"

Ivy felt Stang and the Sons of Tyr looking about the canoe yard with the visitors: at Stang's big old barn with its streaks of rust and pigeon shit; at the yard light shining on the listing beer keg, the chewed-up ax target, the spent fireworks and the remote-control toy trucks; at the fenced enclosure with its clots of river flotsam hanging in the chain link; at the fleet of beached and battered canoes; at Larry Czappa who just now emerged from the barn and looked disgusted; at the vast starry sky and looming coulee walls that made it all seem small and dark and nothing.

The man in the athletic suit panned his gaze across the posing Sons of Tyr until he found Stang, who blurted, "We welcome you!" and shoved Ivy forward.

The tray nearly flipped off Ivy's hand when Stang lifted the Patrón bottle. He poured two shots. He handed one to the guest. "We honor you!" he was saying, beginning a toast, but before Stang could claim his shot, the woman snatched the glass and drained it. She rolled her eyes and said, "You got anything not skank piss?"

The man took her by the armpit and nearly lifted her. "Get back in." With a lunge she bounced the shot glass off the tray and it fell to the ground.

"Oh, I don't even mind! Nine fucking hours! Jesus!"

She slammed the door.

Stang blew into the dirty glass. He repoured both shots. Ivy nearly lost the tray again when the bottle's weight came down.

Stang started over: "We welcome you, honored guest of Sons of Tyr."

They drank. Stang smacked and sighed nervously. "Ahh, numero uno, the best."

The man sniffed his glass—"You think so?"—and set it on the tray.

"Welcome, welcome," Stang repeated.

"Sure," the man said, turning his back. "But save it. I'm the driver."

Czappa laughed in one short burst. The vehicle had two more sets of doors. The driver opened the middle one.

"Out." When nothing happened, he leaned in. "Hey. Buckwheat. You. Out."

Ivy nearly dropped the tray. Here was the reason he had gone down Mr. Pfaff's driveway in the first place. Here was the first brown, the one who left on the motorcycle. This time he looked more like a cool college kid, and kind of an in-between color instead of a brown. He glared feistily about and dropped a look of recognition on Ivy.

"Stay right there," ordered the driver. Then he opened the rearmost door. Out climbed a small, stout, carefully attired young man whose first impression on Ivy was his swooping handlebar mustache, waxed at the tips, then his tidy feedbag beard, then the elevated wedge of oiled hair above the shaved sides of his head. Ivy knew a dandy when he saw one.

"We honor you!" blurted Stang.

But the dandy never looked at Stang. He posed indifferently for a long while, finishing some business on his cell phone. His jeans were cuffed halfway up his shins, revealing polished hobnail boots. His soft little belly pushed open a tweed vest that he wore over a T-shirt that read *Brexit*. Stang poured two more tequila shots while Ivy fought to keep the tray level. The dandy didn't notice.

Then at last he said, "Ciao." He slipped the phone into a vest pocket. "*Ich bin*," he said, looking up, "Crawford Toyle."

He made an open-palmed gesture toward the glowering college kid. "*Heil saelir*. I bring tribute."

The Sons of Tyr stared back spellbound while Crawford Toyle looked around, taking in the scene just like his woman and his driver had. After his inspection, he shrugged to himself. He side-eyed his driver and preened his handlebars to hide a smirk.

Ivy felt Stang start and stop explosively beside him.

Then Toyle lowered his drawl and confided falsely to his driver, making sure everyone could hear. "Jesus Christ, Dewey. Did we turn wrong somewhere?"

When Ivy glanced back at Stang, he had seen that look before, long ago in the Kafka family kitchen, that glint of wild fury before Stang's eyes pinched shut and his lips mashed together as if to hold in an explosion. Then Stang was shaking.

ZING, BOOM, TARARREL!

Sunday, May 20

7:00 a.m.–2:00 p.m.	Troll Hunt (Downtown Farmstead)
7:00 a.m.–9:00 a.m.	Brats and Beer for Breakfast (@ VFW Post 544, 241 First Street)
8:30 a.m.	Royalty Tea (SPECIAL INVITE ONLY @ Bad Axe Good Savior Lutheran Church, 121 First Street)
9:00 a.m.	Parade Participant Lineup (@ Sixth Avenue)
10:00 a.m.	Grand Parade (@ Main Street)
11:00 a.m.–2:00 p.m.	Meatball Supper (@ St. Olaf's Catholic Church, R2764 Ten Hollows Road)
11:00 a.m.–5:00 p.m.	Beer Tent, Food, and Craft Stands (@ Fairgrounds)
11:00 a.m.–5:00 p.m.	Music by DJ Gunnar B (@ Fairgrounds Main Stage)
5:00 p.m.	Volunteer Cleanup (@ Fairgrounds)
6:00 p.m. –?	After Party (@ the Ease Inn, Main Street, and County Hwy Z)

43

She clomped up the gangplank of the *Mississippi Queen* and stood exactly in front of Randall Stone, gripping an oozy Dr Pepper bottle and looking like the kind of river rat or coulee troll that was never allowed aboard Stone's casino boat. He studied her with something between a leer and a frown. To be sure he hadn't recognized her, she waited until he called security.

"It's Heidi Kick," she told him then. "Give me your bus keys and a phone." She paused. The security guy was coming. "And when he gets here call me Darrell."

"Maybe we should just cancel—"

"Do it."

"Real good, then, Darrell, I'll just get the key."

She waited while Stone went through a locked door. His riverboat's parlor was a gaudy hall of mirrors, and from every angle she looked almost too much the part. She had gone home and changed into her heaviest barn clothes and her biggest, muddiest boots. Rather than her own, she had collected one of Harley's dirty hats because she needed more room for her hair. On the yard halfway to the house she had found the old fencing gloves that Opie had used to wrestle the pig. In Opie's room, atop the Amish dawdy costume, she found Opie's red-brown beard. *I'm sorry, sweetheart,* she had muttered as she found a pair of scissors and trimmed the beard to a horrid stubble, fitting for a man who, for example, lived on a houseboat and poached turtles. The beard had stretched and fit her chin tightly and hooked around her ears, hurting like hell on the burned one. She had packed her hair and yanked the hat down. Once she had put on the gloves, the only exposed part of her was down a tunnel of darkness under the hat brim. She had taken the Kick family minivan, completely sprayed with mud from going up and down the driveway. On her way to the *Mississippi Queen*, she had stopped at Pronto, and the girl there had seemed nervous rather than suspicious as she bought a Dr Pepper and a can of wintergreen Skoal. In the Pronto parking lot, she had dumped the Dr Pepper out, installed a pinch, and, squirting into the bottle, had gotten back on the road. Now here she was, a handgun in one pocket and a Taser in the other, ripped on nicotine, fear, and rage, breathing in hot snorts through her nose. The mirrors surrounded her with a grim fact: it wasn't very hard to look like a poor white boy from the country, all beat to shit. It was a type that everybody knew.

Randall Stone reappeared. He gave her a key hanging from a bar coaster and a Tracfone that still smelled like the package. He walked her out to introduce the decommissioned school bus. She had never been inside, where the windows were blacked out and it smelled like alcohol, ashes, and vomit. The passenger space had been gutted and refitted with a slab-wood bar bolted straight down the middle, ten stools on either side. Beer-soaked old couches were bolted to the floor along the sides and the back, and a high-capacity plug-in cooler was anchored behind the driver. A curtain could be closed and secured behind the driver to prevent passengers from seeing out the windshield.

"Tell me what to do."

"Close this curtain after all aboard," Stone told her. "No contact with passengers. Do not discuss the destination. Do not leave the bus when you get there. The whole idea is you never know who you're working for and your passengers never know where they've been."

"If anybody makes me," she warned him, "I'll have you closed down by the end of tomorrow."

Her call came at midnight. She hit TALK and waited.

"Bad Axe Rod and Gun Club," the caller said in a familiar voice-morphed growl.

She put the party bus in gear. It hurt her hands to turn the wheel. She pulled across the *Mississippi Queen* parking lot and left Stone's boat glowing like a cheap cake upon the murky riverscape.

Don't you dare touch me, she heard herself say. These would not—*would not*—be the last words she ever said to Harley.

She turned east off the Great River Road and headed inland on Bible Camp Coulee Road. The Missus Sippy groaned upgrade. Finally on the ridge she heard automatic rifle fire. In a few minutes, a sign at the club's entry read PRIVATE PARTY.

As she pulled around in front of the clubhouse, she could see men shooting skeet lit by truck headlights. In the parking lot were a dozen other trucks and also a large white vehicle with six wheels and Indiana plates that she decided was an SUV limousine. Who was this? She checked herself once more in her mirror, refreshed her chew, cocked her side mirror so it showed her the doorway of the club. She tooted the bus horn twice, then crawled inside her spinning mind and checked for texts or calls from Harley.

I will do anything. . . .

Eventually, familiar men began to board the Missus Sippy. The first few were township VFD guys whom she didn't quite know by name. Then came Royce Underkoffler, the rural real estate dealer, followed by one of her most vocal detractors on the county board, Seth Hefty. All of them were tipsy and fired up, having fun, and none of them seemed the least bit concerned with the troll slouched behind the wheel. The seventh or eighth man aboard, Larry Czappa, gave her a long look, reflected in the windshield. He said to someone ahead of him, "Looks like we might have a soldier." He rattled a beer from the cooler and took a seat.

After that she was stunned to see Albin Metzger, a Vietnam vet and now a prosperous bull breeder, a good guy, she thought. She was a

little less surprised but still disappointed to see a couple guys from the
Rattlers, Harley's baseball team. But they weren't Sons of Tyr, she felt.
Maybe none of these men were. They were going from a gun party to
a fight party. That didn't make them racists or kidnappers.

She shut the door behind the last passenger. She fixed the curtain shut. She hadn't been told where to go yet. She waited, watching an unfamiliar man emerge from the clubhouse while talking on a
cell phone. He was short and soft-looking, hipsterish, with old-timey
clothes, calf-high boots, and a ludicrous handlebar mustache. He was
vaping when she turned the bus headlights on him. He put a hand up
to shield his eyes. *Brexit* read his T-shirt. Who the hell was this? He
backed out of the glare and got into the white SUV limo.

Now the Tracfone buzzed.

She hit TALK and waited.

"Cave Hollow Canoes," said the voice-altered monster.

The men behind cheered as she put the bus in gear.

44

Ivy found where Oklahoma Terry had disappeared to and what he had been doing. Harley Kick was wet all over, and he smelled like piss. No man Ivy knew could soak his own chest and shoulders with piss. But Oklahoma Terry must have swung his dick too close. Harley Kick's feet were not bound, and he wore cleats. No man Ivy knew could cleat his own package. That's why Oklahoma Terry was on his hands and knees a few yards away, dripping vomit.

When he saw Ivy, he struggled upright and staggered away.

Ivy shook himself and got back to business. He had been looking for the key to the handcuffs on Harley Kick. He had just tried the canoe-rental office.

"Hey!" that college kid had yelled as Ivy had found the door locked. "Hey—is someone out there? There's a— Holy shit! Is someone out there?"

Ivy had a blowtorch from the barn's tool room. All he could think of was maybe cut the fence that Harley Kick was cuffed to. Maybe he could do that without being seen, and without burning Harley too much. If he did get seen, or even if he did burn Harley Kick, maybe it would still be OK in the end as long as they got free down the river.

"I couldn't find the key. But I found a torch to cut that fence. I'm gonna leave you gagged because I might burn you a little and you might holler. Just, um, bear with me."

He sparked the torch, then shut it off.

"Wait," he said. "I should get us all set up to first."

He still had the set of keys from Kenny's pocket, and one of those opened the padlock on the back gate to the canoe ramp. He swung the gate until it stuck in sand. He dragged a canoe out of formation, through the gate, and down the ramp until its nose touched the lapping Bad Axe River. The paddle Stang had used was still in the box of the red truck. Ivy carried it down and laid it by the canoe. Back at the truck, he inserted the ignition key and left it. He was done here.

He returned along the outside of the kennel and sparked the torch. He adjusted the gas. "Bend way forward." Harley Kick stiffened and hissed through his gag, but in a minute the sheriff's husband was standing up, his hands still cuffed behind his back to a square foot of chain link, but free enough and solid enough on his feet that Ivy could lead him to the canoe. He grunted, he threw his shoulders around, but he came along.

"Step up and over. There you go. You're in a canoe. Sit. We'll get downstream. Then we'll figure out what to do next."

But when Ivy tried to launch, Harley Kick was too heavy, and the canoe was beached too high ashore. Its nose was in the river, yet Ivy couldn't budge the back end off the sand. He had to solve this in a hurry. Just then two pairs of headlights scorched down Cave Hollow Road, a normal pair followed by massive LED blazes that had to come from Toyle's limo.

Ivy waded into the river to pull the canoe. With his good hand he tugged once. Harley Kick pitched out of balance. The canoe moved two inches.

Ivy stepped back about the same amount deeper, feeling current now, and he tugged again. Harley pitched and crashed. But now the canoe felt lighter, its nose half-lifted and twisting downstream with the current. Now Ivy had to hang on or let the damn thing get pushed back ashore and lose his gains.

Well, shit. He didn't know boats. His feet were slipping on the bottom. He was doing this all one-handed, and wrong.

"Crawl up here, forward."

The sheriff's husband grunted. He couldn't crawl anywhere.

"OK, then maybe I'm gonna . . ."

Ivy let the current take the canoe's nose back ashore. He shoved along with it, helped with the rebeaching.

New plan. He yanked the rear end with Harley Kick out into the river. Just like that the whole canoe swung free, like he wanted, but it caught the current broadside and bowled Ivy over.

He passed under it, underwater. More like the canoe passed over him.

The river choked him. His feet left bottom. His grip let go.

Downstream he hit rocks and crawled painfully ashore.

Harley Kick was gone.

45

There's an arm in here!

Neon Shivers had nearly blurted his discovery to someone rattling the door before he caught himself. He had no idea who might be on his side, if anyone.

He had been searching the office for some way to escape or at least to fight. The severed arm in the desk drawer had startled and pan-icked him: hacked off at the elbow, its sinews curdled and retracted, the purple stain of dead flesh rising under pale skin figured with age spots and sparse gray hairs, wrist bent back by the drawer, fingers forced into a fist. It had to be Augustus Pfaff's arm, taken by Stang Jr. . . . like Hollow Billy's arm, taken by Vernice Freeman. Revenge. And testimony.

Now, when Neon tries to shove the drawer back it sticks. He tries to twist it, lift it, wrench it shut, but he has jammed it, and now he has to let it go.

He finds an expired Texaco credit card and pinches it, trying to work it in behind the door latch, not so much hopeful as desperate—

because through the window bars he can see the limo pulling up outside behind a silver bus. The card is slippery in his hands. He might be getting it.

Then, but not by his efforts, the door opens.

"Mother*fucker*," seethes Stang Jr. with the knob in his grip.

Crawford Toyle, behind him, watches with a twisting lip beneath his handlebar.

"Mother-fucking-fucker!"

Stang lunges in and pops Neon two-handed in the chest. "The fuck you think you're doing?" And pops him again. Neon crashes into the desk. He can smell the arm's sweet rot.

Toyle is amused. "*¿Qué pasa*, Brother Stang? You some kind of Norse cannibal?"

Stang thinks he has to laugh. He tries. Then he snarls. Neon steadies himself. He swipes aside Stang's next shove with a forearm.

"Oh. You wanna fight? Is that what you want? You like to fight?"

"I don't want anything," Neon says. Quickly he changes his mind. He might as well go all in. "I want all this Hollow Billy shit to end. I know what you did, and your dad, and your grandad."

"Fucking idiot. Who the fuck you think you are?"

"Well," says Neon, "I think I'm a great-great-great nephew of your grandma, Vernice Freeman."

"That's a lie."

Stang attacks. Neon throws him back and feels a cold sneer rise. The misbegotten grandson of Billy Skaargaard and Vernice Freeman is too top-heavy, too slow, too sick with drugs and hate—unless he gets help. This thought makes Neon glance at Toyle.

"I know you," he realizes suddenly.

Toyle's chin goes up, his prissy feedbag beard.

"I've seen your picture. Charlottesville. San Francisco. I recognize you from YouTube. I saw you run into a street fight and sucker punch a girl. Then you ran away. You're famous."

Stang launches a roundhouse. Neon slaps it down.

"You're a famous little coward," he tells Toyle. The name fits in place now. "Yeah, I know Crawford Toyle."

"I guess he is a liar," Toyle says coolly. "I guess he does want to fight."

Stang Jr. steps back from Neon and kicks, kicks, kicks the drawer until it screeches shut.

"You will fight," he tells Neon, panting. "Until you're dead."

46

So close to Harley—that was her hope—Sheriff Kick forced herself
to sit still and wait. After she backed the Missus Sippy into the canoe
barn and the tall door rolled shut, she strove to appear sullenly incuri-
ous, swaddled in her dirty barn clothes, a ratty-bearded nobody under
a tugged-down cap brim, spitting Skoal juice into her Dr Pepper bottle and appearing to nod off behind the bus wheel.

But through the bus's big side mirror she saw a shocking pageant
unfold. In that hazy reflection she could see the red-black-and-white
banners, the armed guards, the drunken gamblers, the horrific cage
fights between bloody men who mostly drove tractors and trucks
and motorcycles, mostly sat on café chairs and bar stools, men who
couldn't fight but fought anyway with all their bitter, angry hearts.

She forced herself to wait longer. She couldn't see well enough,
but it was easy to climb onto the roof of a school bus. From there,
among the dark, web-swaddled barn rafters, she watched from flat
on her belly. She knew some of the men. Kevin Boyd kicked a man
twice his age, Clement Haskins, in the side of the head, knocked the
older man to the mat, then dropped his big gut upon Haskins and
rained wild punches until he was pulled off. Boyd stood with a grin
on his gore-smeared face, raising his fists in triumph while Haskins

clambered back to his feet, hugged him like a brother. Then money
was exchanged, and the next bout began. Meanwhile, the Cave Hollow Canoe guy, Rolf Stang Jr., not much on her radar, stalked about,
snarling and barking, infected with some uncontainable excess of rage.
The dandy who came in the limo stayed busy on his phone, hardly
watching. In the next fight, Henry Youngers got Jason Grundwald in
a clinch and kneed him so hard that Grundwald's mouthpiece flew
out, then kneed him again, again, until finally Grundwald collapsed
to the mat like a wet rag and lay there, not moving while the onlookers cheered and someone out of the mob bellowed at the fallen white
man, "Take *that*, boy!"

She watched a few in the crowd move away from the cage and
stand apart, finding one another by the troubled looks they shared.
A fight club, blood sport and gambling, these were expected. But the
aggressive banners, the outsiders in bike gear toting automatic rifles,
the mood of desperate hysteria—and now the suddenly racist intent
of "boy!"—all of this had slipped suddenly downslope and become
another thing entirely.

The bull breeder, Albin Metzger, easy to follow with his cream-
colored ten-gallon hat, seemed to be one of these men, and for that
the sheriff felt some small relief. Metzger stood way back now, scowling as if he hadn't known what he was getting into. Two other guys
she knew pretty well, Rick Themes and Pat Fife from the Farmstead
VFD, looked tense and distressed and talked into each other's ears.
She hoped they would be allies if she needed them.

No Kenny, though. She checked her phone. Nothing.

This whole time she had been tracking Larry Czappa as he moved
about. Now he strode to the fight cage and stripped off his shirt, becoming a pale, hairy slab with tattoos on his shoulders and back that
would have disqualified him from the hiring pool if she had only
known. Then he was inside the cage, fighting a skinny man in leather
pants with his wallet chain flying.

It's time, she told herself. *Go now.*

She dropped down to the barn floor. She fixed her fists around the
weapons inside her jacket. Like this, she roamed the dark outer reaches

of the barn, searching a tool room, a boiler room, a musty subchamber where life jackets and paddles and boat anchors had been stashed out of sight. "Harley!" she tried in a harsh whisper.

"It's me. It's Heidi. Harley!"

The only locked door read OFFICE. She heard someone move inside.

"Harley?"

Silence. But she guessed the office had a window. She found an outside door. She stepped from the hot barn into cool air beneath a sky of coasting clouds. Out here were the motorcycles and trucks of the men who had not come on the bus, who knew where they were, not the special guests but the regulars, the Sons of Tyr. Kenny's truck was here. So where was he?

She put her face to the bars on the grimy office window. The door that had been locked a minute ago was now open, letting in a wedge of light. She whispered loudly at the crack of the window. "Harley! It's me!"

"So, then, uh . . ."

She jumped. From behind her, wheezing and listing, approached Ivy Kafka. "I thought it was you. I heard you calling your husband in the tool room." He staggered toward her.

She fled around the corner of the barn. Here on a bank above the Bad Axe River was a tangle of junk that filled the narrow space between the barn and the fence. She worked through and cornered into more canoes, again arranged in rows. Here was a truck, maybe red, with a trailer, like Neon Shivers said was driven by the man who misdirected him last night, who fit the description of Kenny Kick. Here was a dog kennel, empty, with a hole cut in its fencing. Then a roar of feral glee rose from the barn. She hurried back inside and climbed aboard the bus.

Shaking now, she watched in the mirror as Neon Shivers danced sullenly about inside the cage, a big strong kid, a little soft-looking, but still athletic and quick, a different creature entirely than the hacks and drunks and flabby men who had fought before him. Rolf Stang Jr., runty and muscle-bound, scarred and tattooed, stalked after him.

She knew how this fight would go. *Carlos Castillo*. She had to call for help. But she thought of losing Harley, and she stalled. She watched in mounting guilt and terror as Neon danced and jabbed and mocked Stang and took the first two rounds easily. He was too long, too quick for Stang to hit. He looked angry and arrogant and like he thought he was in control.

Between the second and third rounds he took water. This was the beginning of the end. She saw how it worked. Stang took mace on his gloves. Inside bets were now placed on Stang, and his Sons of Tyr cheered hard. Neon, sluggish and beginning to stagger, took blow after blow, until he was blind on his feet. But he wouldn't fall. She begged him: fall and curl, protect yourself . . . But she had to act. Not like a mother or a wife. Like a sheriff.

She had her phone out, was just touching the screen to call her dispatch when the bus door blew in. Ivy Kafka, large and rangy and wet, farmer-strong, was upon her. "Easy," he panted. "Easy. I ain't what you think." She twisted and fought, desperate to get her hand to her pistol. He clawed her beard away. With his huge right hand, he spun her and trapped her neck inside his elbow.

"Sheriff, easy," he panted into her ear. "I'm sorry. I'm so sorry. But your husband. I know where he is."

She stopped fighting.

Ivy let her go. He was trying to hand her a key.

"This is for Kenny's truck. Kenny's dead."

"Where's Harley?"

"He's downriver."

She heard a noise behind her. Had someone else gotten on the bus? "Downriver?"

"Maybe you can take Kenny's truck and find him."

"What do you mean, he's downriver?"

47

As Ivy explained how he had taken her husband, then tried to free him but lost him, how her husband now floated, hooded and cuffed, down the river, Sheriff Kick slowly opened one gloved hand and accepted her dead brother-in-law's truck key. With her other hand she withdrew a heavy black handgun. Ivy thought that he was dead, and he accepted it. He gave her the center of his bowed head.

Then she was gone.

A few seconds later, startling Ivy out of numbness, there went Oklahoma Terry coming out of the bus, down its steps, empty beer cans spinning in his wake.

Ivy wobbled back toward the fight cage. The brown kid was almost dead, but not quite. Stang had bloodied him, knocked him down and kicked him, and left him curled inside the cage, breathing faintly and bleeding from his mouth.

The fights were over now. The wagering and shouting were over, and the Sons of Tyr and their guests drank and milled about and talked shit. Staggering among them with his head down, Ivy discovered a reddish fake beard snagged in the two-fingered claw of his left hand. He wadded it into his wet hip pocket. Albin Metzger, once a fellow farmer, stepped out and yanked him close in a powerful grip.

"Ivy, are you part of this?"

Ivy teared up and mumbled feebly that he had been. Metzger hung on.

"When's the bus leave. Where's the driver?"

"She's—"

"She?"

"I don't know."

"We had to leave our phones in our vehicles at the Rod and Gun." Metzger shook him. "Do you have a cell?"

The pain was crashing at his fingertips, coming back up his arm, exploding in between his ears.

Under his hat Metzger glared impatiently. "We're in Rolf Stang's canoe barn, am I right?"

Ivy was nodding when he was shoved aside.

"Is there a problem here?"

A Son of Tyr leered in, some pock-faced out-of-town enforcer in leather with gold hoop earrings and an assault rifle bandoliered across his back.

"You gentlemen have a question?"

"Sure do," Metzger said. "When's the bus leave?"

"Mr. Toyle is going to give a talk. After that."

"It's almost four a.m."

"Mr. Toyle is going to give a talk. You'll be encouraged to make a donation. You will be asked to join the march on Farmstead. After that the bus will leave. As in, the bus will leave when Mr. Toyle is done. You feel me, captain? Chill out."

Metzger said in disbelief, "The march on Farmstead?"

Ivy staggered away. He rode his waves of pain past the fight cage. The kid was breathing and his eyes were open. He was a good-size kid, heavy-looking. Ivy had crossed fields with three-hundred-pound calves yoked across his shoulders—but that was in the day, with both hands. If he was going to do anything for the kid, and do it better than he had done for Harley Kick, he had to get more pills.

Stang and Toyle were back in the office. As Ivy stopped outside, he was just able to hear Toyle's cocky drawl. He was shit-talking Stang.

"Not in the least," Toyle was saying. "I am not one bit impressed.

Why would I be? Why would anyone be? You cheated. I saw you. The kid was drugged. You junked-up your gloves."

"I—"

"The fight wasn't real."

"I was—"

"Crawford Toyle is about dealing with the real. The infestation is real. The genocide is real. The fight, Brother Stang, is real. The *diversity*, Brother Stang, is upon us. It's time for strong white men to act. I didn't come here to watch some jerk-off little boy play games."

"I . . . I'm sorry. I didn't intend . . ."

"You'd better intend. Any moment now someone shoots the archduke and it's on. Do you understand what I'm saying? Who is going to shoot the archduke? A little pissant cheat like you? *Nein, meinen kleinen Bruder.* Somebody with a swinging dick is going to assassinate the archduke. A strong white *man.* I came all the way here because I thought you might be one."

Ivy let his face drift past the doorframe. "Sir?"

"What," snapped Toyle.

"No. I mean . . ."

Ivy looked at Stang, sagging shirtless in his desk chair and scowling at his taped hands. Vague dawn at the window lit the office dully, and in this light Ivy saw Stang as that little boy at the Kafka kitchen table long ago, that sullen kid whose mother had left him with his monster of a dad.

"Sir," he started again, swallowing the wrongness of the word, "I might oughta need another pill or two. For the pain, if I'm gonna be of any use to you cleaning up the place. . . ."

Stang yanked his pencil drawer and threw the bottle. Ivy picked it up off the floor.

"Put that coon somewhere. Put him with the hostage."

"I will, sir. I am."

———

Ivy took two pills and waited for the pain to narrow to a steady burn where his fingertips used to be.

By that time, Toyle had begun to give his talk. No one took any notice as Ivy went inside the cage. The kid was limp now, his eyes closed,
his mouth crusted with blood, his breath almost gone. As Ivy carried
him out, Toyle was saying, "This is not easy. Nothing good is ever easy.
Brother Stang, bless his tiny heart, wants things to come easy. Brother
Stang doesn't want to fight, truly fight, because he's afraid to take the
risks and pay the price for what matters to him. . . ."

Ivy hitched and nearly dropped the kid just outside the cage. Like
how he had lost the farm and been so ashamed that he had failed to
fight? Like how he had taken to failure like a duck takes to water? Like
how this had made him a sucker for the bullshit that Stang and Toyle
were selling? That had killed Kenny?

"Hey there, mailman."

Down his two-pill tunnel, Ivy looked at Larry Czappa, a classmate
once, a bully, a man he had disliked and distrusted all his life. Czappa
wore a down vest, shirtless, his hairy arms dangling. He had a beer in
his hand and welt on his face.

"Let's get that kid some proper help."

"Tell me where to put him," Ivy said.

"Put him in my truck," Czappa said. "You know my truck? Red
Silverado, bass boat on a trailer."

"Done deal," Ivy said.

The kid on his shoulders stirred as he moved along. His new line
of thinking continued. The idea came from Crawford Toyle, but it
was right anyway. If something mattered to a fellah, he fought to keep
it, and if he lost it, he fought to get it back. He didn't blame other
people. He didn't mace his gloves and dope the water. He didn't drink
and complain and stash undelivered mail in his subsidized apartment.
Getting hurt and getting up again was the basic work of life. Life was
hard. Hell, farmers always failed. Then they tried again.

"Brother Stang is weak." Toyle was still sermonizing. "Or maybe
he'll surprise us. Maybe he'll be brave. Maybe he'll go big. Make a
statement. Boom! Somebody has to."

Ivy laid the kid on the canoe ramp just above the water. The kid
moaned and his eyes opened.

"What's your name?"

"Neon."

"I'm Francis Kafka the Fourth. You just stay down, Neon. I'm coming back. Then you and me are out of here."

The paddle from his first try had never got aboard that runaway canoe with Harley Kick. It was still there in the sand. He dragged down another canoe. He figured the trick was not to beach the thing square but instead to beach it at a downstream angle so that it wasn't heavy, so the current mostly slipped past while keeping the canoe nudged up against the shore. The trick was to put the paddle in right away, not to think about it later when things were moving and his hands were full. The final trick was to get the passenger aboard on the front seat, over the floating part of the canoe. The weight of the passenger then loosened up the back end.

But not enough. He got Neon in the front. But when Ivy climbed in, when he added his weight to the back, the canoe became firmly stuck ashore.

He got out.

No.

What a fellah should do is wade out a little, push the stubborn bastard, get a little more water underneath it, but not too much, and then a fellah should carefully step in while he . . .

Abruptly this kid, this half-conscious Neon, this faker, was sitting up, entirely alive and alert. He held the paddle two-fisted like a baseball bat. He swung it down full-force on Ivy's hand against the canoe rim, and again harder. When Ivy let go, the kid jammed the paddle through shallow water to the bottom and pushed off.

Ivy staggered after, reaching. The kid hacked his hand away. He back-paddled. The canoe caught the current and began to swing around. Ivy plunged forward to his waist, to his chest. The canoe was straightening out as it drifted. The kid was twisting to take aim. The paddle struck Ivy's head and he went under.

48

Based on what Ivy Kafka had told her about when he lost Harley—
"just before the fights started"—and her guess that a drifting canoe
went about one mile per hour—and her certainty that because the
river meandered, road and river miles were different—Sheriff Kick
powered Kenny's truck across the bridge that carried Cave Hollow
Road over the Bad Axe River just below Stang's.

Across the bridge, she turned left with the current and powered
downstream over the pitted surface of Lower Road until she had trav-
eled two road miles. Then she slowed to a crawl. Kenny illegally shined
deer and for once she was glad for it. She aimed his spotlight where she
could see the river through the tangle of bottomland forest. When the
road swung away and she lost her view, she corked the truck sideways
and set the woods on fire with its high beams. She jumped down and
followed her own long shadow down the crisscrossing alleyways of
light, wading through waist-high stinging nettles. When she found
the river, she screamed her husband's name, and no one answered. The
streambank brush was heavy. The river twisted. She could see almost
nothing in either direction.

She hesitated. Should she go back and take a canoe? Should she
risk it?

Returning to the truck, she thought she heard its door close.

How could that be?

She stood still to listen. She had left the truck running. She could hear that. She thought she heard a crisp metallic click.

She stepped out of the light into the shadow of a tree. The river-bottom forest around her made no sound unless she moved. She stood still. Then she turned and tried to watch the river while she listened, fearing Harley would spin past and she would miss him.

She couldn't see. Only tree trunks and their shadows. Then she heard a clunk and a splash and a grunt and she was running pell-mell back through the nettle thicket, falling over hidden deadwood, getting up and charging forward again until she stood on the bank.

"Harley!"

Nothing. If it had been Harley, he was gone.

She couldn't tell how deep the water was before she stepped in. Before her boots hit bottom the current spun her. She lunged and grabbed an armful of something thorny and in bloom and she hung on, dangling in the cold flow.

Jesus, Heidi.

"Harley!"

She crawled back onto the bank and stood in wet and heavy clothes, surrounded by crazy splinters of Kenny's headlights. Had she really heard something at the truck? She took her phone out—ruined. She drew her gun, and trusting it to work, she started back, trying to stay hidden in the sharp shadows carved by the headlights.

When she could see the truck, she stopped and listened. She saw nothing but the truck's outline and heard only its engine rumbling. She felt impatient then. She was wasting time. Harley had just gone past. She could catch him at the next bridge. She moved into the light. Nothing happened. No one was in the truck cab.

Only when she sat behind the wheel did she see what wasn't there before.

A swollen soda bottle was wedged on its side between the steering wheel and the windshield.

She slid delicately back out, and when she shut the door, the bottle exploded with a hard, shallow pop that crumbled the windshield and sprayed fizzing, gooey shrapnel into every corner of the cab.

Then someone was laughing. Someone who thought she was still inside.

She stepped back to Kenny's tall truck box and used the running board. Terry James Lord crouched beneath the rear window laughing weirdly, wildly, shuddering in his false pleasure, with his hands clapped to his ears. She climbed up and over. The pistol to his skull surprised him.

"Get out."

"Whu—?"

She trapped his head between the oozing rear window and the pistol barrel, and she bore down, wanting to cut it loose.

"Get up. Get out."

She kicked him off the tailgate and he landed badly.

"Stay there. Face down."

She jumped.

"Unless you'd like to get shot"—she put a knee in his back and let him feel the barrel again—"because I'd love to."

"Hey," he said shakily to the dirt road. "Hey, whatever boils your bunny, libtard traitor bitch."

She tried to take a moment to calm herself and think. But that was one more moment with Harley lost downstream.

"I changed my mind," she said. "Get up. Get up and take your clothes off."

He didn't move. She kicked him over.

"I mean it. Get up. Shirt and pants, off. Now."

He lay there trembling until she fired past his head. Then he came unsteadily to his knees with the pistol barrel like a compass point fixed upon his sick brain.

"Clothes off."

"Fuck, lady."

"I'm in a hurry. I want your clothes, and I'd love to have to shoot you for them. Take them off now or I will."

She stayed on him while he stripped off his stupid checked sport shirt and his grandpa pants and white tube socks. She opened Kenny's driver-side door.

"Now wipe it out."

"Eat my dick, woman!"

"For that, you can take your boxers off, motherfucker. Five seconds before I kill you and take them off myself."

She fired past him again. The woods echoed.

"There we go. That's better. Now, I plan to sit in there. I'm gonna use that gear shift and that instrument panel and that steering wheel and this door. I'm gonna touch those floor pedals. I'm gonna look out these windows. Wipe every bit of it out. As fast as you can. Hurry. Now."

When he was done, she left him on the dark road naked with his pile of ruined clothes.

"Now I have to kill you!" Lord shrieked as she pulled away. "You know I will!"

———

She drove on without a windshield, but at least that helped to cut the fumes. It was a different story to search the next section downstream. Since the floods last March, the Mississippi was backed up inland over a hundred thousand acres, drowning fields, submerging roads, driving people from their homes. The road came to a bridge that was underwater and closed. From there downstream, the Bad Axe River was an uncharted morass.

She drove out to the bridge, up to Kenny's axles. She aimed his powerful spotlight. She had hardly heard what Ivy Kafka told her. Now it settled in. Poor dumb Kenny was dead, not quite two months after he'd driven someone else's flag down Main Street. Poor desperate Kenny had put all of this in motion. But surely he hadn't wanted his old teacher Mr. Pfaff to be dead, or his old friend Ivy Kafka to be maimed, or his shining-star little brother to be lost.

The beam upstream was an empty pan across a turgid, backwashed, tree-stumped nothing. She got down from the truck, splashed into the river to her knees and was surprised to feel invisible current still moving west. Maybe Harley had drifted faster and farther than she thought. She unhooked the light and walked it on its cord around Kenny's grille. She shined it downstream toward the Mississippi. Some fool's misplaced deer stand wobbled in the push.

"Harley!"

She screamed her throat raw. Or maybe he was still drifting her way. She stood in knee-deep water, shivering, pointing the light in every direction, for an hour.

Somewhere in the predawn she gave up and drove to Pronto.

"I'm Sheriff Kick," she told the clerk. "Give me your cell phone."

She called Denise, who gave her Morales. She felt her chief deputy's silent dismay, even anger.

"You tried to do this alone."

"I can't lose him," she said nakedly. "They said . . ."

"We're putting up a helicopter," Morales answered her. "As soon as we get light. I'm sending everyone to the river. I'm putting out a call for volunteers."

She had no other idea than to start over upstream. Terry James Lord was gone from the spot where she had left him. Downstream she found no sign of Harley. She returned to the Great River Road. She shined Kenny's light off the highway bridge, and then off the railroad bridge. From there she drove south and turned west across the Guttenberg Dike. From the dike, though the eastern bluffs were etched by early light, she could see nothing but a mile-wide slate of gray river around the black humps and spits that hid a thousand sloughs. With her eyes straining from the dike, she pictured her future without Harley, alone in some new place with three pale and devastated children, their inaccessible grief, and hers.

Just after the helicopter went up—Tri-State Rescue out of Red Wing, a $5,000 launch fee, then $1,000 an hour—she was walking out the pier at Mudcat's Roadhouse and Marina when the Pronto clerk's phone buzzed.

"What the heck is going on?" demanded Bob Check.

"Cancel the parade, Bob."

"We're not going to do that. And, Sheriff, now I hear there's a helicopter. What the sam-heck is going on?"

She told him. Like Morales, Bob Check answered with a grinding silence. Then he said, "This is not how we do things."

"Isn't it?"

"You have all the resources."

"No."

"You have all the support."

"Do I? Larry Czappa, Bob."

"What?"

"Who went against my judgment and hired Larry Czappa, just to dodge a lawsuit? Who showed not only my deputies but the whole damn county that I am not in charge?"

"That was—"

"Czappa's with the white-power crowd, Bob, training for the race war. Bad Axe County gave this guy a job. That's my support?"

"Oh, come on now, Sheriff, I really don't think Larry—"

"It's here, Bob. It's in our community."

"You have all the support."

"Really? Who pooh-poohed flying the Confederate flag on Main Street and said I was making a mountain out of a molehill? Who was determined to believe the Sons of Tyr were harmless?"

She paused as a headache snapped between her eyes. She wanted to believe in innocence too. She was only a step or two ahead of anyone right now. But those were chasm-spanning steps.

"Last night, Bob, who empaneled a bunch of old white men, law enforcement amateurs, to reject my professional opinion that hate had come to town and we needed to act?"

She listened to his rasping breath.

"Didn't you all cut me loose? Why would I think I was anything but alone?"

He still didn't speak.

"I want the Bad Axe to be a good community as much as you do, Bob. Believe me, it's all I think about."

She hung up on him. Denise must have been giving out the number. Opie was calling her.

"Mommy," she said tearfully, "I can't find my beard."

"Oh, honey, I'm so sorry."

"Grammy Belle took me home to get my costume. It's not here. We have to get in line for the parade pretty soon and it's not here. Where is it?"

"I . . . Sweetheart . . ."

She choked on her words, watching a fishing boat curve across the plain of gray water. The helicopter had gone down the Iowa side all the way to the Wisconsin River. She could hear it beating back.

"Mommy, where is Daddy? What happened?"

"It's going to be OK, sweetheart. You can be an Amish boy who doesn't have a beard yet. Or Grammy Belle can stop on the way back into town and you can borrow a dress from Rosie Glick. I'm sure she'll let you. You can be an Amish girl. It's just acting."

"Mommy!"

"Let Grammy Belle help you, Opie. I have to hang up."

49

What woke Ivy was a helicopter going over, concussive sound and streaking shadow cut from high sun.

He hadn't drifted far to the sandbar where he lay. He sloshed against the current for a few hundred feet and staggered up the boat ramp. The vehicles were gone from the canoe yard.

The canoe barn was empty.

The clock in Stang's office read 9:17 a.m. Something smelled dead. The printer pages on Stang's desk expressed a horror that Ivy was slow to understand.

The page on top was a picture of the Syttende Mai parade floats, lined up along the harness track for judging, the way it happened every year. Four clunky-looking floats. One of them was circled with pen. Its banner read: CELEBRATING OUR HERITAGE.

The page beneath that was a closer picture of just that one float, "Celebrating Our Heritage." It was decorated with hay bales and sheaves of cornstalks, potted plants and small trees, colorful blankets, a model tepee, a model round barn, and a model Amish buggy. Within these props posed kids in costumes. He saw their faces: a white, a black, a brown, and a yellow, if you wanted to see it that way. The one kid dressed like an Amish child held up a blue ribbon that read FIRST

PLACE. Ivy raised the page and looked closely. It was a little girl with a reddish beard drawn in colored ink on her face.

He felt hot now. His pain began to flash.

Beneath that printout was a close-up showing mostly the wagon that carried that float and the space beneath the wagon. The next photograph was even closer, a partial wagon wheel and the disappearing vector of its axle. Ivy's heart began to flinch and skip. It hurt.

Or maybe he'll surprise us. Toyle had said that, taunting Stang.

The next picture on Stang's desk was so close, so dark, that Ivy couldn't tell what it was, an idea more than a thing, some notion of underneath the wagon.

Maybe he'll be brave.

Now Ivy's good hand shook. He tried to fold the pages to fit them in his pocket.

Maybe he'll go big. . . . Boom! Somebody has to.

As Ivy jammed the pages down his still-damp pocket he glanced at the window and saw someone approaching—someone naked, limping, wearing only black shoes.

Oklahoma Terry.

He limped straight to the ax target and yanked out an ax with each hand. He turned and headed for the office. Ivy bolted out the back.

———

He left Cave Hollow Canoe the same way he had arrived, pedaling his bicycle. He had just made the first mile north along the river when he came upon the white SUV limousine, pulled over in a turnout where fishermen parked. Crawford Toyle stood beside it with a tall cup of Pronto coffee, gazing over the Mississippi. Ivy squeaked up to him and skidded to a stop.

"He's going to bomb one of the floats!"

Toyle smiled and shrugged. He took a sip of coffee.

"Stang is going to blow up that float! With kids on it!"

"So he's going big." Toyle shrugged again. "I guess our boy is going to man up and kill the archduke, brother. Boom boom."

Ivy had to wait for the breath to say more. The helicopter racketed over the river. A window came down. That bloody-haired woman grinned at him.

"You're all gooney! Shit, look at you, gooney-bird!"

"You—you made him—"

"Me?" Toyle said.

"You dirty sonofabitching coward."

The woman shrieked a laugh.

"Your idea. You said—"

"But speech is free," Toyle said.

Ivy pointed at the man. He pointed. He *pointed*. Toyle shrugged, raised his cup and his eyebrows as he slipped into the limo. The door clicked shut. The limo turned right onto the highway and headed south, out of the Bad Axe.

50

Mudcat's new owner, Julie Vang, was loaning Sheriff Kick a boat. Expertly Julie backed it down the launch ramp, jumped in and released the winch, kicked it off the trailer, and tossed the sheriff a rope. She pulled the trailer up the ramp.

"I called my brothers," Julie said. "I've got five of them, fishermen. They're all out looking."

"Thank you."

"Don't overchoke the engine. You want me to start it for you?"

"I wouldn't mind."

Julie Vang sprang in and ripped the powerful engine to life. Back on the pier, she looked at the sheriff with tears in her eyes, then stepped in and hugged her.

"If anybody's tough and smart enough to survive this," she said, "it's your husband. We *are* going to find him."

As the sheriff climbed aboard the boat, her theory was that Harley had never made it to the Mississippi. If he did, OK, let the helicopter and the fishermen find him. But she was guessing he was stuck somewhere in the vast and inaccessible bog where the big river had backed up into the smaller one.

She sped upstream against the swirling currents. Inside a maze of high-water sloughs, she found the mouth of the Bad Axe. She eased under the railroad bridge, bending double to clear her head. There was more room under the highway bridge, but still she could have reached up and touched the hard-mud swallows' nests. Beyond the bridges, the conjoined river was both wide and treacherous, acres across, clogged with water weeds and flood-swept cornstalks, downed trees and submerged stumps.

She pulled the prop and put down the trolling motor. Was he in here? She felt less sure of it now. But there had to be thousands of places where a canoe could get stuck. If Harley was smart—no, Harley *was* smart—he would let that happen, get stuck somewhere, and just stay put.

At 10:02 a.m., just as the grand parade would be launching down Main Street, the Pronto clerk's phone rang again.

Morales said, "Ivy Kafka just called us."

"And?"

"He's at someone's house, about three miles uphill from the river."

She stopped the trolling motor, reached across the gunnel and held on to the broken limb of a drowned tree. The boat bobbed vaguely in the sluggish mix of currents.

"And?"

"He doesn't trust anyone but you. Voorbrood is the people's name. I'll text the number. It sounds like you'd better call him right away."

She called. As it rang, she scanned the boggy backwater for Harley. A shadow passed over. She looked up to see a buzzard soar under the sun. "Stang!" That was Ivy's voice. Mrs. Voorbrood had transferred the phone.

"Stang is going to bomb the float!"

"What float?"

"With your little girl! In the parade!"

"How do you know?"

After he explained, she hung up, stunned and sick. Harley or Opie. As she turned the boat around, her heart tore apart.

51

Hours ago, when it was still gray-dark, not long after he had paddled out into the big river, Neon Shivers had spotted the other canoe on the Wisconsin side, someone in it, spinning up against a sheer bluff beneath the railroad tracks and the highway.

When he saw that, Neon had been a hundred yards out toward the middle of the river. There was no way he could go crosswise against the current. But he had begun to dig hard with his paddle, angling toward shore.

By the time he could beach the canoe, he was a half mile downriver and couldn't see the bluff anymore. He had bushwhacked inland twenty yards and found he was on an island with a slick of smelly water moving sluggishly backward up the other side. He had paddled around the downstream tip of the island and enjoined the upriver flow, stroking as hard as he could across narrow channels and swampy backwaters. Twice he had portaged over hellish mires of mud and rotted sticks. By then it was morning. There had been a long train heading north. Then a helicopter upriver, blind to his waving arms. He had heard traffic on the highway above. He couldn't see it.

He had been nearly out of strength, but by then the bluff was in sight. The canoe was still trapped there, spinning, tapping the bluff with its nose, rotating, tapping the rock with its tail end, getting re-caught in the swirl and pushed back upriver to start all over again. The man inside it wore some kind white-black-orange uniform, number 7. He was hooded, his hands confined behind his back. Neon had guessed that this man was somehow part of the night's same ugly package.

He had beached again and studied and rested, trying to regain some strength. If the man had use of his hands, and a paddle, he would simply stroke out of the swirl. If Neon could get upstream into it, their escape together would be that easy too. But by then the river had confounded and terrified him. At great cost he had conquered such a tiny, soupy fraction, not enough, and the gap between the two canoes flowed at a billion gallons a minute. But he had kept seeking a solution. Could he get himself bumped right up against the bluff? Could the cracks in the rock, and the twisted shrubs growing out of the cracks, give him handholds? Then could he pull against the current until he too was caught and held by the swirl?

———

In an hour he has accomplished it. He catches the other canoe in a two-hand grip and barely holds on.

"Hey," he gasps. "Hey, man, I'm a friend. You OK? You got help."

The guy grunts. He's in a baseball uniform, dried blood down one arm. He grunts again. Beneath the hood he must be gagged. The two canoes collide, spin, hit the bluff, collide, spin. Neon needs to rest. He doesn't speak anymore. The helicopter gaps past between islands up the center of the river but Neon is hanging on and doesn't have an arm to raise.

In a while he has enough strength to hold the canoes together with just one hand. With the other, he unties his boots and kicks them off. Clumsily, strenuously, ten full minutes in the process, he works his pants off. He uses them to tie the canoes together.

"I'm gonna push us out of here, and we're gonna aim for that slow water a couple hundred yards down."

The man grunts.

"I know you can't see it. But when we get down there and get beached up, we can rest, and that shit comes off your head."

———

But it happens too fast when they enjoin the main current, and Neon can't steer the two canoes. They miss the backwater, miss the whole island, are sweeping out toward midriver.

Then a boat is coming at them. It comes directly, shooting up a rooster tail of water. A man drives standing, a big man with a dark mustache over unshaven whiskers, wearing sunglasses, shirtless under a down vest. He circles them, giving wide berth, rocking them with his wake. Then he cuts downriver and back-motors, aiming, letting them drift alongside. He throws Neon a line. Neon is almost too weak to catch it.

"I gotcha," he says.

He shows a badge.

"Bad Axe County Sheriff's Department, Deputy Larry Czappa."

52

The people at the place where Ivy had stopped to call the sheriff, the tidy house tucked into the hillside along the highway up from the river, the elderly couple, the Voorbroods, didn't know that they knew him from years back, so Ivy had to convince them. They knew his family, his mom and dad, his grandparents, the Kafkas of Bohemian Valley. He was Francis Kafka the Fourth. Four generations of Kafkas. He was good people. They just didn't recognize him now.

"They're gonna bomb a parade float!"

"He seems in a temper," said Mrs. Voorbrood from behind to Mr. Voorbrood, who blocked the screen door with his belly and a TV remote. "Maybe we should call the authorities."

"That's what . . ." Ivy knew he was a sight. He had been one for years. "That's what I'm trying to do!"

Finally, the Voorbroods had let him in. They had stood well back and muted the TV to listen to his phone calls, murmuring behind him as he tried to explain and convince Sheriff Kick. Which float? How did he know?

"I folded up the pictures! I got them! Pictures of under the float! Last night they were setting bombs off! They've got bombs!"

He couldn't say if the sheriff had believed him. He wouldn't blame her if she didn't. He couldn't have imagined it himself. He had to get to Farmstead.

The Voorbroods watched silently as he tried to rise from the chair where their phone was. His heart had seized into a knot. He couldn't breathe and couldn't move.

Mrs. Voorbrood cleared her throat and said, "Ivy, where are you coming from? You came all the from the river? On a bike?"

Mr. Voorbrood said, "You don't look good, fellah. How about you lie down over here on the sofa?"

"No," Ivy managed when his chest felt a little softer and he had enough breath. "I'm fine. I gotta move along."

———

First the road went down a bit, and that gave him a few hundred yards of easy riding. Yet he felt stiff and cold. His left arm hurt. Not the fingers, which pounded dully and incessantly. No, his left arm ached up into the shoulder socket and across the muscles that held the shoulder to his chest, which heaved for air even when he was coasting downhill—and still he couldn't get enough breath. The sun was high and hot, but he felt cold. Then the road started back on its real course, up.

Right away the bike became a thousand pounds, like peddling a John Deere tractor. He got off and pushed. The bike was still a tractor. He was cold.

On the next flat spot, between a gravel pit and a ravine blanketed with purple phlox, Ivy dropped the bike across the double yellow center line and laid himself down.

The asphalt felt warm and soft. It felt like his old bed when he was young and strong on Kafka Acres. He wasn't giving up anymore. He was going back where he was strong. A little rest, he'd be fine.

53

Sheriff Kick roared up Main Street and slammed Kenny's truck to a stop twenty yards in front of the Bad Axe High School marching band, bringing the parade to a halt outside the Norse Nook Café.

The band's lines buckled, and its rat-a-tat version of "America the Beautiful" unraveled and died. More than a few onlookers thought this was Kenny himself, pulling another stunt, and she leaped out into shouts and curses. Except for the beard that Ivy had clawed off, she still wore her troll outfit. She threw the hat off and the protests quickly died.

She got her bearings on the parade. This was the early part of it. The floats were back three or four blocks.

She bolted south down the street, spreading stunned silence. Speeding toward town, she had checked in with Rhino on the clerk's phone.

"We got a Crime Busters tip," he had told her. "Not Ivy Kafka. Same time, different caller. A bomb beneath the kids' float."

She dashed through the leading parade formations as they balked and bunched up, the VFW marching squadron, the 4-H kids leading colts and calves, the Lady Lions, the high school cheerleaders turning interrupted cartwheels. The Farmstead VFD and the EMS ambulance crew were still slinging candy to the kids at the curb. Tootsie Rolls rained off her as she sprinted through.

A Crime Busters call? Rhino's report flashed through her thoughts as she crossed the First Street intersection, where the sidewalks were clogged with adults in lawn chairs. She cut between these startled folks and yesterday's tractor-pull winners, barrel-bodied men with grease-stained hands looking down from their high perches. "Whoa, girl," called Burt Kindergaard over his rutting engine. More Tootsie Rolls bounced off her as she charged across Second Street and came up beside the hay wagon bearing Mr. Pfaff's band, the Principals of Polka. Their polka had broken down. Running alongside them, she shouted, "Play! Keep playing! For Gus! Play!" She dashed past Serenity Detweiler's alternate as Festival Queen, a chubby dark-haired girl in glasses waving from a white convertible.

At the beginning of the next block she began clearing the sidewalks. She heard a siren, one of her deputies screaming into town.

"Move forward! Everybody forward! No, leave your chairs! Leave them! Move all the way forward past Third Street! Until you get to the band! Leave the chairs! Leave the coolers! Move!"

Morales was coming up the opposite sidewalk, herding, pushing people, telling them the same thing: Leave the stuff! Move! She saw with relief that her chief deputy had already severed the parade with his cruiser, inserted his brown Tahoe sideways, isolating the floats while the rest of the parade moved steadily away. And he had cleared the floats.

There was Opie!

Her group of kids from the heritage float huddled together, looking frightened and moving uncertainly up the sidewalk. The sheriff saw a beard drawn on Opie's face. They met eyes and she swept her arm. *Go on, keep going!*

Behind the deserted floats were fifty or so bodies in an ugly scrum, the Sons of Tyr brandishing their pikes and clubs, exchanging shoves and obscenities with the crowd that came to push back. She saw Deputy Bench wrestling and shouting amid them. She pulled her pistol and fired it in the air.

"Get off the street! Now!"

She looked down. A remote-control truck had buzzed up and bumped her boots. Then she saw the county board chair.

Bob Check was on his back beneath the heritage float.

"Bob! Bob, get out of there!"

She dashed, grabbed his ankles, dragged him clear. He looked up at her from his back, his sun-scorched face in a wince and his sharp blue eyes piercing her.

"There's nothing under there, Sheriff."

He rolled over to his hands and knees and stiffly stood.

"There is nothing whatsoever underneath that float."

She looked down again. The toy truck had followed her. It bumped into her heels.

54

Deputy Larry Czappa leans over the side of his boat. He pushes one canoe down until the thick brown current crests its rim and the canoe takes on water. Then he lets go and the two canoes drift downriver, empty, yoked by Neon's knotted pants, sinking.

He grips his throttle. With a surge that throws Neon back, he begins to plow the boat downriver. Its hull slaps the current and bounces in a steady rhythm. Neon, beyond exhausted, fades nearly away, hanging on to one thin thought: *Why would he sink the canoes?*

He jerks awake when the baseball player stomps hard on his foot. He blinks and squints and sees they are peeling away from the Wisconsin side and heading crosscurrent toward the center of the river, closing fast on a thickly wooded island.

That heavy cleat won't stop digging into the top of Neon's foot as the deputy decelerates and tucks his boat up against the island. Now in shade, hugging the island's steep bank, the boat holds in place.

Neon hears the helicopter go over. He examines the deputy, who jockeys carefully to hug the island and stay in the shade. He feels like he has seen this guy before. Where? How?

The deputy uses his cell phone. "I got 'em both. I'll clean up your mess again. But then you stand down and what's mine is mine. You understand?"

The cleats bear down on Neon. Is he supposed to notice something, do something?

"They dumped and drowned," the deputy says. "It's that easy."

Neon looks around the boat. It is set up for fishing. There are rods racked along his side and a pair of heavy-looking tackle boxes under the driver's seat. In the center of the boat ride a gas can and a bucket jammed with dirty life jackets. Behind Neon in the bow space is an anchor, a cooler, and another bucket with minnows spinning inside. Racked along the far side is a long-handled landing net, a short-handled gaff, and a sawed-off baseball bat with a hole drilled through and a leather thong attached.

"You having fun at the parade? Kick a hippie for me."

The cleats dig. Neon looks back at the deputy. This time he recognizes him. In uniform, at the motel, rude to him yesterday morning. Later, at the fight, this is the man who handed him the water bottle.

Neon measures his distances to available weapons, judges their value should he get one in his grip. He can reach behind himself to the anchor. But it's a funky-looking thing with moving parts like a spider, attached to a heavy coil of rope. To get a grip on the bat or the gaff, he would have to leave his seat and take two steps across the boat. With the deputy facing them as he drives, that isn't going to work. But the handle on the landing net is so long that it extends past its side clip all the way to the kneecap of the baseball player. Neon decides that in one motion he might reach across and yank it free.

And then?

He needs the deputy to look elsewhere, to turn around and look behind the boat for two or three seconds. While Neon's watching, he flinches back from the phone, like he's heard something that shocks him.

"Stang? What was that? You there?"

Neon hurls the minnow bucket into the river. The current takes it.

"What the hell?"

He turns to watch the bucket. Before he can turn back, Neon has the deputy's head and shoulders inside the long-handled net. With one jerk the deputy is unbalanced. His arms flail. His phone clatters to the boat bottom. Neon stands for leverage. With one more hard tug on the net handle, the big man pitches overboard.

55

There is no good reason, Ivy tells himself, that he can't get back up, get back on his feet, out of his warm bed, and start over, a new day, try again to do what he loved. That's what farmers do. They get up in the morning.

He should have done some things differently. He should have fought. He will now. What does failing matter? And only two fingers lost? Hell, that was just admission to the farmer club. His two grandfathers had lost six and a half fingers all together. They were happy men.

Cut his hair and shave his face, wash his clothes and his car, milk cows and shovel shit at Vista with the Spanish people, live quietly and save money like they do. Go back to church. Believe in God again. Get his driver's license back; it just takes time. Bankruptcy is a hurt that heals too, people get over it, it's only money and it just takes time, steady time. Build up to a farm again. Try again. Maybe grass-fed beef, organic and expensive like the hippie farmers raise it, steers that feed themselves and self-fertilize. One thing fails, try something else. Try again.

———

So he does. He cleans up and brightens up and tucks away a nest egg and gets a loan and rents some grazing land and hits his price points and pays his loan back and gets a bigger loan, and with that he buys the Larsson place just sitting there with a good well and three hundred acres and things are kind of skinny but he's happy, he's impressive actually, a comeback kid, and Kristi-Jo returns to him, and they do it like they used to, so nice, and they have a son.

Just like that, Ivy rides all the way back up to the top of the hill. His bad past fades behind and below. He is so happy that his heart just stops right there. What a perfect son they have. The fifth Francis Kakfa. Francis Kafka the Fifth. They call him Vee.

56

Sheriff Kick stepped away from the remote-controlled truck.

It revved and jerked after her.

She stepped up on the curb.

It reared its knobby monster tires and climbed right up.

"Somebody knock it off!" barked Bob Check, and he swung a kick, missing as the toy reversed out of reach.

Now the truck was still, waiting. Who controlled it?

By this time Morales had herded everyone up past Second Street except the sheriff, Bob Check, and a smaller group of street fighters who were still engaged a half block in the other direction, scuffling in front of Jake Vig's Coulee Compu-Shack. One more block south was the whole tail end of the stalled parade.

"I'm going to kick that thing through the goalposts," Bob fumed.

The truck closed in on Sheriff Kick again. She bent but failed to grab it as it zipped away. Its little dump box had cargo. There was something taped down inside it.

She understood suddenly. There was never a bomb *on* the float. *This* was the bomb, meant to be guided *under* the float. Now it was for her, Sheriff Snowflake.

She drew her pistol again.

No. Stupid. She holstered.

She stepped back and tried the door of the farm insurance office. But every door on Main Street was closed and locked for the parade. It was a town rule.

No, what she had to do was lead the truck and its bomb away from people. But there were crowds in both directions. She looked toward the Compu-Shack. Maybe this was one of Vig's toys, weaponized and lethal. Was someone inside his store, at a second-story window or on the roof, controlling it from there?

"Get away from me, Bob. Go."

He started. He got ten feet way, then turned and came back at her. "Gosh darn it, Sheriff, you claim you don't make mountains out of molehills—"

She wheeled with her pistol and blew the window out of the insurance office. With her follow-through she tackled Bob Check with all her strength and they fell through the shattering glass just ahead of a bolt of white-hot light and a deafening crack and a concussion of displaced air and shotgun pellets that overturned a desk and shattered pictures on the far wall.

———

Maybe minutes passed. She couldn't say. Her hands hurt. Her face hurt. But she did not feel much more injured than she had been before.

Dazed, she struggled from under Bob Check. "No, I'm fine," she told Morales. "I'm not hurt. Take care of Bob." His old head was bloody, but his eyes were open and he was breathing. She stepped through the glass and over the windowsill, two-fisting her weapon.

No one moved. Farmstead was silent.

She scanned rooftops across Main Street. The blast had scattered pigeons into mile-high specks. The sky's perfect blue flashed in every window. In a reflection, she saw something she had missed. It was behind her in the alley alongside the insurance office: the old red pickup she had seen at Stang's, its door open and its canoe trailer with one canoe jackknifed behind it.

She crossed the street. She pushed the door to Compu-Shack. When it didn't yield, she backed up to the sidewalk, tore a Viking shield from a Son of Tyr and sent it crashing through another plate of glass.

She found Jake Vig dazed on the floor behind his register, bleeding heavily from what looked like a blunt blow to his head. He was in tears.

"I couldn't believe it. I called you guys. I mean, I was doing bombs last night, but I fucking couldn't believe it. Little kids!"

So that was the call. A Son of Tyr with buyer's remorse.

He pointed at his ceiling.

"He's up there?"

Vig nodded.

"There's an apartment up there? Roof access?"

He nodded. She led with her weapon and began to climb his narrow, creaky stairs. There was a landing and a wooden door, locked. Vig labored up behind her, leaving bloody handprints on the wall. He fumbled with a key, then weakly pushed the door until it hit something. She stepped around and shoved it open with her boot. She expected Rolf Stang Jr., but not as she found him, sprawled dead on the floor with an ax stuck halfway through his neck.

Vig said feebly, "Wow . . . so yeah, I called it in. Then this Oklahoma Terry dude comes through the door wearing swimming trunks and swinging axes . . ."

She shoved Vig back onto the landing. Pistol first, she scanned the living room of a very messy efficiency apartment. There wasn't much to cover. Nothing moved.

She stepped over Stang. A single window looked over Main Street. The blind was drawn. She kicked the bathroom door open.

No.

Terry James Lord was on the roof.

57

Emerging from the stairwell, all she saw were stack pipes and vents, with half walls between the two adjacent roofs.

"Lord!" she hollered. "Show your hands and get on the ground!"

Nothing moved. She stepped out warily behind her weapon, fighting to keep her heart inside her body. She should back off.

Should.

She zigzagged across the rooftop, getting angles. At the tile cap on the sidewalk edge, she found the bomb's remote controller and a perfect sight line to where she and Bob Check had stood. EMTs kneeled around Bob. He was sitting up and talking.

And no one else was hurt. Either Ivy or Vig had saved the kids, whoever's tip had come through first. Or maybe Lord had saved them, getting Stang with the ax before he could deploy the bomb. Then, having promised to kill her, he had waited up here with the remote, guessing right that she would show up eventually.

"Lord!"

Suddenly there he was a hundred feet away in the far corner of the roof, rising from behind an HVAC vent with an ax. He was dressed in a tank top and swimming trunks that had to come from lost-and-found at Stang's canoe barn.

"Stop there and drop the ax!"

He cast her a sneer and reeled across the rooftop to the opposite corner, where he tossed the ax ahead and struggled over the half wall onto the roof next door, the old Odeon theater. She heard his footsteps whomping toward Second Street.

She climbed the half wall. The Odeon roof was rounded like a little moon under cracked silver sealant. He might be under the horizon. She was glad he hadn't dropped the ax. She could shoot him this time.

She stalked across the curvature, ready, but he wasn't there. He had made it onto the next roof, above the yarn shop.

That was a ten-foot hang-and-drop onto flat black tar. She landed hard and felt her ankle pop and she had to get up slowly. He could have ambushed her right there. He didn't. He wasn't on this roof either.

There was one more rooftop on the block, over the Whole Stein Tavern at the corner of Second and Main. She holstered, climbed, dangled, and dropped.

Now she limped badly. This was it. On this roof, Terry James Lord would either stick her with an ax, or she would shoot him dead. Goddamn this job, she thought. Goddamn this life.

Toward the far corner of the roof she saw movement—a black shoe flared out behind a crumbling chimney.

She crept to an angle where she could fully see—but it was only a shoe, left to fool her.

She spun. He rose behind a vent and flung the ax.

It seemed to move in slow motion as it cartwheeled toward her head. She saw its rubber grip, its stainless shank, its blunt heel, its glittering blade, then all of these all over again. She ducked it easily and it clattered to the roof behind her.

She was going to shoot him now. They both knew it. He grinned weirdly at her, blew her a kiss, then lunged off the roof.

The sheriff heard screams—an odd, loose concussive sound—then quiet. As she limped for the edge, an engine roared.

By the time she had a view, the white convertible that had carried the alternate Syttende Mai queen was ripping up Main Street, careening through the wagons and tractors, spraying lawn chairs into the storefronts. She looked down. He had jumped onto the Whole Stein Tavern awning and ridden it to the sidewalk.

From beyond where she could see came more screams and then the unmistakable sound of a car crash.

58

By the time the sheriff had worked her way back across the rooftops, past Stang's body, and down through the Compu-Shack building, Morales was nowhere near his Tahoe. Another of her deputies was far away down Main to the south, herding people. And to the north, the band had struck up the "Beer Barrel Polka."

As she made her slow and painful progress that way, toward the car crash, toward the music, some Bad Axers backed against the storefronts and stared. Others streamed forward in front of her, toward the music.

She crossed Second Street. At First and Main, she saw the queen's convertible had crashed into the corner of the *Bad Axe Broadcaster* building.

The car was empty. Deputy Schwem squatted beside an injured woman who sat on the curb.

But Lord was nowhere. She had lost him. After the crash, had he bolted forward, backward, down a cross street? Why hadn't someone stopped him?

She slowed, exhausted and confused.

Why hadn't anyone stopped him?

On the next block, she was baffled to find a hundred people paired up and dancing in a huge swarm to the "Beer Barrel Polka," hopping and twirling and belting out the lyrics as if nothing important had happened, or ever would.

> *Zing, boom, tararrel!*
> *Singing a song of good cheer!*
> *Now it's time to roll out the barrel,*
> *'Cause the gang's all here!*

And Lord was gone.

She stood there in shock. How could this happen? She remembered Augustus Pfaff telling her that *zing, boom, tararrel!* represented the sound of flying bullets as the Nazis closed in, that the lyric was a tribute to strong people who danced defiantly in their dance halls as the world turned darkly against them.

Panic seized her heart. What kind of people were they now?

She couldn't be here. She couldn't do this. No amount of vigilance could make these people safe. Where would she go? What would she do?

Just then Morales took her by the arm. She wanted to punch the smart-ass look off his face. He spoke cheerily into her ear.

"Su marido está a salvo."

What did he think was so funny? She tried to rip her arm away.

"Where the hell is Lord? Why did no one stop him?"

"Heidi!" Morales shook her, pulled her closer. He spoke into her injured ear. "Eh . . . *su marido está*—" He cut himself off and restarted. "Your husband just turned up alive and well on the pier at Mudcat's. Neon Shivers was driving the boat. An ambulance is on the way."

She couldn't speak from relief. But where was Lord? Then Morales was tugging her, grinning even more widely.

"Tienes que ver esto, Heidi!" He spoke rapidly, excitedly. *"Es hermoso!"*

She said helplessly, "What?"

"I'm sorry! When I'm happy, I don't think, I just speak Spanish! You gotta see this! It's beautiful!"

He led her to the hay wagon where the band played, helped her climb up. Royal danced in time so hard the wagon jiggled. From up there she looked out and saw him trapped, odd little bigheaded Terry James Lord in faded swim trunks and a too-tight Bud Light tank top, bolting this way and that, only to be cut off, shouldered hard, stepped on, shoved back. Denise was in there, and she decked him. He scrambled to his feet but was hemmed in by the whirling, bellowing, fierce-faced dancers.

And the gang's . . . all . . . here!

Yes, it was beautiful. "*Sí, es hermoso,*" she agreed.

She moved to the edge of the wagon to jump. As she hesitated at the drop, as Morales reached to help, Lord tried to sneer at up her, throw her one last splash of acid.

She nodded at his effort.

It was so puny. Yet so vast.

But she was one big snowflake, coming down.

EPILOGUE

June 29, 2019

"How many pints do we want?" Harley asked her.

She gave him a happy shrug. "Overdo it," she answered. "You can't have too many strawberries. We can freeze them."

She was channeling her mom, Sheriff Kick realized. Every June, the small but sweet Amish strawberries came on fast, by the millions it seemed, and a person might think, *Too many strawberries!* and hold back, afraid to overcommit, and then they were gone, done, it was too late for strawberries.

"Or make jam like my mom," she added.

Harley raised his eyebrows and smiled at her. Then he and Opie, hand in hand, pulled the wagon over to the back of Eli Glick's buggy to do business. That would be the day, she thought. Heidi Kick slowing down and making jam. That would be the day.

She watched her husband and her oldest child from behind. Harley had his Rattlers uniform on, *Kick 7*, for a doubleheader with the Red Wing Ravens at noon. Opie in boy clothes was a little Harley, the sheriff saw now. Belle had found a photograph of Harley and Kenny as kids, bobber-fishing on the Mississippi with their dad. It was unlike Belle to be sentimental, or to acknowledge Byron Kick in any way. But even she seemed to be growing, bonding, tending to her family tree, such as it was.

In the picture, Harley was eight and Kenny was thirteen, but they were the same size, and the catfish dangling from Harley's fist was twice as big as the one Kenny was thrusting at the camera with a sidelong glance at their dad, who would walk out on the family a few days later. But what the sheriff was seeing in that picture, in her mind's eye now, was Opie standing there in Harley's place, fitting in his outline almost perfectly, the straight-ahead look and easy smile, the sturdy frame, the uncanny way that both of them, against the odds, projected confidence and calm in a storm.

"Make jam out of this stuff," Belle said, suddenly beside the sheriff, handing her an enormous bundle of rhubarb stalks, late and thick. "I got all that off Yoder for a buck."

"Yes, ma'am."

That would be a day that no doubt the sheriff would tally up from and look back on later. *Back 5,271 days ago I made my first jar of jam.*

The twins came racing up. Abe Zook's family was selling iris stalks bundled by the half dozen, brilliant yellows, reds, purples, and she had asked them to pick a bundle that they would take to Uncle Kenny's grave.

"How about this yellow one, Mommy?" Taylor had beaten his brother by a stride. Dylan crashed in with red. "No! Uncle Kenny wants red!"

She sent them back to Zook to pay for both. She put her arm around Belle and drew Kenny's grieving mom close so they both could hide their crumpling faces behind the flowers. "I know, Mom. I know."

There was so much, too, that she didn't know. She didn't know if or how she could have saved Kenny Kick, or Ivy Kafka, or anyone like Kenny and Ivy. She didn't know how or if ever Farmstead and the Bad Axe would recover from the damage done by Rolf Stang Jr. and Larry Czappa with their Sons of Tyr and their fight club, by Terry James Lord with his threats and his acid, by Crawford Toyle with his global inspiration, by Kenny and Ivy and all the other followers. New banners on the light posts seemed to be the plan for now. She didn't know yet if Lord had scarred her for life. Her hands were still shedding layers of dead skin, but it seemed they might be normal again. Her dermatologist said there was a good chance she would be keeping the birthmark-like splotch of pink skin between the corner of her left eye and her left ear. It didn't hurt, and Harley and the kids had been kissing it. And ears were tougher than they looked, she had learned. The tender flesh and inner parts of hers had recovered quickly and completely, except for loss of hearing that she didn't know she had, in a high register she didn't think she would miss.

Royal Strander whooped, "*Eins, zwei, drei!*" and boom, here came "Happy Valley Polka" from the parking-lot bandstand. The remade, post–Pfaff Principals of Polka was a bigger ensemble under Royal's leadership. Two kids from the high school band had joined the old men, a skinny bespectacled girl on cornet and a kid on second tuba who looked well on his way to becoming another roly-poly Gus Pfaff. The darker side of this was Royal still wore the coverall jumpsuit, not the blouse and lederhosen, because Royal went nowhere without a concealed firearm. Observing this, the sheriff didn't know whether the Kick family might be moving on from the Bad Axe soon. She knew she had to think about this, but she didn't know how yet.

Belle pulled away, fumbling money from her scruffy little purse. "Get some for his friend too!" she hollered at the boys, who couldn't hear her for the polka. She meant Ivy Kafka. Belle limped after her grandsons. She would get the flowers for Ivy.

The sheriff didn't know yet whether Waylon "Taz" Kramer had executed Kenny for Stang, or whether he had merely harvested Kenny's valuables after Stang had done it himself, as Taz maintained. Stang was dead and Taz could say what he wanted. She was going to let the DA and courts figure that out. Lord was talking, trying to sing, but he hardly knew anything.

She also didn't know what to do with the severed and decomposing arm they had recovered from a drawer in Stang's canoe-barn office. It had been part of Mr. Pfaff, who was already cremated and fed to the meadow along the Little Bad Axe River behind where his house had been. The FBI wasn't interested because Stang was dead and the arm didn't seem part of what either Crawford Toyle or Lord had done. They liked the part where Toyle and Lord on their separate but related terroristic causes had crossed state lines, and the part where good witnesses like Alban Metzger said Toyle had egged on Stang to the point where he must have decided to bomb a parade float with children on it; they liked that Lord had used the U.S. Postal Service to send threats. They liked to talk about how they were pursuing Toyle overseas. They just didn't care about Mr. Pfaff's arm. His sister didn't want it. So somehow, frozen in its morgue drawer, it belonged to Sheriff Kick.

Here came Opie and Harley with way too many strawberries.

"Whoa, you guys!"

"And he wouldn't let us pay for them," Harley said.

"No way. Go back and make him take the money."

Opie said, "Mom, I took care of it. I gave the money to Rosie, and Rosie snuck it in her grandpa's cash box when he wasn't looking."

The sheriff grinned. *That's my girl*, she nearly said. She didn't know when the language would turn for her. Harley, as Harley would, had already mastered his pronouns.

She hugged Opie. "Here's some money for asparagus, hon. Get a couple pounds. Not super thick ones."

She took Harley's big warm hand and squeezed it. Yeah, as the story usually went, she should have saved him. Not Ivy Kafka, and not Neon Shivers. She should have saved him all herself, to cancel out all her flaws and mistakes and erase all her bad behavior. She had *needed* to save him, to erase *Don't you dare touch me*. She didn't know what to think of the fact that someone else had done it. But maybe there was a message in that somewhere.

"You want to share a morning bratwurst?" she asked Harley now. "Sauerkraut and mustard and everything? Look, they're already on the grill."

He grinned at her. "Dang, woman. You do talk dirty these days."

They carried a very fine specimen oozing in a paper boat over to a picnic table on the courthouse lawn. Wordlessly, comfortably, they traded bites. As it always did eventually, her phone buzzed. Harley stiffened and looked away.

When she answered, Chief Deputy Morales told her, "Dr. Geyer just called. She arrived to open up and found her window smashed in."

Dr. Tina Geyer was a new veterinarian in the Bad Axe. Her clinic was out the highway to the south of Farmstead, across from the Ease Inn, not the best location, given the nature of some Ease Inn clientele.

The sheriff said, "I assume they stole drugs?"

"Everything. Not just the opiates and tranquilizers. Like they'll try stuff later and figure out what it does. Or just sell it and let the chips fall. Dr. Geyer had some cash in a safe. They took the safe too, cast-iron, about five hundred pounds, so there were at least three of them."

The sheriff took a deep, long breath, feeling her pulse come up, tasting sauerkraut on the back of her throat. But she hadn't smoked again or even chewed the gum in a month. She was getting good sleep. She had real energy. She reached across the table and put her hand on top of Harley's.

"Well," she told her chief deputy, "*buena suerte con eso.*"

She put her phone away. She translated for her husband.

"I told him, 'Good luck with that,'" she said.

The fireflies and the mosquitoes appeared together that night. Neon Shivers showed up at the farm on his stepfather's yellow Valkyrie just as Harley was flipping venison steaks on the grill. The first thing the sheriff noticed was that he wore a helmet. Next, as he came toward them across the yard, she noticed the haircut, or more the lack of one. It had been a huge moment in her own life, she knew upon reflection, when she had stopped trying to be cool for other people. She didn't know it then, but she saw it now. It had happened nearly two full years after her parents' deaths, when she was down in Missouri at rehab, the night she had worn flat shoes and loose pants on a date and ate more than the man did. And she had even liked the man.

"Venison, huh?" Neon said, chewing a bite. "I could get used to this."

"Ugh," said Opie, and changed the subject. "Dear parents, may I go to the fireworks?"

Farmstead was doing its Fourth of July on the Saturday before, and Neon had come from Milwaukee to attend a memorial honoring the life of Augustus Pfaff. The sheriff had a huge surprise for him.

"If Rosie is going up to watch from the ridge, and they have room in the buggy, you can go with the Glicks. I'm staying home, and Daddy is under strict orders to keep me here."

After supper she gave Neon a box.

"What is this?"

"I got a warrant to search Ivy Kafka's apartment. That was buried in several hundred pounds of stashed mail. I had to clear possession of it through an entire handbook of postal regulations. It took a while."

"'*A Round Us: Once Upon a Time in the Bad Axe*,'" Neon read in a stunned voice from the top page.

"Then the book was the property of his sister. That also took a while, but eventually she agreed that you could have it."

"'Copyright Augustus Pfaff,'" he read. "Wow."

"He sent it to himself."

"I was going to start all over." Neon looked up with glassy eyes. "I brought a real camera. I was going to find all the round barns, first. Royal's going to drive me around tomorrow. I've got the stuff from my granny's cousin Vernice, and Royal's got a few things, but I was afraid I couldn't put it all together like he did. Now, I can build on this. I mean, I—"

It had once seemed to the sheriff like Neon was born old, but this reminded her that he was still a young man, awkward with his emotions. He fumbled a few more blurry and embarrassed words of thanks and intention. Then he quietly ate his piece of strawberry-rhubarb pie as if nothing had happened, except he glanced at the sheriff and his eyes were slick, and she smiled.

"I made that pie," she said.

After that, she went into the house and turned a speaker toward an open window and blasted a polka record from the collection once owned by Ron and Darlene White. *The Six Fat Dutchmen, Greatest Hits* had been her parents' favorite.

Polka! The twins did a goofy boogie thing. Sheriff Kick took Neon's hands.

"You wanna learn?"

He tried, couldn't get the timing of the bouncy "Heel and Toe Polka." He got his ass worn out and finally quit, out of breath and laughing.

"That is *way* harder than it looks."

A minute later, glancing around to make sure the twins couldn't hear him, he said, "Goddamn, that shit makes me smile."

While the boys played with sparklers, Neon and the sheriff and Harley sat talking comfortably on the front porch. She hadn't told anyone before passing along the manuscript that she had read *A Round Us* all the way through, twice, the second time for law enforcement purposes. The story about Hollow Billy, the terrorist and rapist, later a one-armed ghost, was chilling, and it was central to understanding Stag Jr.'s motive for two murders and related crimes. In a sad footnote to that story, in his dedication, Mr. Pfaff had related his obvious misperception that Rolf Stang Jr. had been "unaware" of his identity and "delighted" to learn of it. She had hoped that Larry Czappa's family would be mentioned in the book, too, hoping that somehow, like Stang Jr.'s, Czappa's eagerness to hate would be explained by some uncomfortable history. But no. She only wished that she could close the book that easily. Czappa's body had been found washed up against the Guttenberg Dike, so she would never know. She hoped that Czappa had not been part of a plan to bomb a parade float or to kill her. She would leave it there.

But what Neon Shivers would learn from Augustus Pfaff about the still-standing round barns, she guessed, was Mr. Pfaff's conviction that they expressed and preserved a connection in the soul. His belief in the way they crossed boundaries and endured, if barely. In his book, Mr. Pfaff would tell Neon Shivers that in their time the round barns sheltered animals, yes, but on people their surprising design worked like music, like dancing, like people hearing the same thing together and reaching out to touch one another, same not different, circles not corners. There was the story. Things were briefly better once, and you might get killed for saying so.

Neon said, "Oh, I forgot to mention. Some guy named Bob Check asked if I would talk to the county board about putting up some new historical markers. Should I do that?"

"Yes," she said. "Yes, you should do that."

The deep green landscape slowly dissolved into a fabric of grays and blacks, pierced by fireflies. The mosquitoes came for everybody's blood. The sky harrumphed for an hour. Then it cut loose. A firmament loaded by the Gulf of Mexico came down upon the Bad Axe.

It rained hard, very hard, and it was beautiful.

A NOTE FROM THE AUTHOR

Alga Shivers, son of a fugitive Tennessee slave, was born in 1889 in Cheyenne Valley, Wisconsin, which had been a far northern stop on the Underground Railroad. For a time, African Americans and immigrants from Norway, Ireland, and Bohemia lived harmoniously in Cheyenne Valley, which once was the largest settlement of African Americans in Wisconsin. Alga Shivers went on to become an architect and a builder, best known for his uniquely designed round barns, several of which still stand in the region today.

All other persons, descriptions, and events in this account are fictional.

READ AN EXCLUSIVE EXCERPT FROM THE NEXT BAD AXE COUNTY NOVEL

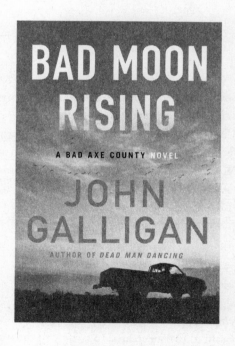

COMING JUNE 2021

CHAPTER 1

1. *Cut several fresh (bright green) dandelion leaves and put them in a clean glass or plastic container. Do not use a metal container.*

2. *Make sure that the leaves, once cut, do not come in contact with sunlight.*

3. *Urinate on the leaves until they are completely submerged.*

4. *After 10 minutes, check for red bumps on the leaves.*

They say that we hear music in the womb.

We hear voices.

We are designed this way.

The wet tympanic membranes, the yielding ossicles, the soft hard-wiring to the brain, these are created to convey to the womb the sweet vibrations of enveloping love. And so, swaddled in supportive sound, we grow.

What could go wrong?

Bad Axe County Sheriff Heidi Kick rolled and gasped beneath her sticky sheets.

What could go wrong?

Seriously?

She lurched up, still three-quarters asleep. Moonlight glistened on her forehead. Night sounds grated at the screen.

It was all too obvious what could go wrong.

We could hear all the wrong things. Anger. Stupidity. The subtracting silence of despair. The pitiless gnashing of time, the thunderous indifference of nature. Surely, along with Mozart and Mommy, we also hear the insanity of the whip-poor-will, the ghoulish wailing of coyotes, the death scream when the owl hits the rabbit.

Or gunshots.

Yes, she had heard a gunshot. Because now she heard another.

From where? Inside herself? Outside?

Two hard cracks echoed across the landscape mapped inside her sheriff's brain, four hundred square miles of farm and forest, ridge and coulee.

Somewhere. Anywhere.

She fell back upon the bed. As her dream resumed, the gunshots echoed. Womb became dirt became a tomb. The Bad Axe soil she had tried to cultivate—her de-thistled pasture, her expanding vegetable and flower gardens, her new acres of alfalfa—poured over her like rain.

Hot. Dry. Black. Rain.

Heavy.

Sheriff Kick groaned and lurched up again, desperate to fully awaken. She wrested over her head and flung away her sweaty T-shirt: BARN HAIR, DON'T CARE. Red-blond strands stuck across her mouth as she pitched onto her side and groped emptily for Harley. *Help me!* But her husband the baseball hero was a hundred miles away representing the Bad Axe Rattlers at a Midwest League all-star event. He had won the home-run derby last night. Today was the game. *Opie, help me!* But her oldest child, the family's wise one, was away at summer camp.

Ten-double-zero! Ten-double-zero! Officer down! All units respond!

The sheriff could not wake up.

Shovel by shovel, the dirt massed upon her. She arched under the weight. She clenched her sheets, drove her hip bones up. Her mouth gaped.

"Unngh!"

She contracted every muscle, exploded upward. Contracted and exploded, sucked air, spit dirt, kicked, clawed.

At last she breached.

Gasped for air.

Cried in jerks and gulps like a baby.

Caught her breath.

Turned on the little rawhide lamp beside her bed.

There it was. Before sleep, she had found her diary from high school, the summer she had turned sixteen, and she had found the page where she had written down the recipe.

Cut several fresh (bright green) dandelion leaves and put them in a clean glass or plastic container . . .

"No," she whispered, touching the clasp on the diary. "I can't be. I'm careful. And we hardly ever even . . ."

But she was seventeen days late.

The recipe for lassies, her Grandma Heinz had advised her, *who don't dare go to the drugstore or the doctor.*

||||||||||

At dawn she endured a stinging bladder as she searched the pantry for an empty Mason jar. When she found one, a pint that once contained strawberry-rhubarb jam, she dropped her cell phone into her robe pocket and hurried outside.

As she started barefoot across the dew-drenched yard, the nightmare clung to her. She tasted dirt. Her body felt sore all over. Her gut retained a sickish tickle of dread. And the dream's special effects seemed to have warped her waking world. The normally clean breath of dawn smelled like kerosene and fish. Birdsong jangled and the sunrise hissed, dissolving shadows with a crackle. She recalled how seven years ago when she carried her twin boys, vanilla ice cream had tasted like socks.

I can't be. Please just let me be sick.

Overnight, two familiar signs—KICK HER OUT and BARRY HER—had appeared on her yard. The election was still three months away, but Barry Rickreiner had been trolling her and spreading rumors since around the Fourth of July. She wondered now, who was Oppo? What did Oppo mean: *Kim Maybee's suicide was a homicide?* Should she fight back with counter-rumors? Maybe. But as much as she loathed Rickreiner, this didn't feel right. Her strategy had been to start campaigning on the first of September, at which time she meant to take the high road. Meanwhile, the heat wave had claimed all her attention.

Hurry, Heidi, before you piss down your leg.

She hastened around the corner of the old farmhouse. So as not to cast a shadow, she sneaked beneath the curtained window of the guest room, where the kids' Grammy Belle Kick slept whenever Harley was gone overnight. Belle had seemed hostile lately, suspicious, as if believing some new gossip.

The sheriff ducked under her clothesline, gave wide berth to the soggy septic drain field, and arrived upon the shady ground beneath the honeysuckle thicket.

Cut several fresh dandelion leaves . . .

Several meant how many? She preferred exact numbers.

She packed nine bright-green leaves, serrated, oozing latex, into the jar. She was ready to cut her bladder loose when she felt the buzz of her phone.

"Sorry, Denise," she blurted into it. "Family stuff. I gotta call you right back."

Her dispatcher and friend Denise Halverson said, "I think we need you now, Heidi."

"I can't—"

She couldn't even finish the sentence. She dropped to a squat, tossed her phone upon the wet lawn, reached beneath her robe, and aimed the jar against herself. Wow. Better.

"OK, go ahead."

Denise spoke distantly from the grass.

"Do you remember that priest from La Crosse who told us homeless men are being picked off the street and never coming back? He was calling the counties a few weeks ago to put us on alert?"

She remembered appreciating the passionate good intentions of the call, but it had left her with questions. The priest had said that five men had disappeared—under suspicious circumstances, he was certain— from the streets of the nearest "big" city. But wasn't the simplest explanation that transients tended to be transient? And why was he so convinced that there was foul play involved?

"Yes, I remember. He thinks someone's offering them farm work. Denise, what happened?"

"A milk truck driver scared some turkey vultures off a body in the ditch on Liberty Hill Road. Deputy Luck just got there. It looks like a homicide. It looks like the victim might have been homeless."

The jar grew warm and heavy in her hand. She heard the gunshot echoes from her dream.

"Sheriff? Are you there?"

"Let me guess," she said. "Shot twice with a small-bore rifle, probably a .22."

The phone went silent for moment.

"And the body's caked in dirt."

"What's going on, Heidi?"

"Am I right?"

"Heidi, what the hell is going on?"

She pulled the jar away and finished into the grass. She raised her face toward the house and saw Grammy Belle staring back at her. The guest room curtain fell closed. She dumped the jar.

"I'm on my way," she said.